"Haven't you ⟨ever done anything⟩ *rash?" Jillian* ⟨asked with⟩ *exasperation.*

"No. I'm not a 'rash' kind of guy," Luke said. "In my line of work, 'rash' equates to dead. The reason I've lived this long is because I play out every scenario...and when all else fails, I trust my gut."

"But your gut may not always be right—"

"Sweetheart," he interrupted. "My gut is *never* wrong."

Luke's smile faded, and she felt the burning intensity of his gaze as he explored her face. They both knew what they were talking about now, and it wasn't undercover police work.

His unspoken message was clear. The affair that they were contemplating was wrong. They shouldn't even be considering it. But, in that moment, she knew she wanted him.

Dear Reader,

It's fall and the kids are going back to school, which means more time for you to read. And you'll need all of it, because you won't want to miss a single one of this month's Silhouette Intimate Moments, starting with *In Broad Daylight*. This latest CAVANAUGH JUSTICE title from award winner Marie Ferrarella matches a badge-on-his-sleeve detective with a heart-on-her-sleeve teacher as they search for a missing student, along with something even rarer: love.

Don't Close Your Eyes as you read Sara Orwig's newest. This latest in her STALLION PASS: TEXAS KNIGHT miniseries features the kind of page-turning suspense no reader will want to resist as Colin Garrick returns to town with danger on his tail—and romance in his future. FAMILY SECRETS: THE NEXT GENERATION continues with *A Touch of the Beast*, by Linda Winstead Jones. Hawk Donovan and Sheryl Eldanis need to solve the mystery of the past or they'll have no shot at all at a future…together. Award-winning Justine Davis's hero has the heroine *In His Sights* in her newest REDSTONE, INCORPORATED title. Suspicion brings this couple together, but it's honesty and passion that will keep them there. A cursed pirate and a modern-day researcher are the unlikely—but perfect—lovers in Nina Bruhns's *Ghost of a Chance*, a book as wonderful as it is unexpected. Finally, welcome new author Lauren Giordano, whose debut novel, *For Her Protection*, tells an opposites-attract story with humor, suspense and plenty of irresistible emotion.

Enjoy them all—then come back next month for more of the best and most exciting romance reading around, only in Silhouette Intimate Moments.

Yours,

Leslie J. Wainger
Executive Editor

Please address questions and book requests to:
Silhouette Reader Service
U.S.: 3010 Walden Ave., P.O. Box 1325, Buffalo, NY 14269
Canadian: P.O. Box 609, Fort Erie, Ont. L2A 5X3

FOR HER PROTECTION

LAUREN GIORDANO

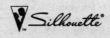

INTIMATE MOMENTS™

Published by Silhouette Books

America's Publisher of Contemporary Romance

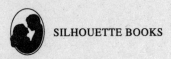 **SILHOUETTE BOOKS**

ISBN 0-373-27390-8

FOR HER PROTECTION

Visit Silhouette Books at www.eHarlequin.com

Printed in U.S.A.

LAUREN GIORDANO

grew up in western Massachusetts, where she spent long summer days imagining she was Nancy Drew. She completed her first novel on a manual Smith-Corona at the age of twelve. These days her imagination still runs wild, but the stories flow easier on her computer. Since she started writing again seven years ago, her romantic suspense stories have won several writing awards. Lauren has also published several non-fiction articles in the area of public safety. She currently works in the field of risk and human resource management, and lives in Virginia with her husband and daughters.

To Mom and Dad,
who always encouraged me to aim for the stars,
and to Dan, who lifted me up so I could reach.

Chapter 1

If only she'd run the red light. Jillian Moseby darted a nervous glance at the man crouched in the passenger seat and willed her heartbeat to slow. The gun was still pointed at her.

"I won't hurt you. Do exactly as I say. No sudden movements and no questions until we're outta here. Got it?"

She nodded mutely. Dear God, don't let him harm them. How could this possibly happen? She'd been in the bloody States for less than a week…and now this.

"Look in your rearview mirror," he instructed. "Tell me what's happening at the building on the corner."

"Which side of the street?" She was surprised. Her voice didn't sound completely terror-stricken. His, on the other hand, had been controlled and unwavering. Whoever he was, he certainly wasn't panicking. Unlike her. And his eyes… Jillian supposed she should be grateful they weren't glassy and wild from drugs or fear. No, the eyes watching her were the gold of molten metal and came with the most intense, scrutinizing stare she'd ever been subjected to.

"My side, one block back. Look close."

"Uh, right." She glanced in the rearview mirror, aware that his gaze followed her every movement. There would be no chance for escape. Not from this man. He wouldn't miss a trick. Her hands tightened on the wheel, her gaze flicking to the back seat. Not that she could ever leave them behind.

It was a miracle how children could sleep through just about anything. Two sandy heads were lolled over, nearly touching in their side-by-side car seats. And James was sprawled out next to them. He was sleeping, too, thank God. She couldn't take a round of his six-year-old's questions right now.

She knew the golden-haired stranger hadn't seen the kids yet. He couldn't have. Why, he'd nearly jerked the door off the hinges when he'd dived into the car. Now he was crouched down so low, he was more on the floor than on the passenger seat. Obviously he didn't want to be seen.

"What d'ya see?"

Jillian adjusted the mirror away from the children and angled it back so she could see the corner. "Three—no, four—men standing outside the building." She winced when he cursed and prayed he would lower his voice. Another shout like that and he'd wake the babies.

"Two of them just crossed to the other side." She bit her lip as the news caused another round of swearing.

"What now? Where are they?"

His tone was angry but not fearful, not really. He sounded more…frustrated that he was relegated to the floor of her hire. She had the awful suspicion he would rather be out there— in the thick of it. She shifted her glance from his tawny eyes back to the mirror. "Goodness. One of them is walking straight up the middle of the street. He's looking into car windows."

"Dammit. Watch the light. As soon as it turns, I want you to step on it. Don't floor it," he ordered, "or we'll attract more attention. And don't let him catch you looking at him or we'll be in big trouble."

"Oh, dear."

"What? What the hell is it?"

His tone was definitely exasperated. She heard him cock the gun in his hand, felt his tension as he readied himself for battle and suppressed a tremor of pure terror. She wasn't ready for the chaos of America. She'd been very happy living outside of London. Far outside, actually. Away from traffic and guns and violence....

Still, it might be best to reassure the lunatic before he started firing the bloody weapon with the babies in the back seat. Only a week ago she'd made a vow to Annie that she would protect them with her life. Who knew she'd be tested so soon? "He's not here yet. He's about four cars away...and he's got a gun, too."

"No kidding."

She kept an eye on the traffic signal. They'd been sitting here forever. It had to change soon. Three seconds later she gunned the engine and the overburdened station wagon groaned, vibrating in protest as it lurched forward. She heard the stranger mutter yet another curse under his breath and was fairly certain his angry glare had something to do with her driving ability.

"You said floor it, so I did." She shot him a scowl as his tension began to rub off on her. It evaporated a moment later when she saw his face twist with pain. "Are you all right? Can I drop you somewhere?" Compassion overrode her fear for an instant. Perhaps if she helped him, he would let them go sooner. "I've got a long way to go today and I really can't afford to get sidetracked."

"You *cahn't*?"

"No, I—" She hesitated when she realized he was poking fun at her.

"Goin' all the way back to England?"

"No. I'm traveling to New Hampshire. I'm starting a new job there." She glanced cautiously to her right. His voice had an edge to it that hadn't been there a few minutes earlier.

"What's wrong, now? You look a little green. Are you feeling all right?"

"No, lady. I'm not having one of my best days. Matter of fact, I feel like hell." He ran one hand along his unshaven jawline as though he were uncertain of what to do next. The white lines around his mouth took on stark relief in his coppery, tanned face.

"I hate to ask, and I hope you'll understand, but I really must know whether you're a good guy or a bad guy." She hesitated a moment and then plunged on before he had time to respond. "And if you *are* a good guy, then could you please point that thing away from me? It's rather nerve-racking."

His eyes registered shock and Jillian wasn't sure if it was at her audacity or if he simply found her question too stupid to respond to. Whatever the reason, it had the desired effect. She heard a little click as he did something to the gun and pointed it at the floor.

"I'm...a good guy, I guess. Although I know I don't look like one. I'm a special agent with the DEA. I'd show you my badge if I had it, but I've been working undercover, so you're gonna have to take my word on it for the moment."

"What's the DEA?"

"Drug Enforcement Agency. What you just experienced back there was a drug bust gone south."

"Gone south?" Her gaze left the road for a moment to slide over his. She still hadn't mastered driving on the wrong side of the road, so she didn't let her eyes rest on him for very long. Just long enough to see the flash of an earring in his ear. A small stud that was nearly hidden by long strands of wavy, golden hair. He reminded her of one of the surfers she'd seen on the telly.

"Yeah, south. Fu— I mean, screwed up. Those guys back there weren't supposed to get away. I thought I had 'em, but something went wrong. I was lucky to get out alive." He shifted uncomfortably on the floor. His frame was so large she simply couldn't imagine how he'd wedged himself in down there to begin with.

"You smell sort of…like you're on fire."

"That was the explosion."

"Explosion? What explosion?"

"Jeez, lady. Try to stay in one lane, okay?"

She righted the car and swallowed hard. Her heart was lodged in her throat again. "I think you can come up now." She checked the rearview mirror.

"Is this your car or a rental?"

"It's a rental. Why?"

"I don't want to get blood all over the seat."

"Blood," she cried as she turned to look down at him. Unfortunately the car moved with her and she careered across a lane of traffic before steadying the wheel. "Good Lord, you're shot!"

"Dammit. Stop doing that or I'll end up with a heart attack."

"I've got to get you to a hospital." Lord only knew what this would do to her schedule.

Jillian bit her lip and carefully glanced down at him. She shouldn't be thinking like that. The poor man was shot. "Tell me where it is and I'll take you there, straightaway."

"No dice. Not till I know what went wrong back there. I can't risk going to the hospital." He stifled a groan as he tried to hoist himself up onto the passenger seat. "Just give me a minute to figure out what to do next."

Her gaze ran over him, searching for the gaping hole she knew had to be somewhere on his body. "Where were you shot?"

The stranger groaned louder and finessed his large frame into the seat. "I suppose I should be grateful. I mean, I wasn't wearing a vest or anything." His sigh was one of relief when he finally eased back against the passenger seat cushions. "But it still hurts."

"Where? You're not going to die on me, are you?"

"No, lady. I don't think I'm that lucky. He shot me in the ass."

It took all the restraint she had not to burst out laughing. But the white line around his mouth and the beads of sweat on his forehead convinced her this was not a laughing matter.

"Who's shot in the ass?"

The stranger nearly flew out of his seat before whirling around to find the voice. The blood had drained from his face when he turned back to face Jillian. "Sweet Jesus! You've got three kids back there. Why didn't you say something?"

"Well, there really hasn't been time yet. I mean, what with the guns and the chase thing going on." She tilted the rear-view mirror back to the rear seat and found James's questioning eyes. "This is James, who is six years old and who is going to be very quiet for the next few minutes, right, love?"

James ignored her, turning to stare at the stranger. "Are you shot in the ass? Is it a big hole? Can I see it?"

"James! Please do not say 'ass' again. If I hear that word come out of your mouth, I will wash it out with soap." She darted a reproving look at the stranger. "I would appreciate it if you could please curse more quietly. James knows better, but Samuel is only three."

The stranger stared at her as though she'd lost her mind. And frankly, perhaps she bloody well had. Jillian had been thinking for the past several days that she truly must be crazy. To give up her comfortable, predictable life back home to face this…wilderness. She'd inherited not only a new country and a new job, but three small children to boot. And in the move, she'd lost Ian. He'd wanted no part of her adventure. Especially not the inheritance part.

"What's his name, Jilly?"

Her thoughts interrupted, she turned startled eyes to the stranger. "Why, I don't—"

"Gianetti. Lucas—Luke Gianetti."

He smiled for the first time, a small, tight smile of pain and frustration. But oh, my. What a smile. Why, he'd be absolutely devastating if he put his mind to it. She'd bet he would clean up well, too. He desperately needed a shave and a haircut, although truthfully, his hair was such a wonderful shade of gold that he looked rather dangerous with it long and wild.

"And you're Jilly?"

"Jillian, actually. Jillian Moseby."

"S'nice to meet you, Jillian." He reached across to shake her hand and she noticed he'd left the gun on the floor. He turned and waved over his shoulder to James. "Nice to meet you, James. What's the other little one's name?"

"That's my baby sister, Sarah. She's only four months old. She cries a lot when she's not sleeping."

Luke's forehead wrinkled at that bit of news and his voice dropped to a whisper. "I see. Well, let's not wake her up, okay?"

James giggled in the back seat and Jillian actually smiled. It was the first time since she'd arrived that she'd heard the little boy laugh or seen him fascinated by anything. Of course, it had taken an armed intruder with a gunshot wound to his buttocks to do it.

Luke's suddenly intent gaze zeroed back in on her. "Okay. Here's what we're gonna do. The closest big city is Charleston. Let's get out to the highway and zip up there. I'll show you where to drop me and then you guys can take off. I'll need your name and address, just in case I have to reach you about this case I'm workin'."

"But what about your...wound? Will you be all right?"

He shrugged it off as though they were discussing a splinter. "I'll be fine. Don't worry about it."

"Wow, Luke, can I see it? Before you leave, I mean?"

Luke shook his head in disbelief. "I dunno, kid. We'll have to wait and see."

Jillian followed his directions and soon they were cruising up the highway, north to Charleston and eventually all the way to New Hampshire. To a new life. One involving far more responsibility than she'd ever been charged with before. A new job and a new mother. To three children. How would she possibly hold it all together?

They'd travelled nearly thirty minutes when she remembered something Luke had said earlier. James had been peppering the poor man with questions nearly nonstop since he'd wakened. And, she was forced to admit, Luke had been very patient, taking the time to answer each one. Unfortunately, each question grew more gory than the last.

"What's it like to shoot someone? Have you ever killed—"

"James, hush for a minute," she interrupted. "What did you mean about that man back there?"

"What about him?" She felt the intensity of his gaze shift to her.

"You said we'd be in trouble if he saw us." She made sure to hold the wheel in place when she turned, her glance seeking confirmation.

Luke's eyes narrowed when he caught her troubled gaze. "And?"

"Well, he saw me looking at him in the rearview mirror."

She sensed him stiffen in the seat beside her. "Are you sure about that?"

She nodded. "Very sure. It was just a tiny peek, actually. But his eyes met mine for a second before I could look away. It's funny…he even looked familiar, but that's rather impossible, don't you think?" She felt the tension vibrating in him, felt it coil around her in the little car and felt her heart speed up in response. Her gaze left the road again. "Is that very bad?"

His face had gone tight, his features hardening like one of those ancient stone carvings her father'd insisted she study as a child. "Get off the highway at the next exit. Do it fast."

"Look, I appreciate your concern—truly, I do. But it was a terribly small glimpse and I simply can't afford to get sidetracked. I'm not exactly sure how far New Hampshire is and I need to get us all settled before I begin my new job."

"Lady, you're not goin' anywhere." He glanced over his shoulder, craning his neck to get a look out the rear window, but not before giving James a nod and a quick smile. Then he rolled down the passenger window and readjusted the side mirror.

"I don't think you understand—"

"Here. Get off here." When she hesitated, he shifted in his seat to face her and she nearly shivered at the expression in his eyes. The mesmerizing golden eyes had turned flat and cold. Luke now appeared ready for battle. He looked...deadly.

"I'm taking you into protective custody. You will do exactly as I tell you until such time that I deem it safe to release you."

"But—"

"Here." He jerked the wheel to the right. "Now move it."

Luke couldn't believe the streak of bad luck he was having. First, the bust had gone haywire for no apparent reason. There had been no screwups on his end, of that he was damn sure. But the vibes had been off from the beginning, starting when he'd woken up this morning. Something had gnawed away at his gut and it hadn't been nerves. He was ready for this op. Hell, it was a piece of cake compared to some of the others.

He'd infiltrated Sloan's group without a hitch. Everything had been building to this day. Every piece of evidence. Every witness. Every damn buy he'd been forced to make. It had been smooth. Maybe that was the hitch. Maybe it had been too easy. Easy that was, until the moment he and Murphy had heard the rumbling of the building coming down around them. Then they'd run like hell. He knew Murphy'd cleared the building, had seen him and the Assistant Special Agent in Charge running for cover—

His thoughts were jarred by the shrill cries of a baby. Oh, yeah. Baby Sarah had quite a set of lungs on her. He shook his head and tried to block out the sound. His butt was on fire. That had been the second thing to go wrong. It was bad enough the bust had gone bad, but then to get shot, and in the ass, no less.

He hobbled into the bathroom and swallowed three more Tylenol. Anything to take the edge off the throbbing pain. The bleeding had stopped, but the bullet was still in there. Had been in there for more than twelve hours now. It had to come out or he'd be in worse trouble. Soon he'd be forced to ask the harried-looking English chick for help. Oh, how he dreaded it.

He limped back out to the main room. Had they been the best of friends or a tight-knit little family, the motel room would've been much too small for the five of them. But they were virtual strangers. The room felt like a closet. He glanced over at Jillian. She was trying to soothe the baby, but her awkward, rocking motions seemed to be jarring Sarah rather than calming her.

"Here. Give her to me. I'll try to shut her up while you make a bottle."

Her glance was grateful, but laced with guilt. He winked at her to take the sting out of his words and was rewarded with a small, wan smile. Mary Poppins looked pooped. Still, she was surprisingly resilient. It couldn't be every day she was waylaid by a federal agent and forced into hiding. So far she seemed to be making the best of it.

He couldn't let them go...not until he knew for sure it was safe. And nothing about this op felt safe, at least not yet. His stomach still felt as though he'd had too much caffeine. He still hadn't made contact with the rest of the team, hadn't been able to reach his partner. Since the explosion, every number was relentlessly busy. Hell, they could be dead for all he knew. Very little was being said on the television news, but he knew for a fact the explosion had collapsed half the building.

Jillian turned to face the next set of clinging hands. Samuel was still awake and rarin' to go. Luke watched in amazement while she settled the rambunctious three-year-old at the tiny kitchenette with a box of crayons that seemingly materialized out of thin air. James was busy mixing the bottle. He wondered about that. Did all kids that age help so much? James seemed far older than six years. Six going on forty. Then again, what did he know?

So far, in his thirty-two years on the planet, all he'd managed to achieve was one former wife. They'd never gotten around to having kids. Never had the chance, he corrected. If it'd been up to him, it would've happened eventually. If Linda had only waited.

His thoughts returned to Jillian. A pretty name, just unusual enough to be memorable. And if her name hadn't caught his attention, her accent would have. He was surprised to learn she'd been born in the States. When he'd asked, she'd said Kansas. Of course, it had come out like ''Cahnsus'' and he'd thought for a second she'd been messing with him.

But her big eyes had gotten all wide and she'd said that no, really, she *had* been born there and moved back to England when she was two. She had pretty eyes, actually—a stormy gray-blue that seemed to change with her moods. He watched her smile at James and tussle his hair. She was lanky and lean, but in a careless, nonathletic sort of way. And she looked nothing at all like her three children, he realized. The kids could've been his, if genetics were based solely on their coloring. They were all blond, pink-cheeked cherubs with hazel eyes, while Jillian's hair was long and brown and untamed.

''You're good at this.'' Jillian appeared again, testing the bottle on her arm. ''She's stopped crying. Have little ones of your own, do you?''

He smiled and continued to bounce Sarah. And wondered if she could see the regret he always felt when he allowed himself to think about it. ''No. Just a lot of practice with my nephews.''

Her smile was genuine when she moved closer to stroke Sarah's fuzzy head. ''Perhaps you can give me lessons? I'm still learning all this.'' She leaned into him, brushing his shoulder as she planted a kiss on Sarah's cheek and lifted the baby from his arms. ''Time for dinner, sweetheart.''

''I'd figure with three of them, you'd be a pro by now.'' Man, she smelled great. A tantalizing aroma of something sweet and fresh washed over him and he had to consciously fight the urge to inhale her scent again. He ignored the tingle of current that shot down his arm, choosing instead to grope for a logical reason. Static electricity. That made sense. Or close quarters. Perfectly good reason.

That, or the fact that it had been a ridiculously long time since he'd been to bed with a woman. He took a long, slow breath. No chance of that happening anytime soon, not with a bullet in his ass. Not with a day-care center at ground zero of their musty-smelling motel room.

''They've only been mine for three days now,'' Jilly admitted as she accepted the baby from Luke's outstretched arms, unsure whether she wanted to delve into such a personal situation with a complete and utter stranger. Since she'd picked the children up at social services, there'd been one ordeal after another to deal with and an absolute mountain of paperwork.

''Wait a minute. I'm confused. Aren't these your kids?'' The poor man seemed to be in agony. Luke hadn't said much, but she could tell by the way he limped that he was in a great deal of pain. For a fleeting moment, though, his grim expression was replaced with one of confusion.

''Well, they are now. I've already filed the papers to adopt them.''

''You flew all the way over here to adopt kids? What made you do that?''

Her gaze shifted to the corner of the room where James sat in a squeaky armchair, his eyes glued to the telly. In three days James hadn't so much as mentioned his mum. But she knew Annie's death had hit him hard. Good Lord, she was still reeling herself. But instinct told her he would speak of

Annie when he was ready. Still a complete novice at the motherhood thing, she'd cautiously followed his lead.

Luke's gaze travelled to James before returning to settle on her. She hoisted Sarah awkwardly onto her shoulder. "M-my sister. She passed away two weeks—"

"I didn't mean to pry," he interrupted, clearly uneasy. "I'm very sorry to hear that."

The flash of compassion in his eyes nearly undid her composure. Her gaze still on James, she blinked back the tears that lately seemed to be too readily available. Lowering her voice, she continued. "I promised my sister I'd come over here and—"

He held up one hand. "I get the picture. I'm really sorry. I didn't mean to upset you."

When she allowed herself to think about it, Annie's death was like a raw gaping wound. Not that she'd had all that much time to think about anything. For once, she was grateful when Sarah began fussing. There was nothing like a hungry baby to get her mind refocused on priorities. She would have a lifetime to grieve for all she'd lost. A lifetime to wonder over what might have been. If she'd only come sooner.

Crossing to the bed, she sat and slid across the spread to lean back against the headboard. She snuggled Sarah into one arm before slipping the bottle into her mouth. Her sweet little face unscrunched immediately as she began happily sucking. And Jillian sighed with relief.

"She's a noisy little thing, this one. I wonder if all babies are this loud."

"I wouldn't be the right person to ask that question. But if I remember correctly, my nephews' screams came damn close to shattering glass when they were hungry." Luke sat hesitantly on the edge of a chair, wincing when his rear end made contact with the vinyl. "I guess that's nature's way of ensuring they get what they need."

"So what happens now, Mr. Gianetti? Have you made contact with your captain, or whatever he is?" Sarah's eyes seemed to follow the sound of her voice and she giggled in spite of her exhaustion. Lord, she felt like a limp dish rag. No wonder Nanny Margaret had always been so foul come suppertime. After all these years, she finally understood why Nanny's evening sherry had been such a sacred event. She'd probably been bloody worn out after endless days spent chasing around after her and Annie.

"He's called a SAC...not a captain."

"What's a sack?" Leave it to the Yanks to abbreviate everything. Why did everything have to be shortened to initials? What was their damn hurry?

"Not sack," he answered patiently. "SAC—Special Agent in Charge. He's the boss. Then there's an ASAC—Assistant Special Agent in Charge. Then way down the totem pole, there's me."

"And what initials are you?" she interrupted.

"I'm just an SA... Special Agent. Actually I'm a UCSA."

"A what?"

A fleeting smile crossed his features. "An Undercover SA."

It was a code she'd have to break. Why, it would probably be even worse on a college campus. Kids today spoke a completely different language. With any luck, she'd be able to hide out in her library. Although she doubted it. She'd been thrilled to accept Dartmouth's offer. Archiving one of the finest collections of eighteenth-century papers was a dream come true. But then Rosemary had gone and ruined it. Her mother's catty reminder of their lineage had planted a niggling worry in her mind. Had they only wanted her because of who she was?

Sarah gurgled, catching her attention, and Jilly was content to let her suspicions slide away. Rosemary wouldn't ruin this for her. She would prove to Dartmouth—and to herself—that they'd made an excellent choice.

"So, SA Luke, were you able to reach any of your initial friends?" She tore her gaze from Sarah and glanced around their meager room. The furniture was threadbare and probably decades old. And the overriding scent was one of mildew. The smell reminded her of the ancient castles her father had dragged his daughters across the continent to visit. Every school holiday had been spent "appreciating" another dreary estate. The only difference now was the temperature. The castles had been cold and dank. Here in the States, it was warm and far too humid for her taste.

"When can we leave this fine establishment?"

"I still don't know yet." Agent Gianetti's tone was clearly defensive.

"We simply can't stay here indefinitely." She raised one eyebrow when Sarah belched indelicately. "Well, excuse you, young lady."

That got a smile out of Luke. "She's not half bad. With a little practice, she just may have a future."

"Mr. Gianetti, please. Sarah is going to wear dresses and have tea parties, not learn to burp and spit." She narrowed her eyes. "Now, please tell me what's going on."

"The good news is that we're safe—temporarily."

"Safe? From what? You said no one followed us." He settled back in his chair and then sucked in a sharp breath of pain. "Are you all right?"

He gritted his teeth and nodded. "I'm okay."

"You don't look okay," she persisted.

"I just need to stand up." His eyes glazed with pain, he grasped the table and hoisted himself from the chair. "The bad news is that I haven't reached anyone on the team. It's like the call won't even go through. All the circuits are down, or some damn thing. And my cell phone isn't working."

"You don't think that man will actually look for us, do you?"

How much did he risk telling her? For the moment she was calm, rational. And Luke wanted to keep it that way. The last thing he needed was a hysterical woman on his hands. Hell, yes, Sloan would be looking for them. He was probably searching right now. Sloan abided by the drug dealers' creed. No witnesses.

"Until I'm positive it's safe, we're not going anywhere. As soon as it gets dark, I'll try to contact my partner from the pay phone out front."

Luke was not operating from a position of strength. He had to come up with a plan. They were all dangerously vulnerable to Sloan and his gang of rent-a-thugs. He was saddled not only with the sexy Jillian, but with her three children—babies, actually. A fast escape would be out of the question, so he had to make sure they wouldn't need one. A quick inventory had already confirmed he didn't have much cash and until he connected with his partner and found out what had gone wrong, he wouldn't risk using a credit card. Even his undercover card would be too easy to trace.

He had no surveillance. No survival equipment and only one gun, and even that wasn't a good one. It was a street piece, no serial number—exactly what a small-time dealer would use to protect himself, to delude himself into thinking he was safe. Luke hated being without his pistol, but his government-issue was too easy to spot. Drug dealers were a very suspicious lot.

If Sloan had made Jillian's car, they were in it even deeper. And they wouldn't have much time before the goons came searching. If Luke'd had more time, he could've lifted another car, but Jilly's station wagon had been packed to the rafters. It would have taken half the night to move her stuff. He would feel a whole lot better with another hundred miles between him and Sloan. The bastard was way too close for comfort, but Baby Sarah's shrieks of protest had put an end to their travels. He shook his head in memory. The kid's voice could've registered on the Richter scale.

He'd finally settled on this dump because it was off the main road. He'd parked the station wagon around back. The gravel lot backed up to a tobacco field. No one would be able to see the rental car without skulking around to find it. Visibility from the room allowed him a full hundred and eighty degrees. He'd see anyone coming in.

If Sloan was on to them, he'd already be scouting the highway, knowing that was the easiest escape route. He would already have found the rental company and—

He'd already know Jillian's name. "Jill—what address did you use on the car rental application?" He felt her hesitation, watched her frown as though he'd asked her to solve an algebra problem without a calculator.

"It was out of Raleigh."

"Why'd you go way up there?"

"Well, I needed a flight fast and everything out of London to the east coast was already booked. Raleigh was the closest city I could get to South Carolina. I wasn't exactly sure how far I'd have to drive to pick up the children. It turned out to be quite a distance after all."

Luke rubbed his eyes with his fingertips. The woman spoke in absolute riddles and he was beginning to suspect the language barrier had nothing to do with it.

"So, what address did you use on the rental app?"

She shook her head in exasperation. "Right, of course. Your original question. Let's see, I wasn't quite sure of my address in New Hampshire, so I used my old address in England. Was that all right? The rental place didn't seem to mind."

"No…no. That's good." Sloan would spin his wheels tracing her back to England and then he'd come up empty-handed unless he found someone there who had her new address. He sighed as he gingerly eased onto a vinyl-coated chair with far too little padding and winced at the now familiar ache.

Problem number two: what to do about the slug? It was still lodged in his right thigh. Extremely upper right thigh. Obviously, it hadn't hit anything too important because he hadn't bled to death yet. He'd barely bled at all from what he could see. Of course, not being a sideshow contortionist, he hadn't been able to see much.

If he only knew for sure they were safe, he could check into a hospital. An agent shot in the line of duty. He was legit. But he still hadn't raised Murphy. Hadn't reached his SAC— or any of the rest of the team. Another bad sign that something was seriously wrong. Which meant no hospital. But the pain would only worsen until he removed the bullet. It had to be soon. He couldn't risk an infection, not with four people's lives in his hands.

It was his fault they'd seen Jillian. The blast had caught him off guard, otherwise he never would've jumped in the car of an innocent bystander. She'd done remarkably well, all things considered. It couldn't be everyday that a wild-eyed stranger hijacked her vehicle at gunpoint. Come to think of it, she'd probably remained calm because of the kids. She'd been praying he wouldn't hurt her children.

Still, she'd had the guts to ask him to lower his gun and to chastise him for cursing in front of James. Luke shook his head, hiding his sudden smile. Oh, yeah, Lady Jillian was an English rose and she had some thorns to her, too. He wondered how wide her eyes would get when he asked her to remove the bullet from his ass.

Chapter 2

"You want me to do what?" Jillian continued backing up until she was all the way in the corner, and still he followed her. Mother of God—he couldn't be serious.

"I know you heard me the first time." Luke's eyes were deadly serious.

"I can't possibly...I don't know the first thing about—"

"Look, we don't have a choice," he interrupted. "The bullet's got to come out. It's already been in there too long. I explained why we can't risk going to a hospital."

"Can't you try to reach your friend again? I mean—" She swallowed hard. "Maybe he got your message. Maybe he's on his way..."

"He's not on his way. He would have contacted me."

His tone was clearly exasperated, but she didn't give a damn. This was simply too much to ask. Perform surgery? Agent Gianetti was stark raving mad. No way in hell was she going to attempt to get a bloody bullet out of his behind. Her stomach roiled at the mere thought. Out of sheer desperation, she glanced around the room. She needed a diversion. Why couldn't Sarah cry now?

"B-but you said your cell phone wasn't working properly. It's probably bodged up. I think you should try the pay phone again."

"I've already taken too much risk. That phone out there can be traced in a heartbeat."

She took another step back and was cornered. Literally. The wall was at her back and a glaring Agent Gianetti stood towering over her. "Are you sure they'll search for us? I mean, I only saw that man for a moment. I don't know that I could identify him."

He gentled his voice at her obvious confusion. She didn't want to believe him. Heck, her safe little world had just been blown wide open. A dangerous drug dealer and his pack of thugs were looking for Mary Poppins and her three charges. He'd be fighting it, too.

"He can't take that chance. And I can't take the chance that he finds you."

"B-but I haven't done anything wrong," she stammered. "I've only been in the States for six days. How can a person get in this much trouble in such a short time?"

Her eyes were big as saucers as she chewed nervously on her lower lip. They were both whispering because the children were finally asleep. James and Samuel were in the double bed and Sarah in the portable crib they'd managed to wedge in the corner.

"If there were any other way, believe me, I'd do it myself. But I can't keep you safe, not feeling like this. If the bullet stays in much longer, I'm gonna get really sick and I won't be able to protect you. I won't be able to protect those babies."

He read the uncertainty in her eyes and realized he was getting nowhere. It might take all night to convince her. Perhaps what she needed was a challenge. "If you're gonna get all squeamish and faint on me, then—"

"No, no. It's not that. It's just…I don't want to hurt you and I see no way around the fact that it's going to hurt dreadfully."

Dreadfully. Yeah. A far more civilized word than he would've chosen. It was gonna hurt like freakin' hell. But there was no other choice. Fourteen hours and he still hadn't reached Murphy or his commander. That fact alone had alarm signals crawling up his spine.

He had to get them out of here…the sooner the better, but he couldn't drive any distance with a bullet in his butt. They were wasting valuable time. It had just gone dark. They should be making tracks instead of talking. "Let's go," he ordered. "Into the bathroom. We can turn on the water to cover our voices." He tugged on her arm, leading her to the closet-size bathroom. "You got any Band Aids in that bag?"

She nodded and immediately went to work, digging through her travel case for supplies. Luke sighed and turned on the faucet. He'd have to sterilize his knife with hot tap water. If he didn't get an infection out of this, it would be nothing short of a miracle. When he turned back, a small mountain of first-aid supplies was stacked on the counter. He blinked and shook his head in amazement. Jillian was prepared for war-zone triage.

"You always carry so much stuff?"

She raised startled eyes to his in the mirror. Her skin was so pale it made her eyes appear even bluer, like the sky just before a storm. "Well, with the children and everything, I thought it best to be well prepared. I bought one of each kind." She blew out a nervous breath. "I'm ready."

He smiled at her reflection in the mirror and watched her pull her hair back in a lopsided ponytail. The color wasn't brown at all but a beautiful cinnamon. It was long and wavy and just a little bit wild. He'd bet the strands would slide like silk between his fingers.

"Okay, tell me what you want me to do."

"All right. In the next minute or so, you're gonna get to

know me real well.'' He paused when her gaze dropped and
noticed the telltale pink flush flare across her cheekbones. He
hadn't thought it possible for a woman her age to blush. ''Try
not to be nervous. It'll hurt, but I swear I won't make a
sound,'' he promised.

''Oh, God.''

Impulsively he grabbed one of her hands. ''Look, if you
hesitate—if you go slow—it'll hurt worse. I want you to make
a crisscross cut over the hole about this big.'' He drew on her
palm while she listened intently, hanging on every word, and
he felt a measure of her tension dissipate.

''It was a small-caliber bullet and it was shot from a pretty
far distance. It can't be in there very far…maybe an inch.
Once you make the cut, I want you to take the edge of the
blade and probe in there like this.'' He pointed the blade down
and gently touched her palm, careful not to press too deep.
''The sooner you find it, the better.''

''What then? When I find it, I mean?''

She blanched again and her eyes carried a hunted look, as
though she knew there was no way to escape. ''As soon as
you feel it, try to get the blade underneath and lever it out
that way. If not, we'll use those evil-looking tweezers you've
got there.''

She jerked her hand from his and raised it to her mouth.
''Ohmigod, Luke—I don't know if I can…''

He reached out and gently pried her fingers from her lips,
giving them a little squeeze. ''You can do this. I know it.''
He waited while she composed herself once again, watching
as she took a shaky breath. ''You need to wash your hands
really well and then I'm gonna lean way over the counter and
you're gonna go to work. Okay?''

She swallowed convulsively and shook her hands, as
though shaking the jitters out of her fingers. ''Right. I'm
ready.''

Luke took a deep breath and unbuttoned and unzipped his
pants. Sweet Jesus, could this be any more awkward? A beau-

tiful woman was about to carve up his butt in the shabby little bathroom of Jethro's Rent-A-Shack. If the guys ever found out about this, he'd never hear the end of it.

He noticed that Jillian played it cool. She'd averted her eyes when he'd dropped his pants and bit her lip when he'd grunted and launched himself up onto the counter. At least he could keep his underwear on...what little was left of the blood-soaked cotton. He tried not to wince as she peeled them away from his right buttock. Once she was finished, he'd cut them off and burn them in the sink. Unfortunately he'd be forced to go commando for a day or so until it was safe to buy underwear.

"How's it look back there?"

She stifled a chuckle. "How exactly do you mean? It's a rather fine-looking butt, if that's what you're hinting at."

Could this get any more embarrassing? He shook his head and tried not to watch her in the mirror. "What I mean is, how does the bullet hole look?"

"Don't clench up. I'm just cleaning the area with alcohol."

Right. She pours something freezing on his ass and she doesn't want him to react? "Well?"

Jillian raised her gaze to meet his in the mirror. "It looks...angry."

"Angry? What the he—" He took a deep breath, blew it out, and tried to remember that she was very nervous. "What does 'angry' mean?"

"It looks red and very tender and much smaller than I thought it would be, actually."

"I'm lucky the shooter was so far away. Otherwise, you'd see a whole lot more damage back there."

"You saw the person who shot you?"

He cocked one eyebrow. "He shot me in the ass, remember?" Her disgruntled sigh was clearly audible. Mary Poppins didn't have much of a sense of humor. If anyone should be pissed about this turn of events, it should be him.

"I'm not a ninny. I meant, how do you know where the person was shooting from?"

Her voice floated up from down near the floor. "The building was caving in...I was running away from it...I just know." In spite of himself, he tensed when she made the first incision. The area was throbbing so badly that it was almost a relief when she made the cut. He heard her take a deep breath before making the cross incision.

"Lord, it's really bleeding now."

Luke gritted his teeth and fought to school the pain. He tasted the sweat beading on his upper lip and experienced the faint, floaty feeling that came with shock. He tightened the muscles in his chest and arms as a countermeasure to the excruciating pain. If he focused on contracting those muscles, he could disassociate from the torture that was sure to come.

"Just swipe it and keep going. It's gonna keep bleeding until you're done."

Jillian took a shaky breath at the pain she heard in his voice. Dear God, if she could only run away. She fought to keep her hands from trembling while sweat trickled down her back and into her jeans. He flinched when she slid the knife in like he'd shown her. She dug in again and heard him bite back a moan. Lord, she was hurting him badly.

On the third try, she felt rather than saw the bullet. She'd found it. Now, to get the blasted thing out. She said a quick prayer to her Maker. If only He'd get the bullet out...she'd never ask for another thing. Just this one favor. Please, Lord.

Unfortunately, He must have been working miracles elsewhere because she came up empty-handed.

"You're stopping?"

She startled at the sound of his voice and paused to stretch the cramped muscles in her back and legs. They were locked with tension. She made the mistake of glancing into the mirror. Dear Lord, his face was gray with agony. "No. I'm...I was...I needed a minute. I'll try again."

She would have bent immediately had he not grabbed her

arm. She noticed then how large his hand was. His fingers gripped her entire forearm with relative ease as he tugged her up to his face.

"You're doing fine. Don't worry about me. It'll be over soon. Just keep goin'."

She blinked back tears as his magnetic eyes willed her to be calm. She took a deep breath and nodded. Luke was still in control. She could be, too. She could do this.

"Right." She squatted again and said another prayer. This time she managed to get his knife under the bullet. She felt the tug of resistance as the bullet rebelled against the blade. This ordeal could be over if she didn't panic. Her gaze still locked on the bullet hole, she reached up with her free hand and groped the countertop. She heard supplies scatter as her fingers wrapped around the tweezers and pulled them down. With one hand lifting the knife blade, she poked through the blood and dug the tweezers into the wound to grab the bullet.

Jillian felt his whole body jerk and then tighten and heard his stifled groan. Ignoring his pain, she blocked it out and concentrated on the sound of running water. Dammit, she had to finish this before she passed out. Or killed him. At last, the tweezers found the bullet. Not daring to release her sweaty grip, she yanked the metal slug out.

It was over.

"I've found the bloody thing." She sagged to the floor, her thigh muscles screaming when they finally unclenched. Nearly light-headed with relief, she waited several seconds before staggering to her feet, her legs still rubbery when she tried to stand.

"Please tell me you got it." His voice was tight with pain.

She loosened her grip on the tweezers and the bullet clanged on the Formica counter. "I've got to clean you up…down there. Then we're through."

"Thank God."

It seemed like forever before the bleeding stopped. When it had slowed to a trickle, she swabbed the area again with alcohol, starting at Luke's sudden indrawn breath. "Sorry about that. I should have warned you."

When he didn't respond, she made a makeshift bandage and taped it down with the neon Band Aids she'd picked up for the children. She managed a half smile and wondered what Agent Gianetti would think if he knew his butt would glow in the dark that night. She suspected he felt much worse than he was planning to let on. He'd been too quiet for the last few minutes. Lord knew she was ready to faint simply from performing the surgery.

"Can you move or are you too weak?"

"I—I'm fine. Once you finish, I...I need a minute to clean up. Just close the door behind you when you leave."

Luke's eyes were closed, his pale, clammy face resting on still-tense forearms, his body straddling the counter. His voice was muffled and miserable and she knew she couldn't risk leaving him alone in the bathroom. He did not have the strength he pretended to have. Jillian eyed the blood-soaked underwear and made a quick decision. She grabbed the scissors and before she could change her mind, swiftly sliced up the sides of his underwear.

"What in the sweet hell are you doing?"

"Don't move or you'll show me far more than you intended." She peeled the underwear off his well-developed and very clenched muscles and pretended not to notice how lean and hard he looked. Dear Lord, this was just his backside. Though she tried desperately not to, she couldn't help but wonder about the rest of him. Forcibly discarding the images, she wet a washcloth with warm water and sponged the dried blood from his skin. Still averting her eyes, she snatched a towel from the rod near his head. Now that she'd stripped him, she was rapidly losing her nerve.

Without meeting his gaze, she wrapped the towel around him and tied it loosely at his waist. Then she dropped to the floor and tugged his jeans from his feet. "I'll wash these in the sink. I can probably get most of the blood out so you'll have something to wear later.''

With another washcloth she carefully rinsed his forehead and face with cool water. He startled when she scooped up his long, golden hair and washed the back of his neck.

''That feels good.''

His mumbled comment sounded faraway and sleepy. When she had done all that she could to make him more comfortable, she dug through the cosmetic bag again while he awkwardly lifted himself from the counter. He staggered a little and she ducked under his arm, forcing his weight onto her.

''Here. Take these before we go out to the bedroom.'' She handed him three blue pills. It wouldn't do much for the agony he must be experiencing, but it was all she had. His face was white with pain and his eyes grim as he scooped them up and brought them to his mouth.

''What the hell are these?''

Jillian felt her face flush with color again. ''They're…you know. They, uh, help with cramps…when I, um, have my monthly. I'm sure they'll take the edge off.''

His eyes bleak, Luke swallowed them without comment. He must have felt terrible, because he didn't even argue when she led him to the empty bed. She didn't dare let go of him as she tugged the bedspread back and snatched the sheets apart. He was very woozy. He just didn't want her to know it. He sat heavily, careful not to put any weight on his right side. She punched up a pillow and gently pushed him back against it. He collapsed onto the pillow and she helped him pull his legs up, pushing them under the covers.

As soon as he was safely in bed, she raced back to the bathroom for a glass of water and the washcloth. She soaked it in cold water and wrung it out before taking it back to Luke. He was still conscious, but just barely. She laid the cloth over his eyes and set the waterglass on the nightstand within his reach.

''Where's my gun?''

"Right here. I'll put it in the drawer."

"No. Gotta have it." His words were slurred, but they were still adamant.

"No. If James or Samuel wakes up and sees—"

"Okay. You're right. Forgot 'bout…kids."

She sighed with relief when he gave in, rolling over onto his side and finally shutting his eyes. A hot shower was next on the list. She was sticky with perspiration and still shaking from the whole ordeal. She stepped away from the bed but was startled again by the strength of his grip when Luke jerked her back to his side. She hadn't even seen him move.

"Wha…what is it? Are you ill?"

His hand was warm where it stroked her wrist, his voice even warmer when he finally spoke. "Thanks for what you did. You're all right, Lady Jillian." His hand slowly dropped away and his breathing deepened. She listened for a moment, absently rubbing her arm where he'd held it before heading back to the overly bright bathroom.

Lady Jillian, indeed. Lady Jillian Moseby would've had the bloody vapors if she'd been asked to remove a bullet. From a man's bum, no less. Agent Gianetti was lucky she'd left Lady Jillian back in Sussex. She was Jilly now. And out of sheer necessity, Jilly would have to learn to be ready for anything. Tonight had proven it. Three children. Good God, how would she do it?

She methodically scrubbed the countertop and put away her supplies. Try as she might, she couldn't find the bullet she'd tossed on the counter. She gave up and began scrubbing Luke's jeans. Once they were dry, the blood stain would barely be noticeable. She held his pants up to the light. The bullet hole was tiny. How could something so small inflict so much damage? She shuddered as she remembered her sister and what Annie had done with a gun in her hands.

Finally she stripped off her clothes and stood under the shower for a long time, letting the warm water sluice over her in an attempt to wash away the horror of the past hour, of the whole day, actually. Dear Lord, it had been bloody awful. Ever since she'd arrived in the States, it had been one nightmare after another. She had absolutely no idea how to be a mother. What if she bodged it up? Three little lives were depending on her.

No one had ever depended on her to do anything. As far as parenting skills, she had none that she knew of. How would she ever live up to her promise to Annie? Jillian was beginning to wonder if she'd ever be anything other than too late. Too late for Annie. Nearly too late for the children...

The terror she'd experienced earlier when Luke had hijacked her car was nothing compared to removing that bullet. Tears sprang to her eyes when she remembered the pain in his eyes. She'd hurt him terribly. The sobs finally came and she allowed herself a good long cry before she methodically conditioned her hair and finally stepped out of the shower. It was nearly midnight. With any luck she could fall into bed for a few hours before Sarah woke her at three. At least that was what the baby had done the previous three nights. She could only assume it would happen every night.

Her eyes were pink when she examined them in the mirror. Her gym shorts and T-shirt would have to suffice for pajamas. It wouldn't be worth the effort of dragging the suitcase in from the car. And where would she put it anyway? The room was ready to explode.

She rinsed out her blouse and brushed her teeth before leaving the claustrophobic bathroom. She left the door slightly open, allowing a crack of light to remain in case the boys got up during the night.

Luke's bulky frame took up most of the bed but she was too tired to pretend she cared about modesty. Lady Jillian or not, there was no way she was sleeping on the floor, not after the day she'd had. And she'd already seen the man's naked butt, for goodness' sake. She shook her head and slipped between the sheets on the other side.

Here she was, across the Atlantic only six days now, and

already in bed with an American stranger. She smothered a giggle as a vision of her mother floated in front of her eyes. Rosemary Moseby would still manage to look dignified and oh, so proper, even with her mouth hanging open and her eyes bugged out. She would be appalled. Her worst nightmare come true: her precious Jillian in bed with a man...and a bloody Yank to boot.

She sighed and settled back against the pillow. If Rosemary only knew. Try as she might, Jilly couldn't picture removing a bullet from Ian's butt. Her fiancé—no, make that ex-fiancé, thank you very much—had been far more like her mother than she'd ever realized. She covered her mouth when another giggle erupted. Ian was so proper and reserved, why he could've simply squeezed his cheeks together and the bullet would've popped out straightaway. Hard to believe she'd contemplated marrying him. Why, they were complete opposites. What could she possibly have been think—

"Are you always like this? First you're cryin' like you lost your best friend, then you're laughing so hard you shake the bed?"

Startled, she rolled over, immediately contrite. "I'm so sorry. I didn't realize—"

"S'all right. It's not every day you pull a slug out of a guy's butt. Least you can laugh about it."

"Oh, no. I wasn't laughing at you—" His deep sigh told her he was nearly asleep again. She didn't bother to finish her sentence as she snuggled under the covers, shivering in the air-conditioned coolness of the room. Her last thought was of Ian. It was one of tremendous relief.

She was still asleep. He'd awakened to find her curled up behind him, her arm wrapped tightly around him, her face pressed into his back. Her soft breathing was hot against his shoulder blade, the curves of her luscious body slowly branding him with the promise of something incredible. Luke wanted desperately to move. He'd been on his left side for hours and his body ached from sleeping in one position. But he didn't want to wake Jillian.

It was murky and gray inside the slumbering room, and he guessed it was still before dawn. He was pretty sure she'd gotten up during the night with the baby. He'd heard Sarah whimper once and then he hadn't heard anything. Jillian must have been waiting, ready to snatch up the baby before she cried and woke everyone up.

He took a deep breath and rolled slowly onto his back, careful not to disturb his bedmate and at the same time, testing how much weight he could tolerate on his butt. The incision had stopped throbbing during the night and now, he discovered with relief, the pain had subsided to a dull ache when he lay back against the pillows. He released the breath he'd been holding and turned his head cautiously toward Jillian. She was lying half on top of him, with one hand pressed over his chest. Her legs were still curled in to his and he confirmed they were just as soft as he'd imagined, like warm satin against his skin.

She had freckles across the bridge of her pale nose and long, sweeping eyelashes that appeared dark against her soft pink skin. A delicate English rose with freckles. The scent of her hair was slowly driving him mad. He'd dreamed of rainstorms and wildflowers. Hell, he knew he shouldn't have taken that cramp medicine. Who knew what was in that chick stuff?

Luke swallowed hard and forced himself to look away from her mouth. One thing was abundantly clear. He still felt like a guy—a guy who hadn't slept with a woman in…forever. Her perfectly shaped lips were parted, her warm breath fanned the side of his neck. Her mouth was soft and pink and ready…

He jerked his thoughts away. He'd better create some distance and quick, before his body took over and did something stupid on his behalf. He slid noiselessly from the bed. Jillian sighed in her sleep and burrowed down under the covers. Forcing himself to refocus, he adjusted his towel and limped into the bathroom. It was time for a security check. And maybe a brisk walk in the cool morning air to clear his head.

The perimeter was secure. The car appeared untouched. He'd shimmied underneath, just to be sure, spending twenty minutes making certain they were safe. But something was off. His gut thrummed with an uneasy sense of warning. Luke just couldn't figure out why.

He scratched his two-day growth of beard and sighed. Maybe it was him. He'd had trouble settling in since he'd arrived from the D.C. office. Usually he fell into the role without a problem, adapted and blended in with his new territory. Maybe he just wasn't cut out for the Southern mentality. It was too peaceful down here, too sleepy. Nothing was as it seemed. There were too many undercurrents. On the surface, things appeared civilized and tidy, while everything underneath had gone to rot. Even the drug deals he'd made held an air of casualness, of laid-back Southern hospitality that had seemed unfamiliar.

He'd been edgy since the op started a month ago. And he'd worked too many years off his intuition, it had saved his hide too many times to question the feeling. He was highly trained, certainly. But it went deeper than that. Luke had taken that training and internalized it, until it became so ingrained it was second nature. He'd learned to never discount his gut. And his gut told him something was wrong.

He pushed off the stucco wall where he leaned, careful to avoid the huge puddle of water that had accumulated under the wheezing air conditioner. The parking lot was quiet, dark and cool, even the birds still silent despite the pink slivers of dawn that crept through the trees on the far side of the lot. He'd quietly checked each motel unit, just in case. There were only seven cars in the lot. And judging by the whine of the air conditioners, there were seven rooms accounted for.

"Maybe some coffee will help," he muttered. There'd been a hot plate in the office when he'd registered the day before and the sign had claimed the office was open 24/7. He just hoped they actually brewed a fresh pot each day. He walked silently around the L-shaped motel, cautious when he passed a room where the AC was running. Occupied units. He heard the steady drip of water as he slipped by each one.

He winced when a cow bell clanged noisily against the office door and he reached up to silence it. His head already ached from the musty, permeating smell of this dump. The night clerk must've decided on a nap because the front counter was quiet. He sniffed the air as he headed across the lobby. Coffee didn't smell scorched.. He poured a second cup for Jilly and paused to tuck some stale-looking cookies into a napkin. There wouldn't be time for the kids to eat breakfast.

He'd already kicked himself for sleeping the whole night. As soon as he got back, he was gonna wake 'em all up. Not knowing what had happened to Sloan was driving him crazy. Had the team managed to arrest him? Why hadn't he been able to reach Murphy? Something about the bust was eating away at him. It was almost as though Sloan had been expecting him—or worse. As though he'd been expecting narcs.

His senses were screaming to make some tracks. He wanted out of here, and fast. He crammed the napkin into his shirt pocket and felt for the gun hidden at the small of his back. He hesitated. If he carried coffee to Jilly, his hands would be full. He wouldn't be able to reach for his gun. Of course, if he didn't bring her coffee he'd be labeled insensitive, or some other female variation of cad. "Insensitive" had been one of Linda's favorites.

Either way, he'd be in trouble. Luke rolled his neck to loosen his tight shoulders and then hoisted the cups. He let himself out, taking care not to clang the damn cowbell. He was halfway to the parking lot when he stopped in his tracks, staring at the seven cars in the lot. *Seven.* And their car was parked out back. That made eight. The hair on the back of his neck stood at attention.

Maybe there was nothing to worry about. Maybe a family

was staying at the Fleabag Inn and they'd arrived in two cars. Yeah, right. Or maybe he'd better go back and check out that office again. His gut notched up to red alert. He retraced his steps and slipped inside. The cowbell didn't even budge. Luke set the coffee on the counter and vaulted over the locked half-door. There was a light burning in the paneled office down the hallway, but no signs of life.

He withdrew his gun and crept into the office. His hand shook slightly when he nudged the body on the floor by the desk. The night clerk's body was still warm.

The phone call.

A sizzle of warning crawled down his spine. His phone call to Murphy. One little phone call and now a man was dead. The clerk's only crime was being in the wrong place at the wrong time. The hit had Sloan written all over it. Why pay for a room you wouldn't be using long when it was so much easier to shoot someone? The bastard didn't care who got killed, so long as he achieved results. Anyone unfortunate enough to be in his way—nuns, small children, innocent motel clerks—was expendable. They were treated equally. Equally ruthlessly.

Luke scanned the hallway and quickly hustled back to the counter. He paused to take stock of the missing keys. One of them belonged to a killer.

A killer who was looking for him.

His stance resolute, he tucked his gun back in the waistband of his jeans and pulled his shirt free to cover the bulk. Luke hoisted the coffee and left the office. He forced himself to stroll along the sidewalk, taking care not to look directly at the motel rooms, keeping his gaze to the ground while he checked the water under each air conditioning unit.

Number six. Only four doors away from theirs. There was barely a drip from the AC. Probably because it had only been turned on recently. He wondered how many goons waited, sweating behind the door. Knowing Sloan, he'd probably only sent one or two. A dealer of Luke's caliber wouldn't have been worthy of more effort. But regardless of his rank in the organization, regardless of the magnitude of the slight, Sloan would've dealt with the double-cross. It was one of the rules of the game.

He tensed when he noticed the minuscule twitch of the curtain and forced himself to take a careless sip of the scalding coffee.

It was going down now. Luke felt the certainty pump through him like a shot of adrenaline. They would take him out and then they'd walk four doors down, where Jilly lay tangled in the sheets. And they'd take her out, too.

He jerked his thoughts away from the kids. They were all in big trouble. He took another sip of the coffee and grimaced as it burned all the way down his throat. He heard the door creak open and said a silent prayer as he slowly turned around.

Chapter 3

Jillian bolted upright when the door bounced back against the wall. Sunlight streamed into the room, blinding her for a moment. When she opened her eyes, a large shadow blocked the doorway. She hadn't even caught her breath before he was on her, shaking her, pulling her from the bed.

"What! What is it?"

He jerked her face up, trapping it between two very large hands. Hands that were spattered with blood. She opened her mouth to scream and he quickly clapped his fingers over her lips.

"Not a sound," he breathed in her ear. She nodded and he slowly removed his hand.

"Luke, for God's sake! What the hell is going on? You scared—"

He put his hand back over her mouth. "Not now. There's no time. I need you to listen. Can you do that?" She nodded again.

"We're leaving. Right now."

"But why—"

He held up his hand in warning. "Later. Get the kids up. I'm gonna move the car. When I pull in front of the door, you haul ass out there and toss 'em in to me. Got it?"

"They need to dress and brush their teeth—"

"Screw their teeth! Do you see this blood? I didn't cut myself shaving."

Jillian felt her blood pressure skyrocket. "Well, fine, then. You're in such a blasted hurry. Go get the car." She hadn't been awake two minutes and he'd already managed to make her lose her temper. What kind of mother woke her children and threw them into a car? With no breakfast? Without a washup? Why, the child authorities would be all over her in no time.

"And take the overnight bag with you. It'll save a trip."

"How soon can you be ready?"

She stripped off her gym shorts right in front of him. If he was going to make her rush, well then, dammit, she would show him a thing or two. She flung the shorts into the overnight bag and yanked out her jeans. Without stopping to put them on, she turned back to the dresser and with a scowl, swept all the kids' loose items into the duffel, clearing the top in a heartbeat. She zipped the bag angrily and hurled it across the bed at Luke, who caught it in the chest, watching her with something close to shock in his eyes.

"How about two minutes? Is that bloody quick enough?"

"Look, there's no need to go off."

"Go off? You burst in here, scare the daylights out of me. It's not even dawn yet and I am *so* not a morning pers—"

He held up one hand and the look in his eyes was enough to silence her. "Not now. You can chew me out in the car. Get the kids up."

His grim, no-nonsense stare made her bite back the argument she wanted badly to start. She glared at him as she shimmied into her jeans and rammed her T-shirt into the waistband. He was still watching her when she pulled her hair back into a lopsided ponytail.

"You can have three minutes," he countered.

"Your generosity knows no bounds." Luke's eyes narrowed at her waspish tone and she sensed that he was barely hanging on to his temper.

"Look, honey, I don't need this right now. I just took out two guys who were about ten minutes from breakin' down the door and killing all of us." He nodded at her startled gasp. "Yeah, that's right, Your Highness. So if it ain't too friggin' much trouble, I'd like to get the hell outta here as soon as possible."

Jilly swallowed hard. Lord, she'd really gotten into it this time. "Luke...I—I'm sorry."

"Forget it." He turned on his heel and strode to the window, stopping to peer cautiously through the curtain before he cracked the door open. "Three minutes," he reminded her.

"Whatever," she muttered, irritated all over again at his orders. "You're the one with the blasted stopwatch."

It had been more than an hour and she still hadn't spoken. It was just as well, Luke conceded. He needed to concentrate. They'd cleared the motel without any incidents. Well, if one considered neutralizing two enemies and pissing off Jillian as incident-free, then he was golden. He still hadn't quite recovered from her impromptu striptease. Damn, she was hot. Burning hot. She had legs that went on for miles—legs that ended with a tiny pair of bikini panties that barely managed to cover her curvy butt. Along with those million-dollar legs however, went a very cranky morning disposition.

He took a deep breath and blew it out. Focus. He had to stay focused. They were safe for now. The road was clear behind them, and there wasn't a single car in sight up ahead. He hadn't seen anything to indicate they were being tailed. Another hour and they'd cross into North Carolina. Then he'd try Murphy again. Try Duncan. Hell, try anyone. Pretty soon they'd have to ditch their ride and find another.

As much as he was dreading it, he'd have to ask Mary

Poppins how much money she carried. He prayed it was a lot—and that she'd converted her cash at the airport. If they were forced to convert British pounds or Euros to cash, they'd stand out like a sore thumb. And right now, he didn't want to be remembered by anyone.

Hopefully, it would only be another day or so. There was a DEA office in Charlotte. He'd contact the agent in charge and request a safe house...just until he found out what the hell had happened down in Spartaville. Nothing since yesterday morning had gone according to procedure. And he'd just thrown the rulebook out the window back there at the Fleabag Inn.

Just as he'd suspected, Sloan had sent a couple of goons after him. One little explosion, and all of a sudden, Billy T. Lathrop, drug dealer extraordinaire, had been expendable. Luke knew Sloan had been growing suspicious of him, had sensed a distinct wariness on the supplier's part over the last week or so. What he couldn't figure out was why. Why now?

As far as he knew, his cover was solid. Murphy's, too. They'd tag-teamed Sloan from the beginning but he and his partner had never even been seen together. There hadn't been any outward signs to indicate he'd been made. But suppliers were an edgy bunch, and for good reason. There was always someone looking to take their place.

Luke had done everything Sloan had asked, passed every test. As Billy Lathrop, he had painstakingly won his trust. It was what the Gianetti boys did best. Luke had discovered long ago that he had the ability to persuade just about anyone to do just about anything. Well, he conceded, maybe not everyone. It hadn't worked on Linda, at least not at the end.

Jillian was a piece of cake. She was wide open to suggestion. It hadn't taken ten minutes before he'd convinced her she could perform surgery. And damn if she hadn't risen to the challenge. He made a mental note to thank her later. Of course, she was miles apart from his former wife. Jilly was clearly somewhat of a free spirit. Even if she was a little scatterbrained, she'd jumped on a plane and crossed the ocean for those kids, and he'd be willing to bet the trip hadn't been planned for a year—like Linda would've done. That's assuming Linda would've actually taken a trip anywhere. In the end, she'd been afraid of her own shadow.

He risked a sideways glance at the free spirit and discovered she'd fallen asleep. No wonder she hadn't given him a piece of her mind yet. He smiled then. Jilly trusted him, all right, but she sure didn't like him very much. She'd managed to get the kids into their car seats without stirring them. He still couldn't believe that one. Only James had awakened, and then only briefly. She'd calmly shushed him back to sleep with a kiss and a pat on the head. Then she'd made sure Luke caught her scowl of disapproval before fastening her seat belt and turning toward the window.

"Where are we?" The sleepy voice came from the back seat.

"Almost to North Carolina. You getting hungry, James?"

"Kinda. I guess I am." Luke watched in the rearview mirror as his little friend rubbed the sleep from his eyes. "But you don't hafta stop for me. Wait till Sarah gets to crying. Then you'll hafta stop anyway."

"Sarah will need her nappie changed. I should've seen to it before we left." Luke heard the husky thread of sleepiness in Jilly's voice and resolutely chose to ignore the jolt of awareness that crawled through his system.

"It's a diaper, Jilly. Not a nappie. If you're gonna live here, you gotta learn to talk like us."

Out of the corner of his eye, Luke saw her wince, but then she straightened and smiled. "Good morning to you, too, James. I'm simply divine. Thank you ever so much for asking."

The little man received her message loud and clear. James scowled and his cheeks got pink, but he muttered a surly good morning under his breath.

"Good morning to you, too, Luke. I feel I must apologize

for my rude behavior earlier. I should have warned you that I tend to be rather foul in the mornings, especially before I've had any caffeine.''

He knew the coffee thing would come back to haunt him. He glanced over and was surprised to discover the halfhearted smile that had formed when she began lecturing James had broadened by the time her gaze met his. Her eyes were smiling, too.

"Perhaps we can start over. I promise I'll be much less grumpy for the rest of the day.''

"You're forgiven. In the future I'll try not to wake you like I did this morning.'' He shot a careful glance to the rearview mirror. Jilly caught his look and nodded slightly. With James awake, their talk would have to wait until later.

"We'll need to stop soon for gas. I promise I'll get you a big cup of coffee then. I had one for you this morning but I spilled it on my way back to the room.''

Flung, actually. Into the face of one of the hitmen Sloan had sent to track him down. Sadly, Luke's cup had spilled into the crotch of the other moron who'd made the huge mistake of going for his gun. The wheezing air conditioner had covered the sound of his screams. That and the pillow he'd pushed into his face before knocking them both out for good. On the plus side, he'd gained two more weapons. A Glock 9 mm and a relatively decent-looking .45. He just hoped he wouldn't end up needing to use them.

They'd left too many bodies behind at the motel. Only one dead one, but that would be enough to trigger an all-out manhunt as soon as the night clerk was discovered. The agency would be there by now. Sloan's thugs were long gone, but Luke sensed they wouldn't give up anytime soon. If there was one rule in the drug-running handbook it was that witnesses couldn't live. Sloan's failure to kill him this morning had only upped the stakes. But he didn't waste time worrying about that. By tonight the whole thing would be over. Jillian and the kids would be safe. And as for him...if Sloan found him, so be it. He didn't particularly care one way or the other.

He shot a quick glance at Jilly. She was humming softly as she gazed out the window. He found it incredible that she wasn't mad anymore. It made him wonder how she let go of her anger so quickly. How it disappeared—leaving no bitterness, no sarcastic aftereffects to keep it brewing. No cold shoulder that would take on a life of its own. Hell, nearly every argument he'd ever had with Linda had ended in a silent treatment that lingered so long he eventually forgot what the original disagreement had been about.

"How come we got up so early?" James's voice had him glancing in the mirror again.

Luke shot a subtle warning look at Jilly. "I don't know about you, kid, but I like driving in the morning. The road's clear and it's nice an' quiet."

James thought about it for a minute before slowly nodding his head. "Yeah, you're right, Luke. Me, too." He yawned again and then directed his attention at the back of Jilly's head. "Jilly, I think we should drive in the mornin' when we go to New York."

"You're probably right," she agreed as she glanced at Luke. "As soon as Mr. Gianetti says we're able to leave, we'll get up very early and drive while it's still dark, like we did today."

"Cool. Maybe I could sit up front? You'll need a good copilot."

Jilly appeared shocked, but then quickly flushed with pleasure at his suggestion. Luke noticed she didn't correct him on the New Hampshire part. He'd sensed the resentment James had toward her, and was curious as to the cause.

"Why, I'd love to have you as my copilot, James. You can hold the maps for me."

"Mama? I need go potty. I gotta go real bad."

Luke adjusted the mirror to include Samuel's sleepy face. His eyes were wide and blue, the color not unlike Jill's. The poor kid musta had six different cowlicks to go along with his morning bedhead.

"She's not our mother, stupid!" James's voice went from friendly to enraged in half a second.

"I not 'tupid."

"James, he's half asleep, for goodness' sake. He made a mistake. Leave him alone," Jilly instructed gently. She glanced at Luke for confirmation before turning to smile at Samuel. "Can you hold it, lovey? Just for a few minutes?" She grinned when he nodded his head. "Luke will be stopping just as soon as he spots a safe place."

"You're not our mom. You're n-nothing like M-Mommy." James gulped in a rush of air. "She was beautiful an...and..."

Luke watched her eyes soften as she directed her attention to James, who had started sniffling. She tried to hand him a tissue, but he turned away.

"James, I know I'm not your mum. I know you miss her. I miss her, too. But someone has to take care of you three and I'm the only one here to do that."

"There's my dad! If he kn-knew what you'd d-done...he'd come get me. He'd come for me, I know he would have. If you h-hadn't made us leave." James was crying in earnest now. "Now he'll never find me. I hate you!"

Jilly's eyes filled with tears and she quickly scrubbed them away as she turned back to face the front. Luke shot her an inquiring look, but she refused to meet it. "James, please...try and keep your voice down. Let's not wake up Sarah. We can talk about it when we stop in a few minutes."

"I don't wanna t-talk to you. I wanna live with my d-daddy."

"Hey, buddy. Let's cut her some slack, okay?" Luke paused for a moment, unsure whether or not he should interfere. But frankly, he had enough to deal with just keeping them all alive. He'd get a monster-size headache if he had to listen to wailing kids. "Listen, pal, Jilly's just trying to protect you."

"I don't need protectin'."

"Maybe not," he conceded. "But what about your brother? What about your baby sister?" He didn't give James another chance to argue. "Since you're the oldest, I thought maybe you could help me."

"You want my help? Is this like…with bad guys?"

He did a quick mental shrug. If it gained him some quiet time, who was he to argue? "Sort of," he said cautiously. "This mission involves driving you guys and Jilly to a safe place…and we need to get there as soon as possible. And we need to keep it secret."

"You mean, like spies?"

"Yeah, we need to move quickly and quietly. So I need your help keeping your brother occupied." He glanced at James in the rearview mirror. "That way, no one will notice us very much."

"You gonna show me that bullet hole in your ass?" he asked as he sniffed away the last of his tears.

"James! For the last time, if I hear any more cursing out of you, you'll be chewing on a bar of soap." Jilly's eyes snapped with temper.

Luke tried hard not to crack up. He swallowed the laughter that threatened to erupt from his chest. His lips still twitching, he forced himself to look out the window. The kid was funny as hell, yet still so innocent. And Jillian, with her very proper British accent sounded like she was ready to explode. Sweet Jesus… Just what kind of mess had he gotten himself into this time?

"You know, James, I'd listen to her if I were you. I've had the soap-in-the-mouth treatment." He slid his glance over to Jillian and found that her frown included him. "And it really suck— It's pretty bad," he quickly corrected as she rolled her eyes.

"I can see it worked like a bloody charm on you," she

muttered under her breath. "Every other word out of your mouth is foul."

"Trust me. You're not gonna like it," he finished, ignoring her. "Tell you what." He paused to see if Mary Poppins was listening. "I'll do it, too."

James's eyes got huge in the rearview mirror when Jillian burst out laughing. "You will? For real, Luke?"

"Yeah. If I say a bad word, then Jilly can wash my mouth out with soap, too. Is that a fair deal?"

"Do I still get to look at your a—your bullet hole?"

The kid had a one-track mind. "Yes, James. When we stop, I'll let you see the bullet hole, all right?"

"Actually, now that you mention it, I need to take a look, too. Your bandage probably needs to be changed."

Mary Poppins's words were spoken crisply and matter-of-factly but he could see the color rise in her cheeks. Little Miss Efficient. If it were possible, she was dreading the task even more than he was. "That's okay. I think I can handle it from here. You give me the stuff and I'll take care of it."

"How will you reach—"

"Jill, I said I'll handle it."

"Very well then." He nearly grinned when she nodded and abruptly turned to the window, suddenly fascinated by the endless miles of green pasture that blurred past the window.

They all felt considerably better after the rest stop. Samuel got to pee, Sarah got a fresh diaper and Jilly finally got her coffee, which she sipped gratefully, waiting for the caffeine to make its presence known. Even James had declared a truce with her, albeit a grudging one. She wondered how long it would take to break through his stony silence, how long before he trusted that she wouldn't leave them. Before he trusted anyone to stay.

Despite the considerable distance they'd covered, Agent Gianetti still appeared to be rather cautious. He'd insisted they get their breakfast to take away, choosing to head for a de-

serted park down the street from the fast-food place rather
than eat inside the restaurant. Inadvertently he'd scored high
points with James and Samuel who were thrilled to eat outside.

"Just because we're eating at a picnic table doesn't mean
you should chew with your mouth open, Samuel." Over the
past three days she'd begun the arduous task of instilling in
the children the most basic of table manners and the boys
hadn't been eager to embrace her instruction. Good Lord, if
Rosemary Moseby could see them now, she would surely die
of the shame.

"Jilly? Can we go play on the swings?"

"I'm sorry, did you ask that question with your mouth
full?" She hid her smile as she bent over Sarah on the blanket
she'd spread on the ground near the table. Even the little one
appeared thrilled to be out of her car seat.

James chewed vigorously, swallowing the lump of biscuit
in one gulp. "No, it's gone, see?" He opened his mouth wide
for her perusal and she shuddered visibly. Behind her, Luke
smothered a chuckle.

Rome wasn't built in a day, she reminded herself. At least
he'd asked her permission. She glanced at Luke for confirmation and he nodded. "Very well then, James. You may
take your brother over to the swingset for a little while."

"Just a couple minutes, okay, guys?"

"Uh-huh. Thanks, Luke."

"Take Samuel's hand so he doesn't fall," she reminded
James. He grabbed his brother's hand, nearly jerking him off
his feet, and launched across the field toward the swings.

"Did you make contact with your friend?" Her gaze still
on Sarah, who was kicking up a storm, she heard Luke slide
down the picnic table bench.

"Yeah, finally. Murphy—he's my partner—said we left behind a big mess. Two guys are dead and two more are in
custody. Said all hell—heck—broke out," he quickly corrected when she smiled. "Somehow a transformer blew and

the power grid went out for almost twenty blocks. That's why I couldn't reach anyone by phone.''

"How many bars of soap is that now?" She glanced up, shading her eyes to search the deserted playground for Samuel and James.

"I'm doing pretty well so far," he countered.

She shot him a reproving look. "It's only been two hours and you're on at least your third bar."

He grinned. "Like I said, I'm doing pretty well."

"What happens now? Are we free to leave? Can we continue north or must we go all the way back to South Carolina?" She picked up her coffee, took a sip and then carefully set it back on the table near the blanket. "Can we drop you off in Charlotte, like you said earlier?"

"For now it looks like Charlotte," he answered. "I'm not going back to Spartaville yet. At least not with the four of you in tow." Luke set his juice down on the edge of the picnic table and smiled over the hopeful tone of her voice. "Murphy's setting up a meeting with the SAC in Charlotte to take your statement."

"But I don't *have* a statement. I barely saw the man. I couldn't possibly recognize him."

"I know you're eager to hit the road." He hesitated, appearing to choose his words carefully. "I know this is inconvenient, but I still don't like it. Duncan, my boss, seems to think this thing is under control. But those guys this morning…" He shook his head. "There're too many missing pieces, if you ask me."

"What exactly *did* happen this morning? Are we still in danger?" It didn't feel as though they were. Yet when he'd burst through the motel room door this morning, she'd been terrified. His demeanor had been that of a warrior, the expression in his eyes deadly serious. And the intensity of his aura had been enough to make her skin prickle with fear.

"I don't know. That's why I'm being so cautious," he admitted. "Ever since the explosion yesterday, nothing has gone according to plan. Now someone's after us. Most likely it's Sloan or someone who works for him."

"Sloan is the drug dealer?" She picked up a rattle and gently shook it over Sarah's face.

"Yeah. He's pretty nasty on a good day, but he's unbelievable when his plans get fouled up. Right now, he's ticked at me."

"Because you were trying to arrest him?"

"Sloan is one of the biggest heroin dealers in the southeast. Yeah, I was trying to nail him. If I hook him then I can finally get a lead on the supplier. There's one guy—one freakin' guy running this ring and we can't figure out who he is. Goes by the name of Castillo. I don't know if it's really his name or if it's a place—nothing. Whoever he is, people sure as hell fear him."

"Well, did you get him—this Sloan person?"

"No. Murphy said we got a couple of his flunkies, but Sloan disappeared."

Luke was clearly displeased with the outcome of his mission thus far. "Once we drop you off in Charlotte, we should be safe enough, right? I mean, if he's after you…" She felt guilty even voicing the statement. Here he was, protecting them and all. But dammit, she hadn't asked for any of this.

"Maybe." To his credit, Luke didn't appear angered over her disloyalty.

"Then we can go?"

"We'll see." His noncommittal response sent angry heat to her cheeks.

"What does that mean? You can't hold us indefinitely."

"I cahn't?"

"Stop teasing," she ordered. "Why can't we leave?"

"Are you forgetting that you saw him, too? I can't be sure that he's only after me. If I let you leave, he could just as easily send someone after you."

"Well, if he's on the run like you say—"

"It doesn't mean a thing," he interrupted. "Last night two

men were ordered to take me out," he emphasized. Several seconds passed before he spoke again. "Those orders may have included you."

"But that means we're in danger whether we're with you or not."

The sun shone warm on the back of her neck, mocking the shiver that jolted up her spine. The sound of mingled laughter carried across the field from the swingset, blending with the birds chirping in the magnolia tree behind them. It felt completely safe.

Yet the blood on his hands had been incredibly real. The spatters on his shirt defied the illusion of safety. "Your shirt...I mean the, um, blood and everything. Those men— Did you...I mean, you didn't have to—"

Jillian glanced up, her expression clearly anxious. Christ, she was actually worried that he'd killed those scumbags. It was the typical bleeding-heart reaction Luke saw all too often and he could feel his blood pressure rising. Drugs and drug dealers were a plague that needed to be dealt with harshly. Drug abuse was not a feel-good social cause. Period. Luke mused that Jillian was probably one of those types who thought addicts should be coddled rather than tossed into jail. Her Ladyship didn't want to believe those guys would've killed her in a heartbeat. She didn't seem to appreciate the fact that he'd probably saved her royal ass.

"You weren't hurt again, were you?"

Hold everything. She was worried...for him? "Nah, I'm fine. And I didn't have to—you know, kill anyone." He paused then and frowned. He shouldn't be telling this woman anything. He had a job to do, no matter what it took to accomplish it. Why was he wasting time trying to reassure her?

"But the blood on your—"

"I just had to disable them. There's a big difference." It probably wasn't a good time to tell her about the desk clerk's fate. Or how close they'd come to meeting the same end. He glanced down at the front of his shirt, noticing the faint spatters of blood for the first time. "Is it really noticeable from where you're sitting?"

She squinted up at him, shading her eyes from the sun that rose behind him. Luke's nerve endings felt her perusal all the way to the top of his head and he mentally cursed himself for being so stupid. Hands down, when this op was over, he was gonna find himself a woman. The dry spell had obviously gone on for much too long.

"No," she said finally. "It's sort of faded and brown. Looks more like you spilled something all over you." Her expression changed to doubt as she wrinkled up her nose. "I have an old shirt that might fit you. My suitcase is in the boot. Before we start up again, I'll look for it."

"I can't imagine you'd have anything that would fit me." Not with that body. She was built like a dream. He stood and stretched his legs, dispelling his fantasy and draining the last of his juice before he tossed the cup in the trash can.

"I've got a few of Ian's old shirts. They might work." Jilly picked up a plastic key ring and shook it as Sarah cooed.

His interest perked up another notch. "Who's Ian?"

She sighed and he noticed that she seemed to want to look everywhere except at him, instead choosing to scan the playground for the boys. "Oh, that's a long story. He's an old friend."

Luke sat gingerly on the end of the picnic table and forced himself to drop it. This girl was none of his business. He didn't want to know anything about her or the kids. Only what he needed to keep them alive. In the grand scheme of things, it didn't matter how many damn boyfriends she'd had. It didn't matter one freakin' bit.

After tonight, Jillian would spend a day or so in Charlotte for debriefing. Then they'd head north to resume life in what was probably a quaint little New Hampshire town. And he'd never see any of them again. The days they'd spent with him would fade in their memories until it became just another funny story of Jilly's adventures.

But just because they were safe for the moment, didn't mean he could afford to let down his guard. He needed to stay focused. Nothing about this op had been routine. Even Murphy had been reluctant to start the final reports on the failed mission. Something wasn't right. He just didn't know what. But his gut still strummed on red alert, telling him to keep them out of sight. He'd never ignored his gut before. He sure as hell wasn't about to start now.

Annoyed with himself, he readjusted his position on the end of the table. Despite the gauze padding and the glow-in-the-dark Band-Aids, his butt was still pretty sore. What he really needed was underwear. When James had discovered in the men's room that Luke wasn't wearing any briefs, he'd wanted to rid himself of his Spider-Man underpants. And Samuel would've followed right along. A trio of men going commando. Now wouldn't Her Ladyship have appreciated that?

She glanced over just in time to see him wince. "What is it? Is your wound hurting? I knew you should've let me clean it."

"What is it with this fascination for my butt? You took one look at it and now that's all you can think about," he said, forgetting that he was trying to maintain a professional distance. Something about that British accent made him want to prod her. So cool on the outside…so prim and proper. But just under the surface—lava, baby.

She pressed her lips together and frowned. "Yes…well, as fascinating as I found your backside, it simply didn't stop traffic for me—if you know what I mean." She finally turned to stare at him. "I realize it's probably not possible, but if you could be serious for a single moment…"

"Sure. Try me."

"I'm trying to determine whether or not you're in pain. I have more of those pills."

"The chick stuff?" He shook his head. "You know, all of a sudden, my cramps are much better." Her Ladyship had a damn fine temper, he noted. He couldn't tell whether she wanted to laugh or haul off and smack him.

"Is your injury hurting worse?"

"Oh, that." He waved away her concern. "Nah, it's fine. Just a little sore, that's all. It's draining okay and I cleaned it with the stuff you gave me. Stop worrying about it."

"It sounds like you've had some experience. Have you been shot before?"

He limped over to the blanket and gingerly sat down, and before he realized it, he'd reached out a finger and was tickling Sarah's belly. "Only a few times."

Her eyes were incredulous. "*Only* a few? Good Lord. What does your wife think about your line of work?"

He smiled at the now chortling Sarah. "Not very much. She, uh, left me four years ago."

Jilly tsked under her breath. "I'm sorry about that. Were you married long? You don't look very old."

"Six years. We met in college." He glanced up, reading the sympathy in her eyes. She really was way too soft.

"And how long have you been doing this drug thing— chasing dangerous criminals?"

"This thing I've been doing is called drug enforcement and I've been doing it for ten years, since I graduated from college." He knelt down on the blanket and made a face at Sarah and was rewarded with a smile.

"Well, you must be pretty good at it," she answered as she tucked a strand of hair back into her ponytail. "Or I guess you would've gotten yourself killed by now."

Luke did a double take and then realized she wasn't being sarcastic, only direct. "Yeah, I guess you could say that. What about you?" he challenged. "Ever been married?"

She made a face as though she'd just sipped bitter lemonade and wanted to spit it out. "No, thank goodness. I almost did, though. What a mistake that would've been." She shook her head ruefully. "How's that for absurd? I'm twenty-seven years old and I still have trouble saying no. My mum nearly had me talked into marrying the man *she* wanted. In her eyes, he was bloody perfect.''

He smiled over her disgruntled expression. It wasn't hard to believe at all. Jillian struck him as the kind of girl who leaped first and then thought about looking when it was too late. "So, what stopped you?"

The gray-blue eyes grew very wide, almost startled. "Why, the children, of course. I mean, I was going to break it off anyway. We were so completely different," she added absently. "But then I got the call about my sister."

Her voice catching, he watched her eyes grow suspiciously misty. Warning bells jangled in his gut. Somehow he'd managed to push the wrong conversational button. She rubbed her arms, as though she'd suddenly realized she was cold.

"She...passed away two weeks ago," she said, her voice starting to break. "I only learned of it, um, a week ago, Tuesday."

Ten days ago. And she'd already been here a week. Luke rocked back on his heels, stunned by the enormity of what she'd been through, surprised by the courage it must have taken to hop on a plane and fly halfway around the world to tend to her sister's children. He watched as she took a deep breath and forced back the tears that threatened to spill over. Watched in amazement when she regained control almost instantly.

Jillian hadn't just learned that trick on the transatlantic flight. He recognized a control freak when he saw one—he'd had the misfortune of living with one—and realized that his initial impression of her was probably wrong. Despite her flighty exterior, Mary Poppins was very tightly wrapped.

"How come you're here alone? Isn't there anyone who could help you?"

"My mum—she's...busy with things back home." Jilly averted her eyes and he knew instinctively that it was with shame. His thoughts drifted to his own family. For the most part, the Gianettis were a traditional Italian-American family, but due to the sheer volume of them, there was definitely a strong dysfunctional element. Yet he couldn't help wondering what the hell had gone down in the white-picket-fence Moseby house. Judging by the way her eyes were swimming, this was definitely the wrong time to ask.

"So what happened with the guy? The one your mother picked out for you."

"Oh, Ian didn't want— He thought three chil—" Jilly clamped her mouth shut and suddenly stood, her movements jerky. "We broke up."

This was getting interesting. He settled himself more comfortably on the blanket. So Ian was an ex-fiancé…not simply the old friend she'd claimed.

"Uh, could you watch Sarah for a minute? I really should fetch the boys back over here."

"Sure. Tell 'em they've got five more minutes." He watched her walk away while his brain automatically began processing what he'd just learned. His mind filtered everything as though it were a giant puzzle, the unfortunate by-product of too many years as an operative. He couldn't shut it off, so he'd learned to use it to his benefit. Once a puzzle piece fell into place, everything else became sharper, more focused.

For some strange reason, Jilly's mother hadn't thought her dead daughter worth the effort of an overseas trip. Nor, apparently, her three grandchildren. And loverboy Ian didn't want to be saddled with someone else's kids. Luke was willing to bet they'd both applied pressure on Jilly, tried to convince her to stay home. And she'd still chosen to go it alone. With that piece of information, he added "stubborn" to the mental column marked Jillian.

He checked his cell phone for the millionth time, grateful the damn thing was finally working. His fingers itched to call his partner. He wondered if Murphy had come up with any new information to fill in some of the holes in the investigation. Anything that would take the edge off his jumpy stomach.

According to Murphy, the junkie grapevine was abuzz with news. Notorious for both good information and bad, the top story today was about Billy T. Lathrop. Word on the street had him on the run with a price on his head, a damn high price, now that he thought about it, and that he was as good as dead.

Sarah chose that moment to grin up at him, cooing as she reached for his finger. The tiny little tug on his finger caused an even stronger tug in his chest, in the vicinity where his heart had once resided. He would've sworn on a stack of bibles that Sarah was looking straight into his eyes when she smiled. He jerked back in reaction.

The sooner he got back to the streets, the better. He'd dealt his hand in life. And he meant to play it out until the end. The faces on his cards were pushers and pimps, not angelic children, not beautiful women who would need him too much.

Dammit to hell! He didn't want to be interested—in any of them.

But there were still too many unanswered questions. Like why Sloan had seemed to know the bust was coming? Or, where the hell the backup team had been when the building had blown to smithereens? As he replayed the takedown in his mind, he fingered the slug in his shirt pocket, a growing sense of uneasiness trickling through his brain.

Who the hell had shot him?

Chapter 4

"Are you boys nearly ready? Luke says we're leaving in five minutes."

Jillian strode over to the swingset and flopped down in the empty swing near Samuel. Dear Lord, she must be crazy. Why had she prattled on about her life to Luke? His questions were deceptively simple and before she knew it, she was talking too much. It was painful enough to realize—to finally admit—that her mum didn't give a damn about Annie. That Rosemary Moseby had considered her eldest daughter dead years earlier when she'd had the cheek to leave them all behind for the wilds of America.

"She must've written me off now, as well," she muttered to herself as she pushed off the ground and pumped her legs. James hopped on the other swing and immediately followed suit while Samuel followed their progress with his eyes.

Her mother had all but demanded that she remain in England…that heading to America would be to her peril. That Jillian would be "on her own." That Rosemary would not come traipsing across the ocean to look for her.

"Thank God for that." Jillian smiled sadly and shook her head, letting the breeze catch her hair as the swing climbed higher. It was about time. Anyone would've thought that she was still a child. The parental noose had only cinched tighter after Annie'd made her escape all those years ago. Jilly had been thirteen...but thanks to Annie's stunt, she'd been relegated to the status of an eight-year-old—and a juvenile delinquent one at that, kept on a tight leash and under constant surveillance.

"Jilly, look at me!"

She shook off the memory as she turned toward James. Her eyes widened in shock when she realized how high he was climbing. "James, slow down," she cried.

Lord, he was so high, he was going to flip off the bloody swing. Jilly immediately quit pumping her legs, trying to slow down enough to jump off. The wind whistled in her ears as her hair blew in her face.

"I'm higher than you are. I'm higher than you are."

"Honey, stop. You're going to fall." She was too afraid to wait any longer. Without thinking, she threw herself from the swing, surprised at how long she was airborne before she crashed to the ground in a heap. She ignored the wrenching pain in her shoulder and staggered to her feet, not bothering to brush off the mulch. When she hobbled back toward his swing, she noticed for the first time that Samuel was staring at her, his mouth dropped open.

"What in the sweet hell did you think you were doing?"

Luke jogged over to her side with Sarah perched in his arm like a sack of groceries. The baby was laughing and waving her arms in the air. He'd clearly run across the park, yet he wasn't the least bit out of breath. She hadn't run anywhere and she was gasping for air as though someone had held her head under water.

"Are you blind? Look at James. He's going to fly off that thing and break a leg." She shaded her eyes to watch James as he slowed down before calmly jumping from the swing. He landed in one piece on the ground in front of them.

"The only one at risk for a broken leg was you," Luke answered. "And from the look of your swan dive, you're lucky it wasn't your neck. Don't you know you're supposed to slow down before you jump off a swing?"

"I bloody well know how to swing, dammit." She swung on Luke, prepared to project all of her fear for James onto him. "Didn't you see him?"

James snickered and winked at Samuel. "Gee, Luke, we shoulda had Jilly in on our bet. She just said da—"

"I know what I said, young man. That's about enough out of you." She wheeled around to face him. "In the future, I would appreciate it if you could try not to scare the life out of me."

James scowled at her angry words. "Well, if you're scared by something that stupid then I'll never be able to do any—"

Luke moved so quickly that she never even saw the motion. He stepped behind James and clapped his free hand over the little boy's mouth.

"He's very sorry. He won't do it again." Luke tilted James's head up to look at him. "Right?"

Even from where she stood, she could see James grinning behind his large hand. And when Luke nodded James's head up and down for him, she heard him laugh with glee. The little bugger wasn't the least bit upset. In fact, he was rather enjoying the fireworks. Sarah was all but hurtling herself into Luke, trying to get him to jostle her as he had when they'd run.

Releasing James's mouth, he strode across the mulch to where Samuel sat mesmerized on the swing and lifted him into his free arm.

"Come on, little guy. Time to hit the trail." Much to Samuel's delight, Luke swung him in a wide circle before setting him on his feet again. He watched them scramble across the grass before turning back to face her.

She rolled her eyes heavenward. He'd been with the kids for twenty-four hours and he'd won them over completely. She'd been with them for a week and she still felt utterly inadequate.

"You okay? You're limping." His expression was carefully neutral, but she knew he wanted to laugh. The man was bloody impossible.

"I'm perfectly well, thank you." She hobbled toward him, edging closer, not stopping until she could see the beautiful flecks of gold that ringed his curious eyes. She froze when he leaned over and plucked a twig from her hair.

"You sure? You sorta went ass over teakettle off that swing." His smile indicated that he knew he was annoying her. And he didn't give a damn.

Well, two could play at this game. She wet her lips with her tongue and saw that his gaze followed the action. Then she reached up and threaded her fingers into his long, golden hair and tugged his head down to hers. She leaned in closer still and watched his eyes widen in surprise, heard the subtle acceleration to his breathing.

"Jillian, what are you...the kids..."

She kept her face expressionless, even when she felt his lean body go rigid with stunned anticipation. Then she deliberately brushed against him, lifting on her toes so her mouth was a whisper away from his ear.

"That 'ass over teakettle' remark just earned you another bar of soap, Agent Gianetti." She released him and took a step back before turning on her heel and marching away.

"Is this really necessary? I think I can probably get away with the shirt I'm wearing."

Jillian sensed Luke's impatience as she dug through the suitcases in the trunk.

"I'll just turn it inside out," he suggested hopefully.

"You can't wear a shirt inside-out. It'll look peculiar." She heard his sigh of exasperation. "Who the hell is going to notice?"

Her muffled voice surfaced from the depths of the trunk. "I know I've got one here, somewhere." She wrestled the faded gray shirt from the bag and zipped the case closed. She turned to find him scrutinizing her, clearly biting back the comment he wished to make. "Here. Try this on."

Giving up, he yanked the shirt he'd been wearing over his head. Balling it up, he threw it on top of the luggage before accepting the one she held. "So...if you dumped Ian, why do you still have his shirts?"

Why indeed? Nothing she'd ever given him had been good enough. If it hadn't been custom-tailored on Savile Row, Lord Ian wasn't interested. She should have returned the damned shirts and donated the money to charity—the Fund for the Hopelessly Priggish. Instead she'd persisted, buying him clothes that became increasingly outrageous, knowing all the while that he would continue to refuse them, but also secretly hoping he would be appalled with her, as well. And it had worked like a charm. Ian's complaints had been predictable. How could she act so commonly? How could she turn her back on her breeding?

"They're not his shirts," she corrected. "They're mine. They were gifts I selected that weren't quite posh enough." She raised defiant eyes to meet his gaze. "But I liked them, so I kept them. Is there a problem?"

Luke's eyebrows raised in question. "Nope. No, ma'am. No problem whatsoever."

"Good." It had grown to the point that she'd looked forward to disappointing Ian. She'd known virtually from the start of their relationship that Ian Dunstable was not the sort of man she wished to marry. Lord, the very thought gave her the shudders. Why, she'd have morphed into a stilted British housewife in no time at all, expected to lunch at the bloody club with Rosemary twice a week.

Ian hadn't seemed to notice he was exceedingly dull and

that she was exceedingly bored. She'd begun to wonder just what it would take for him to realize they had absolutely nothing in common. After six agonizing months in his company, she'd finally accepted that, clearly, Ian would never reach that conclusion. Because in his mind—and her meddling mother's—compatibility and marriage did not necessarily have to coexist.

Luke glanced at the U.K. soccer logo, shrugged and pulled it on over his head. "It fits pretty decent." He stretched his arms to loosen it up. "Thanks."

"You're very welcome." At least someone appreciated her efforts.

"Now can we finally get going?"

She closed the trunk and saluted. "Yes, sir."

Luke waited, damn patiently he thought, while she gathered the kids up and got them strapped into their car seats. He wanted to hit the road. His gut was edgy to move and, frankly, the sooner they reached Charlotte, the better. Jillian was too damn appealing. He'd be grateful for some distance. With those big expressive eyes, he didn't have to be a genius to know what she was feeling. He smiled then. Hell, she pretty much told you. There wasn't much guessing involved.

Ian had to be the biggest idiot in all of England. How much would it have hurt to wear the damn stuff she bought? He couldn't remember the last time Linda'd bought him anything. In the old days she'd gone shopping all the time. But if he'd made the mistake of asking her to pick up some underwear for him, all hell had broken loose. That error in judgment had triggered one of the many "I'm not your servant" lectures.

Here was a female who actually wanted to buy stuff for her boyfriend. And Sir Wimp was too stupid to appreciate it. Why the hell would a guy risk pissing off his girlfriend? Over clothes? Get real. A free shirt was a free shirt. As long as it wasn't pink, who gave a rat's ass what it looked like? His cell phone rang and he pulled it from his belt to check the number. Murphy again.

"Murph? What've you got?" The warm feeling lasted only seconds, his smile fading the moment his brain processed his partner's words. "Are you sure about that?"

His heart pumping with certainty, he didn't wait for the answer Murphy couldn't yet provide. "We're leaving now. Once you've got it set up, call me later with the directions." His stomach lurched to DEFCON 2.

Jillian rounded the car, a question in her eyes. "What is it?"

"It's time to go."

She glanced up, wary. "What's wrong?"

How would he explain it to her? That Murphy's sixth sense was telling him they were in danger? That one of his informants had just confided that the word on the street was they'd been burned? None of that helped much until he knew who'd sold them out. A million questions sizzled through his brain. Who'd blown their cover? And why? Until they learned the answer to those questions, the only safe thing to do was to keep moving.

"We need to hit the road," he explained. "Just as a precaution, Murphy's arranged a safe house for us to stay in tonight. Then, tomorrow we'll meet with the Agent in Charge in Charlotte. I told Murphy we'd be there this afternoon."

"Why do we need a safe house? Is this a normal procedure?"

He mentally crossed his fingers. "Just a precaution. We're all witnesses and until we get everyone in custody, or at least until we get you debriefed, the agency doesn't want to take any chances."

"What else?" Her eyes narrowed with suspicion. "Is there something you're not telling me? Because I don't like not knowing what's going on."

"Nothing. Just a feeling." How could he tell her when he didn't know himself? He was beginning to suspect that Mary Poppins had quite a temper when she got riled. If she decided to storm off on her own, he'd be hard-pressed to stop her without any cuffs. And that wouldn't go over very well with the kids—or the agency. And he sure as hell didn't have time to go chasing after her if she left. Damn, the mess would just get deeper.

Murphy was calling in favors left and right. If his suspicions were right and they'd been burned, then he and Murph would have to develop a plan to deal with it. But operating blind was not his specialty. In fact, he sucked at it. He hated surprises. He'd built his entire career around not being blindsided. He was used to planning every step of the op…running through all the ways their cover might be blown and then mentally prepping a solution for each scenario.

"Something *is* wrong. I knew it!"

He winced when her voice shrilled up an octave and then glanced over his shoulder into the car. The kids were strapped in, waiting to go. James gave him a questioning look. "The kids are watching," he reminded her.

"We're in danger, aren't we?" She brought a hand up to her forehead. "I've already been through one bloody custody battle, and it's only been a week. If these children get hurt—" Her eyes lasered in on him. "I'm already an unfit mother and I've just barely gotten started."

A meltdown was the last thing he needed right now. "For Pete's sake, you're not an unfit mother. You're relocating, that's all."

"That's easy for you to say."

"They're not living in this car," he reminded. "It's just a road trip."

Her eyes narrowed as she advanced on him and his gut tightened with warning. What now? "Can we please discuss this in the car?"

Her reaction only confirmed his decision to wait. He couldn't react when he didn't know what was going on and he sure as hell didn't want her going off the deep end. Jillian could wait, he decided, until Murphy had more details. "As soon as I know something, you'll know something. There's no need to panic." Yet.

She'd begun wringing her hands as their conversation deteriorated. He grabbed them to calm her down. She had the same expression on her face she'd had the previous evening when he'd convinced her to remove a bullet from his ass. "Jill—I promise I'll protect you. There's no need to panic. If I sense any danger, I'll be the first one to get you out of the way. The last thing I want is for any of you to get hurt."

She took a deep breath and released it slowly. "All right. I—I won't panic. But you have to promise me that you'll keep me informed of what the hell is going on."

"I will." He relaxed a notch. Crisis averted. Then she surprised him, anger flaring in the smoky depths of her eyes.

"I don't like secrets," she blurted out. "I'm not made of bloody glass. I'm so tired of everyone always thinking they need to protect me. I—I can handle bad news, dammit."

The frustrated words hung in the air between them and he wondered again what her life had been like. Smothering. Overprotected. And he wondered why. "Uh, right. I never thought you couldn't handle it." Dismay trailed across her features and he was left with the distinct impression she regretted her outburst.

"All right, then. Just as long as we've got that settled." She tugged her hands free of his and jerked open the car door. "Let's go."

"So, how far is it to Charlotte?" Jilly finally broke the silence in the station wagon. Sarah and Samuel had gone back to sleep and James had slipped his headphones on, his head bobbing back and forth to the music.

"Couple or three hours, give or take a little." Luke yawned and stretched back in the seat. She watched him roll his shoulders in an attempt to stay limber. Along with his magnificently shaped butt, the rest of him appeared to be in equally prime physical condition.

"Would you like me to drive a while? I just realized that you've been at the wheel since yesterday."

He gave her a slow appraising look. She noticed he'd been wary of her since her stunt in the park. She knew she'd been playing with fire by flirting with him. But something about him seemed to push her buttons. He'd stared at her with a combination of disbelief and perhaps just a little frustration before giving in to the humor that never seemed to be far from the surface. And his long, slow smile had made her stomach tingle with a sudden awareness that hadn't been there before.

"I guess that would be okay." He glanced at the mile marker on the nearly deserted road and slowed down considerably before moving to the shoulder. "Actually, I wouldn't mind riding shotgun for a little while. Things seem pretty quiet. Maybe I could catch a quick nap. I'm probably gonna want to stay up tonight."

"I can't imagine anything's going to happen now," she said hopefully.

"Yeah, it's been three whole hours since those guys tried to take us out."

Ignoring his sarcasm, she tried again. "Still, I'd feel better if I didn't think you had been stuck with all the driving." She waited for him to stop completely before she unlocked her door and slid out.

"You sure you feel all right? You landed pretty hard back there."

She glanced at him and was surprised to find that he genuinely appeared to be serious. "No, I'm fine. Just a little sore, actually. It's really only my pride that got bruised."

"Hey, you were trying to do the right thing. It's good that you're protective of them."

"Yes, well, they haven't had a lot of that, I'm afraid." She adjusted the mirrors and fastened her seat belt before she glanced over at him.

"I take it they had a pretty tough life with your sister?"

Luke glanced over his shoulder to confirm that James was still listening to music. Then he settled back in the seat and carefully adjusted the side mirror.

"Yes." She swallowed hard. "Annie, my sister, had a substance abuse problem."

"Drugs or alcohol?"

She glanced over at him and then guiltily forced her gaze back to the road. "Both actually. For a long time. But it was the drugs that finally killed her." She took a deep breath and let it out. Still not quite sure she wouldn't cry, she bit down on her lip. Luke waited patiently for her to continue. "She left home when she turned eighteen. Came over here." She shook her head. "I don't even know how she managed to secure passage. I was only thirteen."

"That must've been tough," he murmured.

She nodded, not taking her gaze from the road. "My mum...she sort of...gave up on her. I—I didn't. I guess I was too young to know how serious the problem was." She checked her speed and slowed down a little. "I came over here a few years ago when Samuel was born. I wanted to give Annie a hand, you know? Help her with James and the baby."

She blinked back the tears, determined not to fall apart in front of this enigmatic stranger. "I was finally old enough to do something. I was working. I had money. I was twenty-four and I guess I thought I could fix everything. Bring the whole family back together."

Luke's lips tightened and he turned to stare at her. She sensed that he already knew it would end badly. "Of course that didn't happen. She was much worse by that time. Far worse than she'd been with James—"

"Where's the kids' father during all of this?"

She felt the blush creep up her cheekbones and she resolutely kept her eyes on the road. "They, um, Annie...sort of...had trouble settling down with one man." Her gaze drifted to the rearview mirror where she checked on James again. She lowered her voice just the same. "Each of the kids has a different father. None of them ever stayed around long enough to meet their children.''

''That's not uncommon, you know.''

The intensity of his gaze sent awareness crawling through her system. Her pulse quickened and she swallowed hard around the sudden urge to flee. Something told her to keep her eyes on the road. Even a glimmer of compassion from Luke would have her weeping.

''Junkies throw everything away, eventually. Their morality goes first, followed by their sense of protection for themselves and even their kids. Then their pride. Soon, nothing matters except the next fix.''

She risked a sideways glance and was shocked to see the grim expression in his eyes. ''I realize that now. Annie was so far gone when I was here last.'' She shuddered as she remembered the squalor she'd found her sister living in. ''But she still had pride. She wouldn't let me help…wouldn't let me help James and the baby.''

She startled when Luke gave her arm a little squeeze. ''I— I couldn't believe what she'd become. Yet, she still fought me.''

''What happened?''

She winced. ''She disappeared. With James and Samuel. She refused to let me stay with her. And when I came back the next day with food and supplies, she'd taken off.'' She reached up to wipe her eyes. ''I stayed for a week—came back each day—and she still wouldn't come home. I knew she was somewhere close by.'' She shook her head derisively. ''She was probably watching me.''

''Hey, you still okay to drive?''

Luke's whispered voice reached out to caress her. She heard the concern, heard just a glimmer of caring, of compassion, for what she'd experienced. ''I—I'm fine. Really. You must see this sort of thing every day.''

''Unfortunately, I see it everywhere. Most people have the illusion that drugs are a problem of poverty, a lower-class issue that doesn't apply to them. They think that way until they find it right under their own noses. Drugs aren't selective in who they destroy."

He shifted again in his seat, favoring his left side, she noticed.

"Hell, in some of the jungles I've been sent to, the drug runners are treated like gods. They're the saviors who rescue the local farmers from a life of poverty."

"My mum...I guess she could see that. Annie gave her so much trouble before she finally left...got kicked out of schools all over England. I guess I wasn't really aware of how bad the situation was."

"How could you? You were just a kid."

"I always thought Mum was too harsh about the whole thing," she admitted. "I wanted her to fly to America and bring Annie back. But she never—"

"You can't rationalize the problem, Jilly. Once drugs take over, nothing else matters. Nothing. Not even family." He turned in the passenger seat to smile at James who stopped bopping long enough to wave at him. "I bet you felt differently about her when you visited a few years ago, right?"

She nodded reluctantly. "I was angry...and frustrated. Here I'd spent all that money to come over and then she took off on me. It was as though she'd become a complete stranger."

"What you're doing now for these kids is incredible. You can't change the past, but you can help direct the future. Be thankful they're young enough to forget where they've been." Luke yawned and closed his eyes as he settled back in his seat.

"Luke?" She glanced over and was surprised at how much younger he looked when he relaxed.

"Mmm?"

"Thanks for listening. I appreciate it."

"Stay on this road. Watch for signs that say Charlotte." He folded his arms across his chest and sank deeper into the seat. "Shouldn't be more 'n a couple hours or so. And don't let me sleep too long."

Well, they'd bloody well gone more than two hours. And no Charlotte. Jillian bit her lip in frustration and glanced over at Luke. He was still sound asleep, sprawled out in the seat next to her. And it had been nearly three hours.

She'd seen signs for the damn place hours ago. And she'd kept going and going and…nothing. It was as though the city didn't exist. They were still on the endlessly boring backroad they'd been on all day. Were there any towns in this blasted state?

"Luke?"

She rolled her shoulders and winced at the stiffness in her neck. How the heck would she ever drive all the way to New Hampshire? Already she was nearly crippled and they were probably a million miles from their final destination. Perhaps she'd settle somewhere else…somewhere closer. She could simply call Dartmouth and inform them that she'd had a change of plans. Either that, or maybe she'd fly the children the rest of the way. Her savings would take a bashing, but it would bloody well be worth it.

She'd have to wake Luke. They were nearly out of gas and she had to pee again. James had fallen asleep out of sheer boredom, but Samuel was awake and making noises about being hungry again. Her stomach tightened a notch when she heard Sarah start to softly fuss. Lord, there wasn't much time before that noise became a full-blown wail.

"Luke, wake up." She reached out to shake him and he came awake with a start, bolting up in his seat.

"What? Where are we?"

"Good question. I'm beginning to think Charlotte doesn't exist."

Luke sat up straighter and glanced at his watch. "Where the hell are we? Why'd you let me sleep so long?"

Her eyes narrowed with frustration and the pressure of her

nearly full bladder. "Look, don't start lecturing me. I stayed on this road just like you instructed. It simply has to be the wrong one because Charlotte never materialized."

Luke didn't take the bait, his gaze now fully concentrated on the road signs. "Pull over at that gas station up there."

She was only too happy to comply. Thankfully, the place looked civilized. She'd be able to pick up some groceries to restock the cooler. Maybe Luke would let the kids run around for a while. She pulled up to the pumps and hustled to the loo while he took care of the fuel.

"So, where are we?" she asked as she recrossed the parking lot. Luke had already gotten the kids out to run around in the grass behind the gas station. He balanced Sarah in one arm as he rummaged in the cooler for a bottle. If he hadn't been looking at her as though he wanted to strangle her, Jillian would have smiled. Luscious Luke, the big, bad drug agent looked like the poster model for bloody Father of the Year.

"Jilly, we were on the right road when I went to sleep." His arm surfaced from the cooler with a dripping bottle and Sarah's legs started kicking in anticipation.

"And?" She calmly took the baby from his arms and laid her in the grass to change her nappie.

"And now we're not. We're so far off course it's not even funny. What the hell were you doing? Were you paying attention?" He rolled his eyes in exasperation. "Didn't you notice the scenery changing, the mountains popping up all around you?"

She gasped at his insult. "I'm not the one who had to have a nap. I don't even bloody well live here. We're out in the back of beyond, and I'm supposed to know we're going the wrong way?"

Luke thrust the map in her face and jabbed at a spot in the northwest corner of North Carolina. "Do you see this? That's where we are."

"So what?" She felt her spine stiffen with anger as she watched his finger drag halfway across the map.

"And this is where we were supposed to end up…way over here."

"Fine. I made a mistake. My sense of direction isn't perfect."

"Your sense of direction sucks."

Her hand clenched into a fist at her side. "Very well, then. I suppose this means you'll have to shoot me?"

"Very funny. Do you know how many phone calls it'll take to reschedule all this?"

She studiously ignored him as she finished taping Sarah's nappie. But that didn't stop Luke from lecturing. She continued to freeze him out as she wrapped the soiled one for the trash.

"Do you have any idea how much trouble your mistake is gonna cause me?"

How much trouble it would cause *him?* That did it. She rose to her feet, nearly knocking Luke over in her haste. "How much trouble? Let me see… Probably about as much trouble as it was for me when you jumped in my bloody car in the first place."

"Oh, sure, bring that up." His eyes unsure, he took a step back, clearly preparing for the worst.

"Probably about as much trouble as it's been for me to be on the lam with you ever since."

"On the lam?" He shook his head derisively. "You've seen too many movies."

After everything else, now he was laughing at her. She advanced on him as pure frustration surged through her veins. "I can assure you that I've never been chased by thugs before. I've never had government agencies pursuing me—" Well, that one wasn't quite true. Those damn security agents had made her life hell. But Luke didn't need to know that. "Why, I've never been in a spot of trouble until I met you."

He snorted at that. "Trust me, sweetheart. You are nothin' but trouble." He tugged one hand through his hair in an obvious effort to calm himself down. But all he succeeded in doing was make the top stand up at attention. "This is gonna be a big pain in the ass to fix."

Hands on her hips, she slowly advanced on him. "Big deal. So you're stuck with us for another night."

"Not if we hit the road—" His eyes lit up at the possibility.

"Oh, no. Not a chance." She shook her head adamantly. "I'm not getting back in that blasted car again. I can't take any more driving. My neck is killing me. I'm tired—"

"We'd only have to backtrack two hours."

"I don't give a flip. The kids need a rest and so do I." Anger spurted through her as he rolled his eyes in exasperation. "We've been living in that bloody car for two days now."

"Look, Jilly. Let's be reasonable about this. We hop in the car, we're there in, like, three hours." He waved his arms for emphasis, probably in the hope that she would see just how inconsiderate she was being.

"Why don't you just leave us here? You can go to Charlotte and fix everything."

"Dammit, Jill. You know I can't do that. Whether you like it or not, we're together for the duration."

"Well then, tough. You can take us to this blasted safe house place tomorrow."

Luke jerked his head around. "Shh. Keep your voice down, for God's sake. We're makin' enough of a scene as it is."

She stood her ground. "I want a hotel. I want take-away food and air-conditioning and I want to sleep for more than two hours straight. Maybe a place with a pool so the boys can go swimming."

"This isn't a freakin' vacation. We have to stay out of sight." He looked like he wanted to pull his hair out. Either that, or he was contemplating gagging her and throwing her in the boot of the car.

"Then find us a place where they can play." The fight went out of her as she realized the futility of her request. She turned away, absently rubbing the back of her stiff neck as she walked back to flop in the grass with Sarah. She pulled her knees up and laid her head on her folded arms.

Lord, she was tired. She felt completely hollow inside. Too much had happened. In the past ten days her cushiony, sheltered world had exploded. And she was kidding herself to think that this nightmare was going to end anytime soon. What had she been thinking? She'd left her home, her family, her country, for God's sake. And in a matter of days, she'd become a fugitive on the run from drug dealers and killers. What a fine mother she was turning out to be.

"Jilly?"

"Forget it, all right? I'm sorry I bodged it up and got us lost." She closed her eyes and took a deep breath. "Let's pack up and get this over with. Tie me up, throw me in the boot. I don't care anymore what you do with us." Her voice was tight with the strain of not screaming…of not melting down. She wanted badly to do it—to break down sobbing and never stop—to throw herself in Luke's arms and pretend she was someone else, someone fun and interesting. What had started out as an adventure had turned into an odyssey through hell.

She startled at the feel of his warm hands at the base of her neck. Luke moved so silently all the time, it seemed as though he floated on the air above the ground. His fingers were gentle but firm as he massaged the knots of tension from her shoulders.

"You didn't bodge it up, whatever the hell that means." He sighed as his hands continued to work her muscles. "Look, we'll…we'll do it your way. I'll talk to Murphy. He'll call the SAC in Charlotte and fix it for tomorrow. I'll tell him we've run into a snag and can't make it tonight. I guess one more day won't kill us."

"Can't I just run away from you? We'll pretend that you lost us. That way, it's not your fault." She heard him chuckle as she groaned out the question. Dear Lord, he had the most incredible hands. They were large and calloused. Tough, work-hardened hands that felt absolutely delightful at the back of her neck. She couldn't help wondering what they would feel like on the rest of her. She shivered with sudden awareness and tried to cover the reaction with a fit of coughing.

How humiliating. If he kept stroking her like that, she would simply dissolve into a puddle at his feet. That, or she'd end up stripping him out of his clothes and taking him right there in the parking lot.

"You don't think I'd get in trouble for losing four people?"

"I'll tell them it's my fault," she insisted.

"Besides that," he continued as though she hadn't spoken, "you're in protective custody. You don't have the option to leave," he explained.

"Really. And just what would happen if I tried?"

"Then I'd have to shoot you."

"Lord, that feels good. You'd better stop before I embarrass myself." His hands paused for a fraction of a second and Jillian cursed herself. Bloody hell, he didn't need to know that. She felt the color rise in her cheeks and made sure to keep her gaze on the baby when Luke slowly removed his hands from her shoulders. Sarah had flipped over onto her hands and knees and was grunting with the effort to push herself through the grass.

"Is your neck better?"

"Much better, thank you." She averted her eyes when his gaze lingered. His smug expression told her he was clearly aware of her growing interest in him. Damn him. Apparently when it came to matters of sex, Agent Heartthrob didn't miss a bloody trick.

Chapter 5

"Okay, here's what we're gonna do." Luke cut the engine and turned to face her. "You go inside and get us a room for tonight. Better yet, get us a suite. We need a little space. How much cash are you carrying?"

Jillian wrinkled up her nose and hesitated a moment. "Quite a lot actually, what with rental deposits and such."

"Pounds or dollars?"

"No, it's all American. I converted it at the airport."

He let out the breath he had been holding and thanked God for small favors. At this point, he'd take anything he could get. "Good, because I'm running low. Pay in cash, but don't register under your name."

She looked up from counting the money in her wallet. "Well, whose name should I use? Yours?"

"No, definitely not mine. Make something up—Johnson, Stone, whatever. And don't be too specific when he asks for your plate number. Pretend that you forgot what it is."

"I don't know what it is. Who notices things like that?" she muttered.

He waved his hand to catch her attention. "I know. Tell him you'll come back in later to give him the information on your car."

"Why would I do that?"

"Well, for one thing, I'm sorta thinking we may need to ditch this car tonight and get another one. We've been driving it too long and I don't want to take any chances. Not the way Sloan's guys picked up on us so quick back there."

"I don't suppose we're going to be able to turn this one back in at the rental company?"

"Nope. We'll have to stash it somewhere and I'll see that it's returned later."

"But…"

"Jill," he interrupted. "If we turn it in, they'll be on us."

"They? Who? Good guys or bad guys?"

"Maybe both, but I can't afford to risk it yet. Once I get an update from Murphy, we might have more options available. But until I know what we're facing, I don't want to take any chances."

He thought of yet another problem. "I'm gonna need some clothes, too. All I've got is what I'm wearing." And he was tired of going commando. Luke pressed his fingertips to his eyelids in an effort to stave off the headache he felt coming on. He hated operating like this. His mind was jumping around from one thing to another. He liked logic. He liked planning. This make-it-up-as-you-go-along way of doing things was a great way to get them all killed.

"Damn. I just thought of something else. I don't want the desk clerk hearing your voice."

"Why not? What's wrong with it?"

He shook his head when he saw the heat flare up in her eyes. "It's British, that's what. Nothing memorable, remember? We don't want anyone to remember seeing us. We can't afford to stick out in the crowd."

"How about if I go in with her, Luke?" James's voice piped up from the back seat. "I'll tell the guy that my mom has a sore throat—that she can't talk. You know…what do they call that?''

He swivelled in his seat to stare at James. ''Laryngitis.'' He paused for a moment, mentally playing out the scene. ''You think you could pull it off?'' James nodded eagerly.

''I'm not quite sure I agree that James should lie.''

''Aw, come on, Jilly. It's to help us, not to do something bad.''

Luke rolled his eyes heavenward. Now was not the time to be playing Mary Poppins. She'd have the rest of her life to instill them with honesty. ''It's a pretty good plan, Jilly.''

''I don't know. I suppose…'' She hesitated, clearly torn between doing the right thing and looking the other way. Still, she looked pretty determined.

''I can probably come up with something else, but it's gonna take some time.'' He carefully winked at James. ''You could be upstairs—'' he raised his eyes to the second floor units ''—lying in air-conditioned comfort on one of those big double beds.''

Her eyes narrowed into what was becoming a familiar expression—one that told him she knew he was playing her, but that she'd go along with it. ''All right. But only this once.'' Her gaze locked on James. ''Just this one time, James. Do you understand?''

''I got it. I got it.'' He made the mistake of smirking.

''If I learn otherwise, you will get the bar-of-soap treatment for lying, as well.''

''Don't you Brits know any other form of torture?'' Luke smiled when she grimaced. Hell, by the end of this op, he'd be burping soap bubbles for the next six months.

''We're not a creative lot. We stick with what works.''

''Okay. Now that we've got that settled…'' He glanced her way before turning back to James. ''When you talk to the clerk, don't try too hard. It's gotta sound real. You can't over-act, or it'll look weird.''

Jillian shifted in her seat and he shot her a look. ''Think

it'd work? Maybe if you fake like you're trying to talk at first. You know, whisper and hold your throat. Then James jumps in and talks for you. How's that sound?''

"I think we could do that." She nodded slowly. "James, are you sure you can do this?"

"Yeah sure, piece a cake," he bragged, his eyes excited.

Luke thought of one last thing as they stepped out of the car. "Oh, yeah. Tell 'em the room is for four, not five." At their curious expressions, he continued. "I want the guy to remember a family of four. Just one more thing to throw people off. We can sneak Sarah's crib in after we get settled in the room."

"Gotcha, Luke. I can handle it, no sweat. It'll be cool."

He gave him a quick thumbs-up. "Be cool, James. Be way cool."

James was more than cool. He was great. The registration went off like clockwork. Luke noticed that Jillian played up the story big-time and even he enjoyed how proud James was at being able to contribute. Of course it hadn't hurt that they'd registered at a motel out in the middle of nowhere—or the "back of beyond," as Mary Poppins called it.

Murphy had finally called with an update and he'd informed him of their unscheduled change in plans. When his partner finished laughing, Murphy'd said the streets were quiet, that his informants hadn't overturned anything new. That could be good news—or not. While it wasn't quite encouraging, their situation didn't appear to be life-threatening, either. Duncan, their ASAC, was pretty confident they'd haul Sloan in over the next forty-eight hours. Luke had difficulty believing that logic—especially since Duncan didn't know where to find him. But he'd experienced that sort of blind enthusiasm in the past. It seemed to run rampant in the ranks of ASACs and SACs. Once they were promoted from the field, the reality of undercover work quickly took a back seat in the equation. Their knowledge of the intricacies of field operations seemed to evaporate. The attitudes of the newly promoted swiftly became Just Get It Done.

Luke reentered the hotel room and closed his phone. His earlier recon of the motel hadn't turned up anything suspicious. But his training couldn't be shaken so easily. He'd probably check the perimeter half a dozen times over the next several hours. But for the moment, his gut was settled.

Jillian, however, looked drained. Thanks to his nap, he was feeling pretty good. But she hadn't really had a rest all day. And after burying a dead sister and a week spent baby-sitting three grieving kids, she had to be feeling emotionally and physically exhausted. Before he could stop himself, he'd offered to take James and Samuel out for a stroll in the woods behind the motel.

"Are you sure?" She yawned as she cut the tags off his new clothes.

Finally, new underwear. She'd even bought him a pair of jeans. Luke felt strange spending her money, but until this was over, he wouldn't risk blowing their cover by using his credit cards. Not even his undercover card. His gut was telling him to be cautious. But the thought of clean clothes had been too good to pass up. Even though Jilly refused to hand over the receipt, he was mentally keeping track of the expenses so the agency could reimburse her.

"Yeah, what the hel—heck." Another security check wouldn't hurt. He may as well kill two birds with one stone. He wanted to exhaust the boys so they'd get to sleep early. With any luck, by this time tomorrow he'd be rid of all of them.

"Figure out what you want for dinner and we'll order when I get back," he added.

"Right. Is everything okay with your partner?" She laid down the scissors and flopped back on the couch, closing her eyes.

"Yeah. It's cool. Just had to reschedule a few things." At least tonight they had a little more space. The sitting room was tiny, but there were two rooms. The boys had already spread their toys out on one of the beds in the next room.

"What about your boss? Doesn't he need to know what you're up to?"

"Not really. Usually when you plan an op, you cut through all the red tape up front. Once we receive our orders, the op is officially under way. We're basically on our own until it's done. We get help from the team when we need it."

"What kind of help?" She yawned again.

"You know, surveillance, intelligence, backup, research."

"What about a situation like this one?"

"Yeah. Well, when something goes wrong, then we all have to get creative." After the update from Murphy, he'd checked in with their handler. Duncan confirmed that the desk clerk's body had been discovered that morning, around the time he'd checked in with Charlotte the first time. The ballistics lab already had the slug that killed the clerk and with any luck would have the results in the morning.

Luke didn't hold out any hope the bullet would incriminate Sloan. The supplier simply wasn't that stupid. On the other hand, he was dying to get the slug from his butt analyzed. Aside from all the jokes he'd have to endure, the information could prove valuable.

The question of who'd shot him had been niggling his brain for nearly two days. His mind had replayed the scene a hundred times and something still bothered him. He just couldn't figure out what. The warehouse had already begun to collapse—he and Murphy had been running from the building. There was no way one of Sloan's thugs had taken the time to get off a shot with the damn building falling down around them. They'd cleared the building by at least a hundred yards before he'd felt the sting in his leg.

He closed his eyes and tried to picture the warehouse. The trajectory of the shot would have been from an angle to the south. But the freaking surveillance team had been sitting right there. How the hell could there have been a shooter there and them not see him?

The kids were growing louder by the second. Giving up his mental picture, he opened his eyes. "Come on, guys, let's go outside for a little while."

"So what exactly makes a safe house so safe? Is it underground or hidden away somewhere?" She rose up on one elbow, her eyes still at half-mast and winced when James began arguing with Samuel.

"Nah, nothing that complicated, although it could be. Basically it's like hiding you in plain sight. We put you in an average house in a quiet neighborhood, with heavily armed guards in all the rooms." And constant surveillance. And no privacy. And absolute secrecy. Each DEA office had its own stash of safe houses. And their location was kept strictly confidential. Even the staff didn't know where they were located.

Her eyes widened at that bit of information. "And you truly feel all of this is still necessary?"

"Hey, chill out, guys," he interrupted. "We'll take turns being the leader," he announced in an attempt to break up the argument. Both boys turned to stare at him and promptly stopped fighting. He smiled as Jilly rolled her eyes in mock despair and casually shoved a clip into his 9 mm, slipping it into the waistband of his jeans at the small of his back. Then he carefully tugged Ian's old shirt out of his pants so it concealed the gun. He finally acknowledged her shocked expression in the mirror. "Do I think it's necessary? Yeah, I do."

"So, Jimmy, I notice you take real good care of your brother and sister." Samuel was thrashing along the trails ahead of him while James walked by his side.

"I take care of Sarah better'n Jilly does." His slender chest puffed out with pride. "She's not too good with babies and she talks kinda funny."

"That's because she's from England. They all talk like that over there." Luke stuck his hands in his back pockets as they strolled along the overgrown path. "She'll learn how to handle Sarah. She wants to take good care of all of you."

"Yeah, she says that now. She thinks she's gonna be our mother," he announced, as if it was some sort of joke. "But she'll end up leavin'."

Luke stopped in his tracks, rooted to the spot, his heart wrenching at James's matter-of-fact tone. "What do you mean?"

"Grown-ups always leave. Especially when Sarah gets crying. She's so loud." James picked up a stick and started snapping off dry branches. "Even Mommy. She left us all the time. Then she'd come back and she'd start cryin'. She'd say she wasn't ever gonna do it again…but she always did."

"She, uh, left you alone?" He swallowed hard, stunned at the magnitude of what he was hearing. He didn't know why the blatant disregard for children still had the power to shock him. In the real world it happened every day. Luke dealt with the adult by-products of neglect every freakin' day. Drug addicts, alcoholics and criminals. It was what he knew best.

"Yeah, but she was always sorry she had to go. She knew I'd take care of Samuel and Sarah for her."

"You—how long would she leave you?"

James pursed his lips in thought, his hazel eyes serious. "Oh, I don't know. Usually it was just a day or so. But, you know what?" His voice rose an octave and Luke cringed at what he was about to learn.

"Once, she an' Slow left us for four whole days. I had to change Sarah's diapers, like a million times." James scrunched up his nose. "Even the poopy ones. Man, did they smell bad. But I didn't want her little bottom to get sore, so I used powder and everything."

Samuel scampered back up the trail toward them, his eyes wide with panic. "Luke, I gots to pee."

"Don't worry, sport." He motioned to the heavily wooded area they were standing in. "If you promise not to tell Jilly, I'll show you where guys can pee in an emergency."

James's nose scrunched. "Is this an emergency?"

"Jimmy, when your brother can't make it back to the motel, that qualifies as an emergency." He carefully explained the circumstances under which a boy could use the outdoors as his very own bathroom—emphasizing the most important one—that Jillian never find out he'd been the one to teach them.

He smiled even though he felt like weeping. Life was so damn cruel. There was a time when he and Linda had wanted children desperately. And this woman, Jillian's sister, had had three. Three beautiful children she'd proceeded to neglect…all for the chance to get high. They'd never known their fathers and now, thanks to Annie's addiction, they'd never know her. If James were really lucky, he wouldn't even remember Annie, wouldn't remember what she'd done to him.

As for him, it was already too late. As a husband, he'd failed dismally, falling far short of Linda's expectations. In college, she'd claimed his desire to work for the DEA—stemming the flow of drugs, putting dealers behind bars—was a noble cause. But after his third or fourth op had taken him away from D.C., her feelings changed. It wasn't glamorous anymore, just inconvenient. He was off seeing the world as she put it, and Linda was left to lug groceries up four flights of stairs.

Luke really couldn't blame her, actually. He'd been all over the globe fighting the drug war…gone for weeks, sometimes months at a time. And while the end of a mission was always a relief, it was difficult, too. He found it hard to turn the job on and off—to forget the things he'd seen, the experiences he'd lived—and simply pick up with the romantic-married-couple thing when he eventually returned home.

And it became tougher as Linda became increasingly unhappy. After a year or so, she'd started playing the guilt card. If he loved her, he should've wanted to give up the job. Linda required safety above all else. She'd wanted the comfort and reliability that came with nine to five. She wanted Luke by her side—all the time.

His wife had worked her way to scorn by their third year together. According to her, he'd screwed up their life in every way possible. The very least he could do was get her pregnant…so when he got killed in "some godforsaken jungle," Linda wouldn't be left alone.

Somehow he'd managed to fail at that, too.

"Why'd you call me Jimmy? My name isn't Jimmy."

"Huh?" Thoughts of his former marriage dissipated when Luke bent his head to duck the low-lying branch that was about to snap into his eyes.

"James. My name is James."

"Yeah, I know. But Jimmy is a nickname for James."

"What's a nickname?"

He was startled by the earnest expression in the kid's hazel eyes. Didn't he play with other kids? Didn't he go to school? "A nickname is a…I don't know, it's like a fun version of your real name. Like my name. My name is Lucas, but everyone calls me Luke."

"So what names could I have?"

James's expression was quizzical now, his interest sparked. Luke smiled and gave him the once-over, pretending to size him up. "Well, there's Jimmy or Jim or Jimbo—"

"Jimbo?"

"Yeah." He wrinkled up his nose. "Maybe you'd grow into it." The little guy shook his head and the sun glinted off the red-gold cowlicks. "Maybe when you're older they'll call you Red. You know, because of your hair."

James's head shot up at that. "They? Who's they?"

Luke felt a sinking feeling in the pit of his stomach. What the hell kind of childhood had the poor kid had? He managed to keep his expression neutral. "Why, your friends, of course."

James's smile was slow, puzzled even. But when it finally came, it lit up his entire face, causing the stoic, serious little boy to vanish before his eyes and reveal the glimmer of a hellion in the making. Luke felt a wild rush of relief and just the smallest spark of happiness ignite inside his chest. For this one, it wasn't too late.

James would grow up. And Samuel and little Sarah. With Jilly. She was their future. And he'd be damned if he was gonna let anyone or anything get in the way of it.

"I think, for now, I'd like Jimmy, okay?"

"Sure, kid. Jimmy it is."

Luke stepped out of the bathroom, still rubbing a towel through his hair. Jillian glanced up as she collected trash from their makeshift dining table. For lack of space, the empty pizza box was balanced on the television set.

"Kids asleep yet?" he whispered.

She nodded to the darkened bedroom as she crossed the room toward the shaft of light from the bathroom. "Are you finished in here?"

"Yup. It's all yours."

"Good. I'm dying for a shower." She rolled her neck in anticipation, not sure which she looked forward to more, washing away the stickiness of the day or bawling her eyes out under the comforting white noise of the shower. She'd never been much for tears before, but since she'd arrived in the States, crying had become a nightly ritual. Between grieving for Annie and the emotional strain of caring for three children, she'd found it a necessary release each night. She'd learned how to hold it together each day, handling Sarah's constant demands and Samuel's clinginess and even James's obvious disdain, so long as she could have ten minutes a night to herself.

"I won't be long," she promised.

"Good. Then we'll hit the sack. I wanna get an early start tomorrow." Luke crossed the room, heading for the door. "I'll make a run to the Dumpster with the trash. It smells like a pizzeria in here."

She inhaled deeply and smiled. "I could think of lots of worse things."

He grinned as he picked up the overflowing trash can and grabbed the pizza box from its perch on the TV. "Yeah, I'll take this smell over one of Sarah's diapers. Be back in two shakes."

"Should I wait, or can I take my shower?"

"Go ahead. I'll take the key. Just make sure the door's locked," he reminded her.

She checked and rechecked the door after he left before heading into the bathroom and stripping out of her clothes. She sighed with pleasure as the warm water pounded into her aching neck and shoulders. Probably a result of her stupid fall from the swing—her "swan dive," as Luke had called it.

Despite her exhaustion, she didn't feel quite as stressed as she had the previous night. Perhaps she was growing accustomed to this motherhood thing. Of course, it helped immensely that she hadn't been required to surgically remove any bullets this evening.

The memory of bullets turned her thoughts to her sister and she said a quick prayer in the fervent hope that Annie had found the peace that had so eluded her on earth. She tried not to think about how she'd died. How awful it must have been. She wondered if Annie had known her killer. Wondered if the shots had taken her instantly.

She shuddered as the tears sprang to her eyes. Her sister's death hadn't been completely in vain. She'd protected her children, God love her. Annie's mind hadn't been so clouded with drugs and fear that she'd forgotten her babies. At least she'd called Jilly.

And Jillian had responded—or tried to, anyway. The blinking message on the answering machine had sent her into a frenzy of overseas calls. But she hadn't been able to locate Annie anywhere. The call with the news of her sister's death had come two days later. She'd hopped on the first flight she could get across the Atlantic.

She'd missed her sister by only thirty days. If it had been one month later, Jillian would've been in the States anyway. She'd received the offer from Dartmouth and had decided to accept it. She'd had high hopes of dragging Annie to New Hampshire where she would've tried to find a treatment center for her sister.

Instead, the day after her arrival, she'd buried her only sister. A day after that, she'd become a mother to three children, one of whom made no secret of the fact that he couldn't stand her. Then there had been the custody hearing in an unfamiliar American court. She hadn't understood most of the words passing over her head. Thankfully, the American solicitor she'd been forced to hire had. Whoever was trying to take Annie's baby away from her hadn't succeeded.

Two days after that drama, she'd become a fugitive, on the run from a powerful enemy, from a gang of faceless drug dealers like the ones who'd killed her sister. Jillian shuddered and dragged in a breath of air. The sobs came in earnest now, and she leaned against the shower wall, her arms wrapped tight around her middle, her eyes screwed shut against the memory of her sister's lifeless face.

Something had gone bloody wrong tonight, she realized as she tried to catch her breath. The ten minutes were supposed to make her feel better, not worse. Tonight, her shower trick wasn't work—

She nearly jumped out of her skin as the bathroom door crashed back against the wall. Her eyes jerked open and widened at the large shadow looming closer to the shower curtain. She opened her mouth to scream as Luke ripped back the curtain and forcefully pulled her into his arms.

"What's wrong? Are you hurt?"

"You! W-what d-do you think you're d-doing?" Luke was prepared for battle. The icy intensity in his eyes made him a frightening stranger, one who was clearly prepared to kill if necessary.

His fingers were still biting into her shoulders when he

froze. He reeled back and averted his eyes, but not before he'd had the chance to thoroughly inspect everything God had given her, she noticed. He dropped the curtain back as though it were on fire.

"Have you g-gone m-mad?" She cringed at the pathetic screech that had become her voice. She sounded like one of those women who'd gone completely 'round the bend. But, Mother of God, she was still trembling. "You've nearly scared the life out of me."

"Damn, Jilly. I—I'm sorry. It was reflex. I came through the door and I heard you howling in here."

"I was not h-howling." She heard the familiar click of his weapon. "Good God, you b-brought your g-gun in here?"

"I thought for a minute that someone… I thought you were hurt."

"I do not howl." She wiped blindly at her eyes and succeeded in getting soap in them. Bloody hell, did that sting. "I can't get a moment's peace around here," she wailed.

"Well, if nothing's wrong, what the hell are you crying about? You were bawling last night, too."

"Last night you had me performing surgery on you, for pity's sake. I'm not allowed a moment to feel frazzled after something like that?"

"Oh, yeah. That reminds me. Thanks for…you know, that. You did a great job."

"Thank you." She stood there behind the curtain, her body trembling, her eyes still screwed shut and bit down hard on her lip. Lord, she was very close to completely melting down. "Now, if you'll…"

"So what are you crying about now?"

"None of your business," she informed him haltingly as she sniffled back more tears. She watched as his shadow retreated a few steps and sucked in a gusty breath in an effort to slow her heart rate from its current gallop.

"Look, a lot's happened to you in the past few days. There's no shame in crying." He'd obviously succeeded in calming himself down, as his voice no longer sounded urgent. In fact, from behind the safety of her curtain, Luke's voice was low and husky. She closed her eyes on the sudden wave of longing that swept through her. Dear Lord, what was she thinking? Clearly she must be losing her mind.

"I don't see you crying."

He hesitated then. "That's different. I'm used to danger. I'm trained for chaos. You're not."

"Well, I've got three children now. I'd better get used to it, shan't I?" Why was she so bloody attracted to him? Why this man? Why now? Didn't she have enough to handle? The very last thing she needed was another complication.

"Jill. All I'm saying is that if you'd like to talk about it…"

She was in real danger of doing something terribly stupid. There was nothing she wanted more at that moment than to throw herself at him, to lose herself in a mindless, shattering release. She could spend the rest of the night in his arms. Feel those tough, work-hardened hands along the length of her body. Feel the steel of his corded muscles wrapped around her. She could experience one night of pure unadulterated lust and at the very same time know a sense of comfort and security that being with Luke would bring. Oh, yes. Agent Luke Gianetti would be incredible.

"You'll be the last person I call, thank you very much." There was no doubt in her mind that what they shared would be unlike anything she'd ever experienced. And there was absolutely no doubt that when tomorrow arrived, it would end.

Luke knew it, also. She'd seen the knowledge in his eyes all day and again as he'd held her a moment ago. And she knew he fought it, too. This was the right thing to do. The logical thing. "Now, get out of here so I can dress. I'm pruning up in here and the water's gone cold."

Jillian sensed his hesitation, even across the bathroom. She peeked around the curtain and found him standing by the door, his hand on the knob, his eyes uncertain as he debated whether or not to believe her.

"Seriously, Jill. You're okay?"

It was the compassion that nearly did her in. He looked so damn approachable. Those beautiful, expressive eyes. It was all she could do not to throw herself into his arms and cry until she'd exhausted all the tears. But in the end, her problems would still be here. And worse, Luke would know how weak she was, how afraid she was that she would foul up everything. And where would that leave her?

"I need help, all right. I'm going to need to have my head examined after this ordeal." She snapped the curtain back in place. "Now, get out."

She cautiously stuck her head around the door a few minutes later, grateful for the darkened room. At least Luke wouldn't be able to witness her embarrassment, wouldn't be able to see her swollen pink eyes and blotchy face. And he wouldn't see her regret.

She glanced up as the door to their room swung silently inward and Luke slipped inside. He reminded her of a cat, moving soundlessly through the night. She wouldn't have been surprised to see his golden eyes glowing in the dark. He bolted the door and stood with his back to her, motionless at the window as he stared out into the darkness.

"Is everything all right?"

He didn't turn around. "Yeah. Just following my gut, being cautious. I don't like leaving anything to chance."

"This place seems pretty quiet, don't you think?"

"Yeah." He finally seemed satisfied that no one was outside that shouldn't be and he turned around. "Sometimes quiet isn't good."

She sat on the end of the sofa near the door and stared at the flickering screen of the muted television. She'd stuck her head into the bedroom and heard the deep, even breathing of the boys. Over the soft whirring of the air conditioner, she caught Sarah's quiet, steady snuffling and her heartbeat tripped a little faster. It had only been a week, but those precious babies had already taken ownership of her heart and she would do anything to keep them safe. She finally raised her gaze to Luke's and smiled. "Sometimes quiet is wonderful."

She sensed rather than heard him as he materialized by the couch and carefully sat beside her. His every movement seemed controlled, almost calculated and she wondered if he ever did anything without first analyzing it from all sides.

His hand drifted slowly over to hers and he slipped his fingers between hers, giving them a little squeeze. "You're right. It can be very peaceful." He sighed as he tightened the grip on her fingers. "Look, about what happened in there. I'm really sorry."

"Forget it. You frightened me, that's all." And saw her stark naked. And made her so damn aware of him that she was ready to self-combust.

"I guess I'm not accustomed to peaceful. I like things predictable, organized. I like to make plans and then stick to them. And everything lately feels so damned disorganized that it makes me edgy. I apologize if you think I'm overreacting."

"I guess in your line of work, you must have to prepare for anything."

"Yeah. You could say that."

Jillian gently slid her fingers from his. Touching him right now was definitely not a good idea. "My whole life has been planned, everything scheduled out for me down to the smallest, most absurd detail." She absently patted Luke's hand on the cushion. "And I'm so bloody sick of it," she admitted with a smile.

"I promised myself when I left home that I would—I don't know, wing it a little." Her smile was halfhearted and she felt her stomach twist with the need to touch him. Lord, he was absolutely stunning. She took a deep breath and looked away.

"You'd already decided to come over here?"

"Yes. I'd accepted the position at Dartmouth before I knew about—" Her grip on his hand tightened convulsively. "Originally, I'd planned to take my time getting to New Hampshire. For the first time in my life I was going to be free. No one telling me what to do or how to do it." She sighed longingly. "I had big plans to explore a bit on my own."

"Dartmouth? No way! Not a professor? You can't possibly be old enough to teach."

She smiled at his stunned expression. "No. Sorry to disappoint you. I'll be working in the library there. I'm an archivist."

"A what?"

"Archives. You know old records and documents? I was hired to catalog the library's collection of rare seventeenth- and eighteenth-century papers."

He appeared to give her the once-over and Jillian felt herself stiffen, despite the teasing smile of disbelief on his face. Why did everyone assume she was a complete ninny? Why, even her own mother thought she was a scatterbrain.

"I am qualified, you know," she said icily. "In spite of the fact that you think I'm completely without a brain, let me assure you I'm one of only a handful of people—"

"Whoa there, honey." Luke sat up straighter on the sofa. "I never said you weren't qualified to do anything."

His tone and his expression were suddenly earnest, all traces of teasing gone. "Perhaps not," she conceded, "but you were thinking it."

"So far, the only thing you stink at is directions."

She turned on him in mock exasperation. "You know, sometimes you need to go with the flow. In your whole life, have you ever done one spontaneous thing? You know, deviated from your master plan, done something frightfully rash?"

He shook his head. "No. I'm not a 'rash' kinda guy. In my line of work, rash equates to dead. The reason I've lived this long is because I play out every scenario. And when all else fails, I trust my gut."

"Your gut can be wrong—"

"Sweetheart," he interrupted, "my gut is never wrong."

"Sometimes veering off course a tiny bit is good for you," she argued.

"And sometimes veering off course is deadly. Like a car wreck."

Luke's smile faded and she felt the searching scrutiny of his gaze as he explored her face, as he delved for secrets she wasn't quite sure were safely hidden. Her pulse quickened when she acknowledged the burning intensity echoed in his beautiful molten eyes.

She swallowed nervously. His message was as clear as if he'd spoken. That it was wrong. That they shouldn't be considering what they were clearly considering. But, dammit, she wanted him anyway. Her nerves were strumming with awareness. If she so much as looked at him…

He released her hand suddenly and shoved himself away from her. "We should get to bed. I want an early start tomorrow."

She glanced up, startled by his sudden movement. "You're right, of course. And Sarah will wake again in a few…"

She forgot the rest of her sentence as their eyes made contact. The thought that had been forming flew out of her head and died on her lips as she met the blast force of desire that was visible in Luke's mesmerizing gaze. Desire that he wasn't bothering to hide from her. Her eyes widened in shock, with the knowledge that he was suffering, too. That he, too, was about to explode. She inhaled a ragged breath and blew it out.

"Jill, this has disaster written all over it."

"I know," she whispered.

"I don't want entanglements. I—I can't do a relationship." His eyes were still desperate, but there was a deliberate edge to his voice, one that clearly told her how it would be. Luke would suffer no illusions on her part. "I won't promise anything."

She nodded in understanding. "I don't think I can handle anything more myself."

He jerked his head back, glancing to the ceiling in sheer frustration. "This is ridiculous. I can't believe we're contemplating..." His gaze swung back to meet hers. "This is a one-shot deal. Tomorrow we're outta here and heading in opposite directions."

"I'm not asking you for...more."

"You're sure about this?"

Jillian nodded carefully in the affirmative, aware that his bone-melting stare missed absolutely nothing. "No, I'm really not."

Then she smiled at his double take, when his eyes belied his confusion over her words. "But I simply can't help—"

She was in his arms so fast she wasn't quite sure who had moved first. And a millisecond later she didn't care, because when Luke's mouth came down on hers—the very moment their lips touched—she went up in flames.

He kissed her hard, his mouth ruthless, as though he'd been pushed to the limit of his control. As though he'd been waiting forever to kiss her. She opened to him on a groan and when his tongue thrust past her lips, she nearly fainted from the exquisite sensation. Just the feel of his lean, strong arms holding her, the sensual aura of danger he exuded, had her reeling. The mere suggestion of what was yet to come made her dizzy with the urge to feel him. He hadn't even touched her yet and she was already so close—so near the edge.

She moaned his name while his mouth moved over hers, when it left her face and traveled down her neck, as his tongue found the pulse beating wildly at the base of her throat. His hands cupped her breasts and when he stroked her sensitized nipples, she bit back a cry of sheer wonder. "Oh, Luke. I can't wait. Please."

He raised his head to stare at her and she read the surprise in his eyes. Surprise that she was already so out of control for him. And he had the nerve to smile. Her eyes widened as his smug smile turned quickly to a grin...and wasn't that devastating? Still, it frosted her that she'd given herself away so quickly. And there he was, not even breaking a sweat.

She gave him a little shove. "Never mind. What I meant was—"

"That you want me inside you?"

Yes! She closed her eyes and bit back a groan while she thought of him thrusting into her. She forced her eyes open when she heard him chuckle. "No, damn you," she croaked. "What I meant was—"

"That you're so hot for me you're ready now?"

That got her blood stirring. The bastard. He was playing with her now. "It's more like, let's get on with it because I'm tired and I'd like to get some sleep."

Luke's grin grew even wider, if that were bloody possible. "Really? So, like, if I were to stroke you right here—" One magnificent hand reached down to glide over her stomach, his fingers slow and lazy as they stroked even lower. For the life of her, Jillian couldn't contain the shudder that ripped through her body, leaving her nearly sobbing for more. She barely managed to summon the will to slap his hand away while the other ninety-nine percent of her brain rebelled, wanting desperately to pull it back.

"That if I did this—" Luke leaned toward her slowly, his gaze never leaving her face until they were mere inches apart. Then his focus dropped to her breasts. He bent his head, nudging her back against the couch and placed his mouth where his hand had just rested. She gasped a breath of air into her lungs and bit down to stop the ragged moan of wonder. She closed her eyes as her brain short-circuited, as a bolt of lightning zagged down from the heavens and detonated inside of her. He took her nipple into his mouth and suckled her, right through her cotton T-shirt and Jillian felt the tugging sensation all the way down to her toes.

"Luke, oh, yes. Yes, don't stop."

He waited until she was on the verge of completely shattering before he raised his head.

"So, you wouldn't come apart in my hands?"

She writhed beneath him on the cushions, then reached up and pulled him down. Her hands were wild in his hair and she tugged him down to her mouth. She opened her eyes then, willing to witness his smug satisfaction if he would just get on with it. "Yes, yes, dammit. Are you happy?"

His grin was still evident, but so was his increasing tension and she smiled with the knowledge. He might be toying with her, but it was damn near killing him to do it. Despite his smile, his eyes burned with the white-hot intensity of the sun. The perspiration that formed at his brow had nothing to do with exertion and everything to do with control. A control that was eroding rapidly.

"Not yet," he rasped, "but I'm pretty sure I will be soon."

It was her turn to smile when she reached out, stroking him through his jeans. She was surprised that she was able to chuckle at his instantaneous reaction. He was hot and hard and so very ready for her. She could barely wait.

"Oh, Jill." He groaned as a shudder ripped through him. "Don't do that."

"So, are you saying that if I did that again—"

Her question was cut off as he scooped her up from the bed and carried her back to the bathroom. Her head fell back as his mouth continued to torture her through her shirt. She wrapped her legs around him as he pushed through the bathroom door, and then leaned back against it until it shut.

"Why are we—" She was surprised that she could formulate words.

"Condoms. In the bag on the counter." He set her on the counter in question and quickly tugged her shirt over her head. She grabbed his face in her hands and brought him back to her mouth. Jillian would have been content to kiss him for the next ten years, right here in the bathroom, with her legs wrapped his waist. Luke however, had other plans. He gently pried her legs apart and took a step back to gaze down at her.

"Jill, you are the hottest-looking woman I've ever seen." He reached out a hand, and damned if it wasn't trembling. He knew she was gonna be great. He couldn't wait to be inside her. It was all he could do not to tear her clothes off and take her right there on the counter. Yet, thankfully, from somewhere deep inside him, another Luke surfaced, another more civilized part of him somehow managed to step in and take over, commanding him to go slow.

Luke wasn't certain it was him controlling his hand as it reached out and cupped her breast. It was as though someone else watched Jillian through his eyes, noticing everything about her, every reaction, every shuddering breath she took through that luscious mouth. He saw her eyes, those beautiful stormy eyes, watched them dilate with passion for him as they first widened with shock and then deepened gray-blue in anticipation of what he would do.

He felt her breast in his hand, felt it swell to his touch, felt the nipple tighten in reaction, felt himself harden in response. This wasn't supposed to be happening. This was about sex. About hot, steamy, wild, way-the-hell-overdue sex. It was about rewarding himself. About finally taking something that he hadn't allowed in so freaking long that he was surprised he could still remember how to do it.

Just for tonight, he wouldn't feel guilty over Linda. Tonight he could finally release the godawful build-up. He would work off years of sexual frustration with this one very willing woman who sat naked and ready in front of his eyes. Jillian— a woman he'd just met, a woman he'd never see again. They could use each other up and then move on.

"Luke, hurry." He felt the smile form on his lips and groaned as she unzipped his jeans. He heard her throaty laughter as she tugged him down for another soul-scorching kiss.

"Here, let me help you with that." Jilly turned slightly to delve into the bag on the counter. He allowed himself a moment to breathe in the soft, fresh perfume that clung to her hair and her skin.

"Baby, you smell so damn good." It was the scent of a spring rain, so clean and new. So innocent. He wrapped his hands around her shoulders and let them slowly drift down her long, slender arms. "You're so soft, so beautiful."

She was still wrestling with the box of condoms and he took the opportunity to kiss the side of her neck, to tug at the fragile skin he found there, to revel in the throaty gasping sound Jilly made in response. It was getting harder to maintain any semblance of control, but the civilized Luke knew if he wasn't gentle, he'd leave a bruise. The civilized Luke knew if he really let loose, he would devour her.

"Got them."

His brain registered her cry of delight at the same moment he felt her hands fumbling with his belt. Damn, she was gorgeous—so healthy and alive. He was dying to get the rest of her clothes off, to thrust himself into her and explode, so deep inside her that it would take the rest of the night to recover. Yet something about this didn't feel right. It didn't feel like a one-night stand. Jillian didn't seem like the kind—

Yeah, right. Like it was every day that a totally hot sexy woman threw herself at him. Was he freakin' nuts? He didn't know anything about this woman. Maybe she'd slept her way across the Atlantic. Her sister obviously had. Who was he to question her motives?

"Luke—what are we waiting for?"

She raised her gaze to his and he swallowed hard. She was the most beautiful woman he'd ever seen. And tonight she was all his. He would take what he could get and—

"Nothin', baby. Nothing at all."

His hands shook as he ripped the foil packet and he groaned with pleasure when she took him into her hands and stroked him. Luke didn't recognize the sandpapery voice that ordered her to stop the exquisite torture.

"Let's get this bloody thing on you. You know I can't afford to get pregnant, but if you wait much longer I'm going to scream."

And just like that, it was over. Luke jerked back away from her, breathing hard, his limbs heavy and weak, as though he'd completed a marathon in record time. The blood roared in his ears, matching the rhythm of his pounding heart.

"I can't do this." His eyes captured the picture of Jilly's eyes widened in bewilderment, as her face registered shock and then slowly drained of color.

"W-what? Luke? What is it?"

"It's nothing. It's me." He turned abruptly, unwilling to face her as she shivered in comprehension, unwilling to see the scorn that would be in her eyes the moment her brain finished processing what had just happened.

"Luke, can't we—"

He zipped his pants and wheeled around to face her. "No, honey, we can't. This was a mistake. There's nothing to discuss." He jerked the door open and strode through it, unwilling to risk catching the disgusted look in her eyes. He crossed the room quickly and flung the chain off the door. The only thing that kept him from slamming it in absolute frustration was the soft, fluttery breathing of the kids. Jilly's three kids. Jeez, what the hell had he been thinking?

He heard the door open ten minutes later as he leaned over the railing outside their room. The parking lot was poorly lit and nearly empty, the pool deserted, save for the sound of the filter humming in the reflective water. The motel rooms had gone dark and still. This was farm country and mountain people retired early, apparently even while on vacation.

"Luke? Are you out here?"

He closed his eyes and dropped his head down to touch the railing. God, he didn't want to have this conversation. "Yeah, I'm here."

He felt her move closer, sensed her hesitation as she stopped a few feet behind him. "You should get to bed. It's getting late."

"Are you coming inside?"

"In a little while." He heard her take another step toward him. "Don't wait up for me." As if he'd dare crawl into bed beside her tonight. As if she'd let him. He was an idiot. Linda had been right. He was completely freakin' useless.

"Luke, please. Can we talk for a minute?"

He opened his mouth to put a quick end to her speech, but her words came tumbling out, almost as if she knew he wouldn't want to listen.

"I just wanted to apologize to you for…" He had to strain to hear her voice. "I made a complete fool of myself…and I'm so sorry."

He winced when she started sniffing. Sweet Jesus, please don't let her cry. He tensed when he felt her hand on the back of his shoulder, her touch tentative, as though she were afraid of what he might do.

"I'm…I've never done that before."

"Had sex with a stranger? So it doesn't run in the family then?" Her hand dropped away and he felt a stab of shame in his chest when he heard her small, startled whimper. Dammit, his raging frustration didn't give him the right to be vicious.

"Jill. I'm sorry. I didn't mean that."

She was quiet for a long minute and he knew she was still absorbing the blow. God, he was such a jerk.

"Um, well, actually, the answer is yes. Unlike my sister, I've never made a habit out of sleeping with strange men."

"Jilly, I—"

"What I meant was that I've never thrown myself at a man like I did tonight."

She plowed over him, apparently determined to clear the air despite his surly attitude. Luke had to give her credit for courage. She moved forward and leaned on the railing, making sure to keep several feet between them. He didn't want to look at her, didn't want to see her face for this discussion. But if she could take it, then so could he. Out of the corner of his eye, he saw her shake her head derisively and he braced himself.

"I don't know what came over me. I'm so awkward and clumsy." Her voice faltered and he watched in near amazement while she fought for control and won. Watched as she bulldozed over the overwhelming hurt she had to be feeling and kept on talking.

"I know I'm not very attractive. I just…" She swallowed hard and leaned farther out over the rail. "With everything that's happened, I just needed someone, that's all."

His body stiffened in absolute disbelief while her words washed over him, as her pain crawled inside him and hurt him, too. "Jill, let's get one thing straight." He closed some of the distance between them. "You are, hands down, the most beautiful woman I've ever met. How could you possibly think that I wouldn't want you."

He shook his head in disbelief. "You're sexy as hell."

"Then why—"

"Look, when I said it was me, I meant it." He didn't want to go there—not tonight, not ever.

"When a man says 'it's me,' he usually means 'it's you,'" she argued. "So at least do me the courtesy of being honest. I came on too strong. I'm sorry."

Luke pushed himself off the railing. He felt claustrophobic in his need to pace and his stomach had tightened into a painful knot of frustration and dread. Why couldn't she just let it go?

"It's me, okay? It's me, dammit." He tried unsuccessfully to unclench his jaw. His head was starting to pound with the effort to maintain his control. "It's not you, all right?"

"Is this about your wife?"

"I don't want to discuss it." He sucked in a jagged breath. "Please, for both our sakes, could you just go inside?"

He saw the tears form in her eyes, saw that she tried to hide them when she quickly turned away. And he wanted to touch her. So badly. He wanted to take her in his arms and just hold her. She was hurting so much and, dammit, so was he.

He sensed her movement, felt her arm when she brushed past him, retracing her steps to their room, and his stomach tightened with regret. He didn't expect her to touch him. And he started when her hand rested briefly on his shoulder.

"Okay," she whispered and her hand fell away.

Before he could stop himself—before he could admit that he didn't want her to leave—he grabbed her hand and pulled her back against him. Luke felt the air whoosh out of her when he hauled her up against his chest, felt her stiffen briefly in surprise. And then, regrettably, felt her body slowly melt against him. She was so soft and compliant in his arms.

No question about it, he was out of his mind. The moment this op was over, he would check himself in for a psych evaluation. She was so alive. So perfect. And he was walking around half dead.

"Look, I'm gonna explain something, and then I want you to go inside and go to bed. Got it?"

He felt her nod her head against his chest. He dragged in another breath before he could continue. Jilly's scent was alive in his senses, overtaking the sharp mountain breeze that danced over them. Overpowering the lilac that wafted up from the garden by the pool.

"I don't want you to say a word. Just listen and understand and then go inside." He felt her body tense slightly and absently began stroking the nape of her neck. If he couldn't have her, then at least he could enjoy touching her for the next minute or so. Because after that, she sure as hell wouldn't be looking at him the same way.

"Okay, here goes." A minute went by and he stood there. Like an idiot. Not speaking. And then his heart started pounding and he began to feel light-headed. Jilly had to be thinking that he'd completely cracked up. He swallowed hard, his throat suddenly drier than any desert.

"Don't." Her whispered voice wafted up from his chest, wrapped around him in the cloak of darkness and forced him to take a shaky breath. "Don't tell me."

"I said no talking," he reminded her. She pulled back, her arms still loosely wrapped around his waist. And he missed the warmth almost immediately. Luke knew in that instant that she'd somehow managed to get under his skin. That the feel of her, the scent of her, was forever burned into his brain.

"I can feel how tense you are. Your heart is going a hundred kilometers an hour."

"That fast, eh?" Luke felt as if he were dying inside.

"I believe you, all right? I believe that it's not me. It was wrong of me to ask." Jilly dropped her arms and smiled up at him in the dark. She raised herself up on her toes and dropped a kiss on his cheek. "I'm going to bed now. Don't stay out too long."

She turned and took a step toward the door.

"I can't get you pregnant," he blurted. "I can't have—we couldn't…"

She stopped in her tracks. He felt the shock radiate out from her in waves, felt himself encircled by them when she turned back to face him.

"That's what this is all about?" She took a step toward him and he saw the disbelief in her eyes. "So when I said that I couldn't afford to get—"

"Yeah. That sorta did it." He was glad it was so dark. He could see her expression clearly, but he prayed she couldn't see his, prayed that he was hidden in shadow.

"But why should that matter so much?"

"It mattered to Linda…to my wife. It mattered a lot."

"I'm sorry you can't have children. But I don't understand." She closed the rest of the distance between them. "When you love someone, it shouldn't matter. You adopt children."

Not according to Linda. If he couldn't produce them for her, he was as good as useless. "Well, anyway—" he cleared his throat awkwardly and winced over the lump in his throat "—now you know. It's not you."

She smiled up at him then and his heart tripped in reaction, first in shock and then something else. Something he didn't dare put a name to. Something that felt a great deal like hope. God, he was pathetic.

"Well, just so *you* know, you're still the sexiest man I've ever seen." Her gaze ran down the length of him and he felt a painful surge of longing. "Definitely worth throwing caution to the wind."

She turned again and opened the door. He could see the flickering white light from the television set. And he watched her shadow hesitate when she stopped and turned back to smile at him. "Definitely worth veering off course for."

The door clicked softly shut behind her. He stared at it for a minute and then shook his head as he swung back to the railing. He took a deep, cleansing breath of the night air. And felt his heart rate slowly revert to normal. He still hadn't released his sexual frustration, but damned if he didn't feel better.

Luke had to admit he was surprised by what he'd observed tonight—or by what he hadn't seen, what he'd thought was inevitable. He hadn't seen frustration. He hadn't seen disgust. He hadn't heard Linda's bitter, angry voice in Jillian. His mind clicked back over what Jilly had said. Maybe she was right. Maybe talking about it would make it better, would make it easier to live with. Maybe after this was over, he'd still have a shot with her.

The door jerked open and he turned to find her framed by the light in the doorway. He tensed immediately while his brain registered her obvious distress. He was already moving toward her when he spoke. "What is it?"

"God, Luke. You'd better see this."

He looked beyond her at the images on the television screen. At the billowing smoke and the secondary explosions that had been captured on film from the fires that raged into the night. He left her to shut the door behind them, his gaze glued to the words running across the bottom of the screen.

"The announcer said something about Charlotte and I—"

"Turn it up," he interrupted. He swore under his breath while his eyes captured the images that had just sealed his fate on another sleepless night. And maybe several more.

"Luke, what is it?"

"That, sweetheart, was our safe house—and three other houses in the neighborhood."

Chapter 6

Jillian swallowed the wave of panic that still had her knees so weak she had flopped down on the end of the bed. He'd been gone for ages. And she'd tried not to worry. She'd tried to get ready for bed, as Luke had instructed. But the night didn't seem friendly and peaceful anymore. The dark seemed claustrophobic without him. The wind blowing outside sounded sinister and dangerous.

Her heart went into overdrive when she heard a faint metallic clink outside the door. She prayed it was Luke's key that was currently working the doorknob. Bolting from the bed, she dove for the connecting door and waited to see who would appear.

"Luke?"

"I thought I told you to get some sleep." He slipped inside noiselessly and slid the lock back into place, then took the time to position a chair under the door handle. He proceeded to the drapes and opened them a fraction, checking the parking lot.

His body was on red-alert status. She recognized the signs

now. His stance was battle-ready, his expression no-nonsense. And she felt a giddy rush of relief that he'd finally returned and that he would protect her and the children. He was theirs now.

"I can't sleep. I tried, really. But all I can see is that fire. Those explosions." She sighed as he finally turned to face her. The room was murky, lit only by the sliver of light from the opening in the bathroom door. Despite all the commotion of the past several hours, the children slept peacefully on, blissfully unaware of her restlessness.

"What's going to happen?" She closed the bedroom door and crossed to the couch. Shivering, she sat, curling her legs underneath her and wished for a blanket to hide under.

"It'll be all right. I made some calls. Duncan was pretty relieved, actually. He thought we were in Charlotte."

"You didn't tell him about my screwup yesterday?" She sensed Luke's movement before she heard him as he finally drifted away from the curtains.

"Nah. I try not to bore him with the details, just the results." He hesitated then, something close to uncertainty flashing in his eyes.

"Remember your promise. Whatever it is, you must tell me."

"My boss wants me—us—to stay low another day or so."

"And?" She felt the cushion sag under his weight when he sat on the edge, staying far away from her, she noticed.

"I'm not so sure I agree with that."

"Why?"

"I don't like waiting. I don't like sitting still," he admitted. "Someone is on to us. And I'm beginning to think it might be someone inside the agency."

A chill sizzled up her spine. "H-how is that p-possible? Who would do that?"

"It's possible if someone's on the take. Hell, Sloan is so powerful, there could be several people on the dole. I just don't know." His arms resting on his knees, he turned to stare at her, his expression grim. "And to make matters worse, my cell phone bit the dust. I don't know if it's our location or if the damn battery is finally drained...but I can't get the freakin' thing to work."

"Could we buy one?"

"Time is a luxury we don't have right now. My gut is telling me we're still in trouble, but damn if I know what to do about it."

"Well, there's always this phone—"

"Too easy to trace," he interrupted.

"The phone booth then. I saw one out front at the end of the drive."

"I can't run an op from a damn phone booth." He ran a hand along his jaw, his tension obvious. "I don't mean to take this out on you. It just feels weird not to have my stuff."

"You've got a gun."

"Yeah, but it's not my gun. And I don't have my tools. I don't have any help."

"What about your partner? Can't you talk with him? Perhaps he'd come here to help you."

"I'm workin' on it, hon. Believe me." He smiled then, closing the small space between them on the couch and she tried not to groan out loud. Lord, he was so sexy. And so strong and capable. She trusted him, she realized, to get them safely out of this mess. She trusted him with all their lives.

"Why do they want us dead?"

His expression was instantly serious. "We don't know that for sure. I think they're after me. You know, you just happened to be in the wrong place at the wrong time."

"But I saw that man in the rearview mirror."

"Yeah, well there's that, too. Drug dealers don't like witnesses."

She felt her heart start thumping again. Lord, were they going to be on the run for the rest of their lives? What about Dartmouth? What about her plans? "I, um, know this sounds sort of silly right now, but how long do you think this will take? Should I call Dartmouth and move back my start date?''

To his credit, Luke didn't snort with disbelief, nor did he laugh at what was clearly insignificant on his list of important things to do. He handled her concern the way he seemed to deal with most things, she realized. He thought about it first.

''Mind you, I'm not trying to sound petty. It's just…they're expecting me. And I wouldn't want them to worry unnecessarily.'' There she was again. Rosemary Moseby's dutiful daughter. No matter how much distance she managed to put between them, she would forever be Lady Jillian Marie Winthrop Moseby—always so bloody concerned with what everyone thought of her. Wouldn't want to smear the family's good name with the Dartmouth crowd. After all, the university thought it was hiring royalty. Now wasn't that a joke?

''No, it's a legitimate concern. I think probably you should call tomorrow and leave a message. We'll keep it quick and vague. I don't want it traceable, just in case.'' He pressed his fingers to his temples as if to stop the pounding in his head.

Luke was clearly distracted and she immediately felt guilty. Here he was, with a million things on his mind. She should've just taken it upon herself to call. Lord, she was a fool. She didn't have to seek permission for every blasted thing.

''I should let you get some rest. Is there anything I can do to help?''

He stifled a yawn with his hand and then stretched his neck and shoulders, temporarily relieving what had to be an eye-popping amount of stress.

''Nah. What I'd like is for you to try to sleep. I'm not completely convinced that we're staying here tomorrow. But I need to think about it for a while.'' He glanced up at her again. ''And I might need you to do some driving.''

''You'd trust my sense of direction after the last go-round?''

''Well, actually, look how it turned out. If we'd made it to Charlotte—''

Her mouth dropped open as the realization hit her. Dear Lord, her mistake had saved them. There was a good chance they would have been inside the safe house. "I hadn't thought about that."

"So, just in case I need you to save us again tomorrow, you should get some sleep tonight."

She nodded reluctantly. The least she could do was to try to stay out of his way. "Okay. You're in charge."

He smiled at her choice of words. "Remember that, Jilly. The next few days could get…difficult. Whatever I tell you to do, you're going to have to do without question. Got it?"

She knew he was deadly serious in spite of his killer smile. And with three beautiful children to protect, she'd sell her very soul if she had to. Still, he didn't have to be so cheeky about it.

"Yes, I've got it. I'll belt up for the sake of the mission." She rose from the end of the couch and was grateful to find her legs much steadier as she crossed the room and opened the bedroom door to check on the boys one last time before bed.

No doubt about it, simply having Luke nearby was soothing. Perhaps it was that aura of invincibility. He exuded confidence, even when things didn't progress the way he wanted them to. He was just so damn capable. In fact, Luke Gianetti seemed ready for anything. Even the children had picked up on his no-nonsense demeanor. James especially. And they seemed to love him for it. He was easygoing and patient with them. But when he announced it was bedtime, the boys seemed to know intuitively that he wouldn't tell them a second time.

She, on the other hand, was getting nowhere with James. He challenged her at every turn. Samuel was young enough to still want mothering. But James…he would be a tough nut to crack. Running for their lives wasn't helping the situation. What he needed in his life was consistency.

She bit back a sigh as she tucked the blankets around Samuel's shoulders. She looked forward to settling down with all of them. James would have his own room, his own bed. She wanted badly for him to have a private sanctuary where he could put something down and have it still be there when he came back for it later.

From what little she'd seen of Annie's life, it had been a succession of dreary little flats occupied by too many people. Along with the children and her man-of-the-moment, Jillian knew there had been transients walking through at all hours of the day and night. Any toys and clothes she'd purchased for her nephew over the years had either been sold for drugs or stolen by her sister's friends. James had simply gotten used to never having anything that he could call his own.

She pulled back the sheets on the bed, nearly delirious at the thought of sleep, then remembered she'd left her glass of water in the living room. She slipped back into the living room and saw that Luke had taken up his position by the windows again. Sighing, she reached for the glass. She glanced up to find Luke watching her closely.

"Somethin' wrong?"

"No. I was thinking about Annie—the message from her, and the call a few days later." She glanced away from the compelling intensity of his stare, afraid of what she might inadvertently reveal.

"What'd she say?"

"The usual. She was in trouble again." She frowned as she remembered their conversations. "I would hear from her once or twice a year, usually when she needed money. This time she sounded very frightened. She said…"

To his credit, Luke waited patiently for her to continue. She swallowed convulsively around the dry lump in her throat. "She said it was really big. Annie wanted me to come over straightaway. And I was to go directly to the apartment downstairs from hers. She said she would meet me there with the kids." She glanced up to find him watching her intently.

"I got the feeling that she was running away and that she was going to leave the children and take off."

"What happened?"

She roped her fingers together to keep them from shaking. "I tried all night to call her back, but I never reached her. The phone rang and rang the first few times and then it was disconnected." She shrugged her shoulders and glanced away. "By morning I was absolutely frantic. I'd already called the airline to change my tickets. The earliest flight I could get on standby was a whole day later."

"It must have been hard to wait."

She nodded, her eyes still focused on a spot on the far wall. If she concentrated then she wouldn't break down. "It was horrible. I felt useless. And then the next day finally arrived, when I could finally do something. I got the call from the police as I was leaving for the airport."

"Who called you?"

"I don't remember. I was in shock, I guess. It was a man. He said my sister was dead. Then he began talking about the children."

"That must have been rough."

"I didn't even know about Sarah. Can you imagine how that felt? I remember the call so vividly. I thought the man was mistaken when he said three children." She shook her head sadly as she glanced over at the crib. "And now I simply can't imagine life without her."

"What is she? Four, five months old?"

Jillian shrugged. "I think closer to five. James seems to think she was born in January. He said it was still winter."

"She should be sleeping through the night by now."

"That's what all the books say, but they also say that babies should be on a schedule." She glanced up and smiled. "We haven't seemed to get that part down yet. And I'm sure…" She hesitated over what she was about to say. Even thinking it seemed disloyal.

"With all of Annie's problems, poor little Sarah probably wasn't on any kind of schedule with her, either."

"Were you two close before her drug problem?"

She shrugged her shoulders. "Close enough, I guess. We were five years apart so I was far more interested in her than she was in me. Annie seemed so grown up and there I was this clumsy, *gormless* twit always wanting to tag along."

Luke smiled at her description as he settled back in his chair, his hand dropping away from the curtain. "Gormless is bad then?"

"Indeed it is." She traced a figure-eight pattern in the condensation on the side of her glass. "I have a picture of her. Would you like to see it?"

She pushed off the door frame and crossed the room, delving into her purse before he had the opportunity to refuse. With her wallet in hand, she retraced her steps. "Here's one from my last trip. Samuel was a tiny babe. See? That's him in Annie's arms and there's James standing near her."

She retreated carefully as he studied the picture, not sure that standing close to Luke Gianetti was a good idea. She had confirmation when he raised his head to stare at her with those magnetic eyes.

"She looks like you. Hair's a little lighter. Same eyes. Same smile." He glanced down at the picture again and back at her before returning it. "She looks old, though. Tired."

"Annie was so pretty. All the boys were in love with her. She broke several hearts when she hightailed it to the States." She tucked the treasured photo back into her wallet. "What about you? Do you have any brothers or sisters?"

"One brother. He's a surgeon in Chicago." He turned off the television and Jillian watched the glow of the set as it faded into darkness. She knew it was a not so subtle hint to belt up and go to sleep.

"Is that where you're from?"

"Yeah. My parents still live there. They're retired. Dad was a cop and my mom owned a bakery with my aunt Loretta."

"That must have been lovely." She smiled in the dark. "I don't think I could've resisted all those sweets."

"I still can't resist my mother's canoli. I don't get home much anymore, but it's the first thing I think of when I step off the plane at O'Hare." He chuckled as he admitted it. "My brother was more of a bread man. For me it was dessert, but for Vinnie it was Italian bread. He could go through a whole loaf in about ten minutes. His wife finally put a stop to that a couple years ago. Said it was bad for business for a heart surgeon to have love handles."

"Older or younger brother?"

"Vin's older by six years."

"A heart surgeon and a secret agent. Your parents must be terribly proud of you."

"It's always nice to have a doctor in the family."

Jillian didn't miss the slight. "Does your brother have children?"

"Three. All boys. Oldest is about ten." He stood and stretched, effectively ending their conversation. "You'd better get to bed. It's nearly morning."

"All right. Good night, Luke." Throwing caution to the wind for the second time that night, she smiled as she pushed through the bedroom door. "I'll save you some room, in case you change your mind."

She'd finally fallen asleep. Her soft, even breathing was deep and undisturbed. Luke knew this because he was standing a mere two feet away. He'd been sitting at the tiny table, perched in an uncomfortable vinyl chair for the better part of the past hour. Watching. Listening. Waiting. Outside, the night was still and quiet save for the occasional gust of wind that wafted past their room gently lifting the cheap patio chairs that stood outside their door. Luke would've almost called it peaceful. Almost.

His gut didn't think so. And for that reason, he couldn't shake his sense of foreboding. He just didn't know what his gut was trying to tell him. For the first time in years, he was afraid. And it wasn't about drug dealers. And it wasn't about death. Those, he could face. Easily.

No. The urgency twisting his insides made him want to run for cover. He glanced down at Jilly's head on the pillow. True to her word, she'd left him plenty of room.

It was her, dammit. He still wanted her. Badly. His need was an ever-present ache. He was cool with the wanting part. It confirmed that he wasn't completely dead inside. It was the thought of wanting more than sex that made his blood run cold.

He took another step closer to the bed. It was the thought of taking a chance, of *even contemplating* it, that had him cursing himself. How stupid could he get? He'd had his heart ripped out a long time ago. As far as he knew, it hadn't grown back.

He reached out a tentative hand and gently stroked the hair back from her face. And closed his eyes on the rush of pleasure that simply touching her gave him. The long, wavy strands were soft and silky as they slipped through his fingers. And the scent of her hair was driving him nuts.

It was the thought of taking her home to meet his family that made his stomach churn with warning. It was the stupid images that had clouded his brain as he'd talked with her. Images of James and Samuel playing with his nephews. Images of him, God help him, his arm around Jillian as he introduced her to his crazy relatives. Of pulling her into his parents' tiny kitchen and kissing her senseless up against their ancient refrigerator.

He jerked his hand back and retreated to his chair by the window. He ran one hand down his face in a futile effort to regain some control and then shook his head derisively.

"Hey, G-Man, you've definitely lost your mind this time." The nickname reminded him of Murphy. Thank God, he'd be here soon. His partner always called him G-Man, partly because it was short for Gianetti and partly as a joke. Luke was as far from a typical government agent as one would ever find. His partner was more by-the-book than he was and Murph never missed the opportunity to remind him that he never would have cut it as a Fed anywhere else. The other agencies were too rigid. Too many rules. He liked the uncertainty of fieldwork too much, liked the freedom of calling his shots, building his cases from scratch and following through to the end—no matter where it led him.

He checked his watch in the still-dark room. Where the hell was Murphy? He needed him here, needed Murph to create some distance between him and Jill before he went and did something really stupid. Against his better judgment, he'd left the phone number to the room on his partner's voice mail. It was either that or keep running to the pay phone. And at two o'clock in the morning, that probably wasn't such a smart move. Talk about obvious. To the locals, it wouldn't take much to raise a red flag of warning. And a strange man using the pay phone in the wee hours of the night would definitely fit the bill.

He trusted Danny Murphy, his partner for more than four years. Post-Linda years, he liked to think of them. Despite its size, working for the DEA was a pretty insular experience. Personal news traveled fast. And everyone had heard about Linda Gianetti. But undercover work had its benefits. Luke was gone so much of the time that the rampant speculation about his wife had gradually faded. Not that Murphy didn't remember what had happened four years earlier. He just knew better than to ever bring it up.

His mind drifted automatically to the puzzle at hand. Why had the safe house been blown? Jilly had raised a valid question. Were they still after him or her? Neither? Nah. He crossed out "neither." There was no such thing as coincidence.

A more troubling question nagging at the back of his brain was the possibility of a leak. How had Sloan and his dopers learned the location of the safe house? That was highly classified information. Either Sloan had a lot more money and manpower than he'd originally estimated or someone pretty high up the chain was getting nervous.

That led him to replay the scenario with the desk clerk. Luke had wondered why the clerk had been killed when it clearly hadn't been necessary. The goons could've rented the room and then taken all of them out with the silencer they'd used on the motel clerk. Sloan was either getting careless or desperate. And for a sleazebag like Sloan to be desperate, then the kingpin at the top of the pipeline had to be a pretty scary individual.

And if there was a leak, was it DEA or local task force? Was it Spartaville or Charlotte? Or somewhere far away from the action? Clearly he was missing something. Something big. He closed his eyes and fell back in the chair, allowing the pieces of the investigation to free associate in his mind. Given time, they would all fall into place. They always did. The question was, how much time did he have left?

He turned to his right and took stock of all the sleeping bodies he was responsible for and felt his heartbeat accelerate a little. Women and children. An operative's worst nightmare.

Luke couldn't afford any mistakes on this one. Personally, he wasn't afraid to die. Most days he didn't particularly care one way or the other. But innocent people dying on his watch? That was a whole different ball game. He couldn't let it happen again.

Out of a sound sleep she bolted up, her heart racing. It was still dark. Jilly was half out of bed when a set of hands pushed her gently back against the pillows. "Sarah?" Her speech sounded heavy and slurred to her own ears.

"Shh. I've got her. She's fine."

"Bottle."

"Honey, she's nearly finished it."

"She can't haf honey...she's not—she's...old enough."

Jillian frowned at the chuckling sound. What was so bloody funny?

She must have spoken out loud, because he laughed again before answering.

"Your accent is very pronounced in the dead of night, lovie."

The deep, masculine voice was husky and soothing to her ears and the warm, stroking hand comforting against her cheek. She turned into his palm and mumbled what she deemed a highly appropriate response before she sighed and slid back in to sleep.

Jillian blinked the sleep from her eyes and glanced over at the window. She slid down between the sheets and sighed with pleasure at the cool crisp feel of cotton against her legs. Sunlight struggled to filter through the heavy drapes. She scrunched up her nose as she tried to remember where she was. "What time is it?"

"Too early. Sleep a few more minutes."

The drowsy voice belonged to Luke. As did the arm that was draped across her stomach. And that was clearly his chest that she was tucked up against. Her heart began beating wildly and she came more fully awake. Dear Lord, those were his long, muscular legs tangled up with hers. And didn't they feel incredible?

"You having a heart attack or are you just happy to see me?"

She couldn't contain the shiver that swept through her at his whispered words. She took in a ragged breath. How could anyone sound so unbelievably sexy this early in the morning?

"I thought you said this was a bad idea." Her voice came out on a squeak and she winced as she cleared her throat. His response was to pull her back against him when she tried to move away.

"I think I've changed my mind. I think the idea has merit."

He dropped a kiss on the side of her neck and chuckled when she bit back a soft moan.

"Stop that. The children will be awake in moments." Jillian knew that it was more of a plea than a demand, but she prayed that he wouldn't hear the panic in her voice.

"Kids can sleep through anything."

"Luke!" She turned to face him then and flattened her hands on his chest in an attempt to put an end to his nonsense. His wavy, surfer-gold hair was tousled from sleep, the color matching the stubble on his cheeks. She rolled her eyes at his lopsided grin and the mischievous glint in his eyes. And in spite of herself, she laughed. "Please, we can't do this," she whispered. "We simply can't."

"Why cahn't we?" He deliberately dragged out his pronunciation to match hers.

"Are you making fun?"

"Would I do that?"

"I'm not the one with the accent. It's all of you—"

He swooped in for a kiss and a moment later, she forgot what they had been talking about. It was all she could do to stay conscious under the violent wave of sensation Luke aroused. Any second now she would spin completely out of control. He was, hands down, the best kiss she'd ever experienced.

Damn him. Why did he have to be so bloody tempting?

It was Luke who finally pulled back. Luke who heard Sarah begin to fuss in her portable crib. Luke who still had his wits about him mere seconds after removing his tongue from her mouth. She, on the other hand, wanted to weep with frustration.

Instead she fell back against the pillows, stunned silent as he padded across the room to scoop Sarah up from her crib.

"Yo, Jill…"

"What?" She lifted herself up on her elbows to meet his gaze. She watched him warily as he crossed the room and tried desperately not to notice how delightful he looked with a sleepy baby nestled against one chiseled shoulder.

"You're right. We definitely shouldn't be doing that with the kids around."

She managed to smile at him despite the longing that grew more insistent with each passing moment. She smiled in spite of the hollow ache in her chest, an ache she was beginning to suspect had nothing to do with wanting him physically. "I'm right?"

The intensity of his gaze forced heat back into her cheeks and she swallowed hard. Jillian didn't know which was worse, when he smiled or when he simply told her with his eyes what he was thinking.

"Yeah. When we finally make love, we are definitely gonna need to be alone."

"We, uh, will?" Not "if." He'd said *when*. Her mouth was so dry she could barely formulate words. And her heart pounded so loud, the racket in her ears nearly drowned out his voice.

The smile returned to his lips and she could tell it was all he could do to keep from grinning. "My gut tells me you're gonna make a lot of noise."

"Your stomach seems to tell you a great deal."

"Not my stomach. My gut."

"Your gut might be wrong, you know." She scowled at him and sat up, swinging her legs over the side of the bed. "In fact, I have it on good authority that your gut is way off on this one."

"Honey, my gut is *never* wrong." He placed Sarah into her outstretched arms, deliberately brushing against her as he made the transfer. At her involuntary shiver of awareness, he nodded in confirmation and lowered his voice. "We'll just have to wait and see."

"So what happens next?" Jillian smiled down into Sarah's cooing face as she changed her diaper. "Have you worked out a plan?"

Luke set down the styrofoam cup of coffee he had been sipping while he studied the notes he'd made during the night. "We sit tight. Murphy'll be here in a couple hours. Then we're gonna split up and—"

"Split up?" She jerked her head up at the news. He was getting rid of them?

"Not us. Me and him," Luke explained. "He's bringing me some gear, thank God, and a couple guys so we can finally run this op like we need to. We'll have communication with the ASAC and once Murph and I fill in the blanks, we'll decide where I'm gonna stash you."

"I'm confused. Are we going up to Charlotte or somewhere else?" She settled Sarah into the portable crib with her toys.

"Don't know yet, lovie." He winked at Samuel, still in his pajamas while he drove his tiny toy cars over each piece of furniture in the spartan room. Samuel paused the roaring engine sound to smile back at Luke.

"Wanna play? I gots more cars."

"Thanks, Sammy. I'll have to take a rain check. How about this afternoon?"

Samuel nodded and drove the car up one of Luke's arms and down the other before continuing along the headboard of the bed.

"Blast! Sarah just spit up on her last clean shirt." Jilly glanced across the room at him. "All right if I run down to the car and get her case?"

His immediate frown clued her in on his thought process. "No, it's not all right. Put her in something dirty."

"I certainly will not do that. She has a dozen outfits in the car."

"After what happened last night, you're not going anywhere, not outside, not down to the car."

"Honestly, Luke, you were out there for half an hour and you didn't turn up any thugs or bombs or anything. What could've happened since then?"

"I just brought you a suitcase," he reminded her in a pa- thetically obvious attempt to change the subject.

"Well, it's the wrong one. I said I wanted the blue one."

"They're all blue."

"I meant my sister's blue one. It'll only take a minute." She rose to her feet.

"When Murph gets here I'll go down to the car and get it." In the blink of an eye, he'd risen from the chair to block her movement toward the door.

"I don't need a damn bodyguard to walk to the car." She strode to the window and thrust the curtain aside. "Right there." She tapped the glass. "That lilac tree. The car's only about twenty feet away." She swung around to meet his gaze. "Take a look. We've practically got the whole motel to our- selves."

"The car is more like a hundred yards away." He shook his head in exasperation. "Remember what I said about obey- ing my orders?"

"I agreed not to argue with you. I don't recall the word 'obey' being part of our discussion."

"And this isn't arguing?" He threw his pencil down on the table and stalked over to the window. "All right. I'll go down to the damn car. Where's the suitcase you need? You've only got like a hundred of them down there."

"I'm not on a bloody vacation, Luke. I moved my entire life across the ocean. It's a miracle I was able to fit everything into the boot of one car."

"Save the tirade for when I come back. I'll be happy to discuss your luggage issues after I've made sure you don't get killed while I'm looking for a damn baby outfit." Once he'd surveyed the perimeter, he turned to glare at her. "Which suitcase?"

Hands on her hips, she bit back the caustic remark she wanted to make. "Since you got rid of my car last night, I don't know where anything is now. I had the boot completely organized and you've gone and piled everything into the new one.''

"What color is it?" His jaw was so rigid he seemed to ask the question through his teeth.

"It's periwinkle."

"What the hell is periwinkle?"

She rolled her eyes in disbelief. "It's blue, dammit. It's a little blue bag and it's got a strap like a diaper bag."

"Jesus, I oughta have my head examined." Luke jerked his gun off the table and checked the clip. Then he strode to the door and jerked it open. "Close this up tight and don't open it for anyone, got it?"

She squeezed his hand as he walked past, well aware that he'd gone stiff with protest. He was probably already regretting his decision. And for that reason, she didn't linger. "Thank you, Luke. I swear we'll be careful."

"Good. If you hear gunfire, I'd suggest you hit the deck and start praying." He yanked the door shut with enough force to make her wince. Belatedly she realized that she probably shouldn't have provoked him. She could have rinsed Sarah's shirt out in the sink and dried it on the towel bar. But bloody hell, she was getting tired of all this cloak-and-dagger nonsense. This was their third day in captivity and there was no foreseeable end in sight. She was beginning to feel like a caged animal at the zoo.

She glanced at James and Samuel who had paused mid-drag race to listen with interest as they argued. "It's all right, boys. Luke's not angry. He's just worried about us."

"Well, you shouldna made him go out for some stupid shirt."

"Thank you, James. I don't believe Sarah would appreciate your comment." She clicked on the television as she smiled at the baby. Sarah probably didn't care that she had formula all down the front of her, but by God, she did. No decent mother would allow her children to traipse around in dirty clothes. And she was getting damn tired of Luke ordering her around as if she were some brainless twit.

"Hey, turn it up. That's Luke!" James cocked his head as he stared at the screen. "Least, I think it's him. He's got short hair."

Her breath caught in her throat as she turned up the volume. And then her heart began to pound when she heard the words "dead" and "motel clerk" and "drug runner" associated with Luke—with the man she thought was Luke. Actually his name was really Billy T. Lathrop. She winced at the familiar pictures of the motel they'd left the previous morning.

Her mind flew back to yesterday, to the blood-spattered shirt Luke had been wearing. She remembered his urgency, his insistence that they leave before dawn. That was why they were still on the run. That was why his DEA partners hadn't shown up and why he didn't have any identification. Luke had a perfectly good reason for not wanting to go to a hospital that first day. He wasn't with the bloody DEA.

Good God, she was supposed to be hiding *from* drug dealers, not *with* them. She swallowed hard and tasted terror as her brain made the connection that they were all in terrible danger. She felt her palms start to sweat and she scrubbed them viciously against her jeans while she made a beeline for the door. And to think that she'd been taken in by him. Why, she'd practically slept with him. Hell, she'd thrown herself at him. And all the while he'd been playing her for a bloody fool.

Dear, sweet Lord. Luke was the enemy.

Chapter 7

"Jilly, what are ya doing?"

"I'm locking the door." She grunted as she pushed the small dining table in front of the door.

"How's Luke gonna get back inside with that big table blockin' it?"

She paused to push the hair out of her eyes. "He's not coming back in here."

"Why not? How's he gonna keep us safe if you lock him out?"

"James, please. Not now. I've got to think of a plan. I have to figure out what I'm going to do."

"What are you talkin' about? Luke's a good guy. He didn't kill nobody." James crossed the room and began tugging on the table to move it out of the way.

"Love, what do you think you're doing? Get away from there this very minute."

"Jilly, he's not a drug dealer. He's too nice." James folded his arms across his slender chest and scowled at her. "He's not like any of the drug dealers I know."

"Oh, really? And just how many drug dealers have you managed to come across in six years?" She nearly jumped a foot when she heard Luke's key turn in the lock. "Bloody hell. He's back already?"

She heard his muffled curse when the door nudged against the table she'd placed in front of it. "Go away," she called. "You're not coming back in here."

"What in the sweet hell is going on in there?"

She threw herself against the table when she felt him try to force the door on the other side. She was pushing so hard that she didn't even feel it when James and Samuel started pulling her from behind. "Dammit, James. Let go of me!"

"Open this freakin' door. What the hell's blocking it?"

"It's Jilly," James cried. "She gone crazy. She saw you on TV and now she's got all the furniture in front of the door."

"Thanks a lot, James. Crazy, indeed." She cringed when Luke let out a string of curses that had the air turning blue and then promptly crashed to the floor when James gave her an almighty pull from behind. From her new spot on the carpet, she watched Luke's feet pace back and forth in front of the door and winced when she heard his tirade about dizzy, overreactive women.

"I am not bloody overreacting. You're the damn enemy." She rose unsteadily to her feet and bit her lip as she watched James struggle to push the table free. "No, James. We can't let—"

Luke kicked the door in just as James slid the table out of the way. The door flung open and reverberated off the wall, bouncing back in time for Luke to close it behind him.

"Here's your damn bag." He tossed the suitcase onto the bed with such force that it bounced off and landed near her on the floor. Then he crouched to lift James from the carpet.

"Now that we've got that settled, you okay, bud?"

"Yeah, I'm good." James accepted his hand and popped up from the floor.

"Thanks for letting me in."

James rolled his eyes toward Jillian before he answered. "Yeah. No problem."

"You okay, Sammy?" She watched, stupefied, as Samuel nodded yes and ran over to hug Luke around the legs.

"And what about you?" She winced when he took three steps into the room and towered over her. "I'm gone five minutes and I come back to hysterics. What the hell is going on?"

"I am *not* hysterical." She noticed he didn't offer her a hand up off the floor. Sarah must have sensed the tension because she began whimpering in her crib. Without taking his gaze from Jilly, Luke reached down to scoop her up and cradled her against his shoulder as he rocked back and forth to comfort her.

"You lied to me. You're not with the DEA. You're a bloody drug dealer. For God's sake…you've killed someone."

"And you learned all of this how?" His stance still clearly angry, Luke refused to budge an inch. He should have been apologizing to her for withholding information. He should have been groveling, admitting that he lied.

"We saw it on TV, Luke." James flounced down on the end of the couch. "Your picture was on. An' you know what? You had real short hair. They said you killed a guy at the hotel, but I didn't believe it."

Samuel nodded in agreement and Jillian groaned as she got to her feet. What was it about him? A complete stranger, possibly a killer at that, and he inspired the children to more loyalty than they felt for her.

Her eyes wary, she stared at him. "Well, what are you going to do with us now?"

"I have half a mind to gag you and throw you in the trunk of the car. But there's already too much luggage in there." Her indignant gasp was cut off when he turned on her, finally letting his anger show. "Just so you know, I could've been shot out there while you're in here playing freakin' games."

"Games? How dare you? You kill some poor, innocent motel clerk and then you're surprised when I try to defend myself?" She launched at him, thrusting her finger into his chest. "What do you take me for?"

"I thought you had some sense in that dizzy head of yours."

"Dizzy! I'm dizzy?" She cringed at the sound of her voice. It would definitely qualify as a shriek. "You bastard!"

"Oops. That was a big one, Jilly." James fell back against the cushions laughing at the sight of her apparent meltdown. Samuel immediately followed suit, despite his lack of understanding of what the commotion was about.

"I distinctly remember you telling me yesterday that you hadn't killed anyone."

"So, you're willing to believe something you heard on TV rather than me?"

"I don't know you from a hole in the wall," she admitted. "If you were telling the truth, you would have mentioned shooting a clerk."

"Oh, really? So now I'm supposed to clue you in on the whole operation?" He folded his arms across his chest and stared down at her, his eyes still glacial.

"You promised to keep me informed. This is my life we're talking about—and the three children I am responsible for—not you."

"I forgot, okay? With everything else going on, I forgot to tell you about the clerk. Would you have felt better? Knowing someone was dead? Knowing that the guys after us are willing to kill you, too?"

"At least I would have been operating with all the facts, Agent Gianetti—if that's really your name."

"Of course it's my freaking name," he snapped. "Why would I make that up?"

Hands on hips, she glared at him. "Is there anything more you're holding back, Billy T.?"

"What we're dealing with is bad enough. I don't need you having a damn breakdown in the middle of it."

"I liked you so much better without the superior attitude, Luke. You know, I might just be able to help."

He snorted. "I don't need you to invite them all up for tea and scones. What are you," he continued, "some kind of British operative?" His smile was tight as he ran his gaze derisively over her. "So tell me, Your Ladyship, what's our plan? I'm all ears."

She was appalled to discover her eyes filling with tears. How could she ever have been attracted to him? How could she have thought him to be kind and decent? Luke was ruthless and hard. And he was cruel.

She swung away quickly, heading for the bedroom. The last thing she needed was for him to see her cry. He'd only use it to humiliate her a little more. She jerked Sarah's suitcase up from the floor and blindly pushed past him.

Luke took a deep breath and sank down onto the end of the couch when he heard the bathroom door click shut. God, he was such an almighty jerk. He'd blown it with her again. Any other time and the situation would have been comical. And incredibly sweet. Jilly'd had the intelligence to react quickly to a threat, one that she perceived to be real. She'd had the gut instinct to protect her children. She'd been willing to fight him even though he was bigger, stronger and better prepared for battle.

And he'd totally overreacted.

All because she hadn't trusted him. He'd been so confident that he'd won her over. That his powers of persuasion and her accepting nature meant that she would do what he asked without question. And it had pissed him off to learn that she wouldn't. Dammit, he'd meant to tell her about the clerk. He'd simply forgotten.

James came over and squeezed next to him on the love

seat. A moment later he felt the cushions sag behind him when Samuel climbed up and leaned against him, his soft little body resting against his back. He closed his eyes for a minute and concentrated on the sweet warm weight leaning against him. How could something so small and so insignificant feel so good? He had Sarah's warm weight on his shoulder, her face snuffling against his neck, James tucked into his side and Sammy behind him.

"She's crying, ya know."

"Yeah, I know." Luke heard the shower turn on and knew he'd really hurt her. She seemed to take showers all the time, and especially when she was at the end of her rope.

James shook his head in understanding. "You shoulda seen her. She went nuts when she saw you on TV. She freaked out and started moving furniture."

"She did the right thing," he admitted. "I was wrong to yell at her. She was trying to protect you guys."

"Yeah, but—"

"No buts, Jimmy. Think about it. How does she know I'm not a drug dealer?"

James tilted his head sideways to give Luke a look that told him he was totally lame. In an odd way it warmed his heart that the kid had such faith in him.

"You're nothing like the dealers we used to have at my house. They were all dirtbags."

He felt the shudder that coursed through James's too thin body and felt his gut tighten to red alert. He shifted on the bed to face James and swung Sarah down from his shoulder to sit in his lap. Very cautiously, he stuck a toe in the water. "What do you mean?"

"My mommy, she, um, took drugs sometimes."

"That must've been tough on you, Jimmy."

"Yeah, not so much on me but Samuel. He's really little and Sarah's just a baby."

Luke felt like crying over his matter-of-fact tone. "So, how do you know about drug dealers?"

"Oh, that. Well, they were in our house all the time." He glanced over Luke's shoulder and dropped his voice to a whisper. "Sam's daddy was a druggie, an' Sarah's daddy, too." He reached out a finger and smiled when Sarah grabbed it and started tugging. "Sarah's daddy was Slow."

"Slow?"

"Yeah. An' he was real mean to us." James wiped his eyes and turned away from him.

Luke's heart wrenched for the kid, for what he'd lived through and for what he would probably never forget. "Hey, pal, it's okay now."

James snuffled away the tears, determined to be tough. "I used to hide the kids from him," he admitted as he wiped his eyes on his sleeve. "He didn't like us very much. He was real bad to my mommy."

He felt his pulse accelerate when James's voice dropped to a whisper. "He hurt her. A lot."

"Did she try to fight him?"

"Uh-huh. They yelled a lot. And then one day he shot her. Him and his friend. They laughed about it."

Luke's heart stopped for a moment as he absorbed the blow. And then he pulled Jimmy roughly against him, tucking him against his chest when the little boy began to sob. "I'm so sorry, Jimmy."

James cried for another minute, an almost silent sound, allowing his grief to show for perhaps the very first time. When he finally pulled out of Luke's arms, he sat up straight and tugged his shirt free, pulling it up to wipe his eyes, his breath still coming in shuddering gasps.

"Mommy got him back, though. She laid there acting like she was dead. Then when Sarah's daddy left with his friend, she crawled into our room and got Samuel and Sarah."

Luke sat in stunned silence while he digested James's story. "What happened then?"

"She took us downstairs to some old lady. Mommy said she was our friend." James hesitated, frowning as he tried to remember. "I can't 'member her name but I 'member Mommy sayin' we'd be safe there."

"And then?"

"I'm not too sure. She told the lady she had to call her sister. I think that was Aunt Jilly. And then she said she knew where a whole bunch a' money was and that she was gonna get it so Aunt Jilly would take care of us."

James's eyes filled with tears and he quickly blinked them back and bit his lip to keep it from quivering. The action reminded him so much of Jilly. The depth of control absolutely floored him. The freakin' kid was six.

"She had a h-hole in her stomach. I tried to help her but she w-wouldn't let me. She said she was gonna go get it fixed. I— She left an' we never saw her again after that."

Luke gave him a little squeeze and kissed the top of his head. In the back of his brain, he heard the shower shut off in the bathroom, heard the water trickling as it drained in the tub. Jilly was through crying, too. Soon it would be time to apologize. And to find out more about Annie Moseby. Why the hell hadn't Jilly told him her only sister had been murdered?

He never got the chance to apologize, Luke realized later. Murphy finally arrived, thank God, and with him came several hours of unruly confusion as they set up a command post in the room next door. By the time Jilly surfaced from the bathroom, there were three more federal agents squeezed into the room. Judging by the scowl on her face, Luke knew she was thinking that he'd invited his co-workers to set up camp in the hotel suite not to save her ass, but simply to prove her wrong.

She'd studiously ignored him after he made the introductions. She liked Murphy, that was pretty clear. Usually everyone did. On the surface, Danny Murphy was Mr. Nice Guy. He knew how to talk to women, knew how to finesse them for what he wanted. Luke usually excelled in that area, too.

It was a necessary part of the job. But nothing about this op had gone according to plan. Not by a long shot.

He clearly hadn't used the right maneuvers to gain Jillian's cooperation. She'd questioned his authority from the start. He tried not to let it bother him while he watched her from the corner of the room. Watched as she cooperated with Murphy. No fits of temper. No complaints. She smiled sweetly at him and did whatever he requested. The other two agents were from Charlotte. One of them was familiar. He'd worked with Josephson before on a few takedowns. The other guy, Petrie, he didn't know at all. But by all appearances, he seemed to be the communications genius that Murphy'd claimed he was.

The ASAC's plan was to lure Sloan out of hiding by dangling Luke as the bait. Duncan hadn't bothered to consult him about the specifics of this strategy. For example, what was he supposed to do with Jilly and the kids while this op went down? But, the cheese had already been planted in the trap and by now Sloan was probably already sniffing around to make sure the bait was genuine and not strychnine.

Their location had been carefully leaked. Now all they had to do was wait him out. According to headquarters, a covert team had planted a transponder on a vehicle believed to be Sloan's. A surveillance team was in place to follow his movement, another to intercept him as he approached their location. No one else would watch the motel. Luke wasn't crazy about that part either, but they'd all agreed that Sloan would be scared away if he caught even a whiff of a possible setup.

The only thing they hadn't been in agreement on was where to stash Jilly and the kids. Murph wanted them out of the way and in another safe house, but something about that left Luke distinctly unsettled. He couldn't forget the series of explosions he'd witnessed on the television the previous night. Nor could he forget that somewhere, somehow, someone had known exactly where they were headed.

He still wasn't completely convinced that Sloan was after only him. What if he really was after Jilly because she was a witness and for the simple reason that she'd seen one of his thugs? His gut was adamant. She and the kids weren't leaving his side.

That left two choices. He could bow out of the op and take them to safety. But he was the bait. Would they really be safe traveling with him? He was no closer to an answer on that question than he'd been two days earlier. If he hit the road with them, he could end up exposing them to even greater danger.

The other option was to keep Jill and the kids out of sight and hope the takedown went like clockwork. In a perfect scenario, no one would get hurt and Sloan would be under arrest. But if the bust went south like it had on Tuesday...

He shook his head. He was pretty much damned no matter which option he chose, because there were no freaking guarantees. More than anything, he wanted the arrest to go flawlessly. He wanted to see Sloan captured with his own eyes. It was the only way to know for sure that Jilly would be safe. It was the only way he could safely set her free.

He crossed the room, signaling Murphy with his eyes. His partner nodded and casually followed him through the connecting door to the next room. Luke smiled at the boys bouncing on the beds. They might not be able to go outside, but at least for the moment, they had more space to play in.

Murphy flopped down at the table by the window and leaned forward, arms resting on the cool surface. "So, G, what's with the hot little number in there? You gotten any action yet or are you still doing the monk routine?"

Luke felt his body go rigid with fury, but forced back the comment he wanted to make. Not cool. If he said anything foul, Murph would be all over him in a heartbeat. He'd never hear the end of it.

"Yeah. We've had nothin' but time to get it on. And with only three kids in the room, it's been a breeze." If he was gonna be angry, it should be with himself. Hell, his partner was right. Jillian was hot. He'd had the chance and he'd blown it. She'd offered herself up on a freaking platter.

"If I hadn't screwed up," he reminded Murphy, "she wouldn't be in danger. The least I can do is try to keep her from getting killed. I'm protecting her and the kids. That's the extent of my interest."

"Well, if you're not interested, Josephson's gonna take a whack at her." Murphy shrugged his shoulders. "Heck, if I weren't married, I'd be thinkin' about it."

Luke launched off the bed and headed for the door. "Joe better keep his hands to himself if he knows what's good for him."

"Well, it's about friggin' time."

He stopped cold at his friend's words. "What the hell is that supposed to mean?"

Murphy smiled and stood, stretching his long legs. "For not bein' interested in her you sure sound interested."

"Lay off, Murphy." He shook his head in an effort to contain his anger and retraced his steps, reminding himself that his friend was deliberately trying to provoke him. And damned if he wasn't falling right into Murphy's trap. His partner didn't know jack about the situation. Frankly, Luke didn't give a damn who Jillian ended up with just as long as it wasn't on his watch. He forced himself to let it go. They had business to attend to. "How about we try and focus on this take-down?"

Murphy shrugged and pulled out the chair again. "Suits me just fine. Didn't mean to upset you."

"I'm not upset," he said through clenched teeth. Murphy's booming laugh made the kids glance in their direction. Luke rubbed his tired eyes and prayed for the strength not to haul off and punch Murphy.

Desperate to change the subject, he grasped for the first thing that came to his mind. "Did you check out that lead on Annie Moseby yet?" The least he could do was find out what had really happened to Jilly's sister. If she ever chose to speak to him again, he'd be able to relate what he'd learned. That was assuming she didn't already know what had happened to Annie and like everything else, she'd been holding out on him.

"Comin' up with nothin' so far. Ya know how it is, one dead addict is just like another."

"This addict was murdered."

"Yeah, well, the task force doesn't have time to slog through a bunch of Jane Does right now." He huffed into a chair and scratched his balding head. "Priority one is luring Sloan out here. But if you ask me, it doesn't look good. I don't think you're a big enough draw."

"I agree." In his gut, he felt the op was a waste of time. He wasn't important enough to draw Sloan out of hiding.

"You know his woman's missing all of a sudden."

"Winnie? What's going on? You think he's hit the road with her?"

"Dunno. Maybe she left him and he's gone after her." He paused, warming to their what-if game. "Maybe he freaked out after Tuesday's close call and *he* took off and left her holding the bag."

"That doesn't sound like him. He's too arrogant. Sloan wouldn't run." Luke shook his head. "He'd want to thumb his nose at us."

"Beats me. It's just funny they're both gone. We've been monitoring their movements for months—why would they leave now? There's a ton of cash missing, too, if you listen to the rumors."

"Where are you hearing this?" Luke straddled the chair opposite his partner.

"Crackheads, dopers, scumbags, you know, the junkie grapevine." Murphy shook his head in disgust. "You can't trust anything they say, so who knows what really happened. Maybe Winnie just got tired of gettin' the crap kicked out of her and she took off."

"Sounds like our boy's had his troubles lately."

"Yeah, first his lieutenant gets blown away and now some-one's made off with his chick and his cash. Gotta hurt." Mur-phy shook his head and smiled.

"Who do you think burned Gomez?"

"Who knows? Probably some other punk in the pecking order." Murphy chuckled. "You know how it works. Only way to get a promotion is to kill someone on the next rung up the ladder."

"Maybe that's why Sloan's sweating."

"Yeah. His friggin' operation's falling apart, he's got the Feds breathin' down his neck and his boss probably ain't too thrilled about the missing money."

Luke glanced up. "What if Mr. Big doesn't know about it?"

Murphy's drumming fingers paused on the table. "Jesus, I wouldn't wanna be Sloan when Castillo finds out. What's he gonna say? 'Gee, my girlfriend left me and my assistant got shot. And, oh yeah, I've misplaced your three hundred grand.'"

"Either he's frantic to cover it up or he's trying to fix it. Maybe to buy more time?"

"You're dreaming. Where's he gonna come up with that kind of cash?" Murphy shook his head. "If you're right, he ain't gonna be able to hide it much longer. The heroin drops have been spaced about ten days apart. You can almost set your watch by them. Castillo's gotta be leaning on Sloan for the money from the last shipment."

"Talk about all hell breaking loose. If Sloan gets taken out, there'll be a helluva war over his turf. The task force better order up a supply of body bags." Luke threw his pencil down, frustrated.

Something still didn't make sense. If the money really was missing then Sloan had to be scrambling. Hell, if he didn't have a price tag on his head yet, he would soon enough. No one messed with Castillo and lived to talk about it.

And if he was on the run, why would he blow resources

chasing them? He wouldn't have time to waste on a dealer like him. Billy T. Lathrop was small-time in comparison. And while Sloan might want to kill Luke for being a narc, at the moment he clearly had bigger fish to fry.

What was making him pursue them? What was the reason he would drive out into the mountains of North Carolina? It couldn't be a vendetta. There had to be something more. Which led him back to Jilly. Was Sloan after her? And if so, why?

Luke rose from his seat and edged closer to the mattress. The boys were jumping wildly on the beds. Any minute now and they'd be airborne. He wouldn't score any points with Jilly if one of them busted his head open.

"I'm gonna have Petrie run a check on Sloan's cash flow. Maybe you hit on something. Maybe he's trying to cover the loss himself until he can find his missing cash." Murphy made a note on a scrap of paper he pulled from his pocket. "Sloan's runnin' out of time. Whoever Castillo is, the big man's gonna find out soon."

Luke mentally shifted gears. "Hey, what do you know about this Petrie guy? Who is he? Where's he work out of?"

His partner shrugged. "I've seen him around. I think he's out of the Philly office originally. He's been involved with the CENTAC task force in other cities, mostly south Florida, I think. I don't know what he was doing for them in Spartaville."

"But you've worked with him? He's good?"

"Everything I've heard about him is great. Electronics wizard…blah, blah, blah."

"Okay." The knots in Luke's stomach loosened just a bit. "If you get a chance check out the Moseby thing."

"Remind me again in a week or two. Right now, we're stretched pretty thin. We lost two CENTAC members in the raid Tuesday," Murphy explained. "No DEA, but a couple of local task force guys. One from Spartaville P.D. and one from the sheriff's department."

"Yeah. Sorry I had to cut out on you and miss everything."

His partner paused to grin. "Hey, G-man, I forgot. How's your ass?"

Luke scowled as he lunged to the edge of the bed, caught Samuel in mid-leap and steadied him. Dammit. Someone had squealed. "How'd you hear about that?"

Murphy stood and cocked his head toward the beds where James and Samuel were whooping it up jumping from one bed to the other. "Jimbo told me about five minutes after we got here. Said you got shot in the ass and you weren't wearing underwear anymore."

"Damn."

"Hey, I was pretty psyched for you. Especially the no underwear part."

Luke ignored his stupid grin. "That reminds me, have this checked out by ballistics when you get a chance." He dropped the slug Jilly had removed into Murphy's hand.

"Wow. Can I keep it? I mean, it's like a part of you." He took his time pocketing the bullet.

"Shove it." His partner cracked up, laughing loud enough for James to pause mid-bounce. "Do you think there's any way we could get that round analyzed by an outside lab?"

Murphy went very still, any trace of humor disappearing. "What do you mean?" He shot a furtive glance over his shoulder and moved away from the connecting door. "You think there's a leak?"

He nodded.

"What makes you think that?"

"The safe house, for one thing." He hesitated, hating the thought that he might be wrong. Hell, he probably *was* wrong. Lowering his voice, he asked the question that had been eating away at the lining of his stomach. "Have you thought about Tuesday? How it went down?"

His partner nodded. "Yeah. Not our usual style. It felt a little weird. I didn't like all the loose ends."

"Like, where was our backup?" Luke asked.

"And why didn't they see the shooters?" Murphy muttered. "I was wondering why Sloan seemed so relaxed, you know, sort of like he was biding his time, sort of like he was waiting for something else to go down."

"Or maybe he was waiting for his own backup," Luke added. "Yeah, I noticed." He swallowed hard. Christ, he hoped he was wrong. Their mission was to shut down a major source of heroin pouring into the southeast by way of Mexico. And while there were several players at Sloan's level, CENTAC had linked them all to only one supplier, Castillo—the infamous mystery man

If there was a leak, then it was someone damn close to the details of the CENTAC task force investigation. And if that were the case, then the leak could be someone on the task force or associated with it. Trouble was that the task force was a huge joint coalition of multistate, multijurisdictional overlapping agencies. The enemy could be anyone…at any level.

Or he could be in the same room.

"About that bullet—" Luke nodded to the next room "—maybe you should keep it to yourself."

"Yeah." Murphy nodded, his eyebrows now drawn down in a scowl. "I think that can be arranged. I'll make a few calls."

"Why didn't you tell me your sister was murdered?"

Jilly tried her best to avoid eye contact with him. Despite the fact that she was still deeply annoyed with Luke for insulting her, her damn heartbeat refused to recognize the fact. It accelerated alarmingly fast every time she had the misfortune of laying eyes on him. Agent Gianetti was surly and rude, and she simply couldn't tolerate the man for another second.

"I told you Annie was killed by drugs. I believe that to be an accurate portrayal."

"It sounds to me like Annie was killed by a bullet. Why didn't you say that?"

She glared at him then, infuriated by his condescending attitude. "What could it possibly matter? She was a drug addict, like thousands of others. If she hadn't been addicted, she wouldn't have been shot. Why do you care how she died?"

"Because it was a murder, Jill. Don't you care who did it?"

"How dare you? Of course I care. She was my sister." She blinked back angry tears as she advanced on him, wanting badly to wipe the incredulous expression from his face. "I can't change the fact that she was murdered. And neither can you, *Agent* Gianetti—not with your bloody guns, not with all your fancy equipment and not with your drug busts. None of that will bring my sister back."

"What about justice?"

"Don't lecture me about principles, Luke. I don't have time for justice." She caught the interested glances from across the room and lowered her voice. "I've got three children to raise. If I can manage to do that, if I can overcome the disruption to their lives—" She swallowed hard around the lump of anguish clogging her throat. "If by some miracle, I can provide stability and try to erase the horror they've lived through, then justice will be served."

"So, you don't care if her killer goes free?" His laser-beam eyes narrowed in disbelief.

"You really do believe I'm completely stupid, don't you?" She clamped her lips together to keep them from trembling. He was the most arrogant, insufferable man she had ever met.

"Do you think I flew over here and buried her in the backyard?" She shook her head in disgust. "The police were involved, Luke. There was an autopsy. I'm sure all the details are buried on some bureaucrat's desk somewhere. If you're so bloody fascinated, you can check it out yourself once you're rid of us. Then you can send me a copy of your report."

She sank down onto the edge of the bed and bit her lip to

keep from crying. Why was he doing this? Why did he persist in upsetting her?

"Jill, perhaps we got off on the wrong foot. I was trying to help, that's all. I figured I could check into it for you and get some details. I didn't mean to hurt you by bringing it up."

"Don't bother. I really don't need to know." The mattress sank when he sat beside her and she winced at the incredible sensation caused by his thigh touching hers. He leaned forward, resting his elbows on his knees.

"Do you have any of her personal effects? Any notes?"

She shook her head. He simply didn't know when to quit. "Just the three suitcases. The children didn't have much."

"That's it? You're sure?"

Still unable to look at him, she shivered at the gruff persistence in his voice. He never gave up. The knowledge made her want to weep. Why couldn't he want her like that? Like she was a war worth winning? He wanted answers. He wanted convictions. He wanted justice. And in the end, he'd probably die fighting for them.

"Look, I said some things earlier that I probably shouldn't have."

"If that's your version of an apology, it's rather pitiful." Jillian felt his hand clamp around her arm and pull her up from the bed and into the far corner of the room.

"Unhand me this instant. You're embarrassing me in front of your friends." Her face heated with anger. How dare he? The room was full of agents. The children were shrieking in the next room. Sarah was fussing. It was bloody chaos.

"I don't give a rat's as— I mean, I don't give a damn." He shook his head in exasperation. "You know what I mean."

"Yes. I can see the bar-of-soap trick is working splendidly. Why, you're truly a changed man."

"You're driving me insane. Do you know that?" He released her arm and took a step back. "I'm sorry. Okay? I was angry and I said things I didn't mean. You reacted to the television report just as you should have. The bottom line is you were protecting your kids and that was the right thing to do.''

"Then why didn't you at least try to see it from my perspective?''

"How about seeing this from my point of view? I left you alone to retrieve a freaking diaper bag of all things.'' He dragged his fingers through his hair, looking as though he wanted to pull it out. "I was a sitting duck out there. If there'd been a sniper in the woods, we'd all be dead. I didn't have time for hysterics—not that you were acting hysterical,'' he quickly amended.

She folded her arms across her chest. "I see.''

"I was pissed, all right?'' He grimaced and lowered his voice. Luke was clearly a man who was unaccustomed to explaining himself and least of all to a female. "I thought you trusted me,'' he said. "So, I apologize. Okay? For hurting your feelings.''

She swallowed hard, her heart suddenly thumping far too fast for its own good. Lord, he was absolutely devastating when he stared at her like that. She could almost pretend that the worry reflected in his eyes was concern for her and that maybe he liked her just a bit. Maybe he really was sorry.

"Look, you need to get over this. I don't want it to affect us.''

"Us?'' Her pulse leaped foolishly into a gallop. He did care. She knew it!

"I don't want to blow this op. When I give an order, you've got to do it without hesitation. Without question. Are we clear on this?''

He didn't care a whit for her. It was simply another ploy to gain her cooperation. Luke Gianetti had to be the greatest undercover operative the DEA had ever known, because he was the best liar she'd ever met. And she was the most pathetic woman on the planet.

"Apology accepted. You have my word I will belt up for the sake of your mission. Now, get away from me."

His eyes widened in confusion. "Now what have I done?"

She glanced beyond his shoulder and pasted on a smile. The agent named Josephson was standing directly behind him. "Yes, Charles? Did you need me?"

Luke's body stiffened and she had confirmation that he was annoyed. He was probably just put out because he'd been interrupted before he'd accomplished his goal. He was just annoyed that she wouldn't fall into step with his plans.

"What d'ya need, Chuck?"

"The baby's starting to fuss and I figured Jilly would want to know."

Luke refused to take his gaze from her. She felt his stare, felt him try to intimidate her with those beautiful eyes and decided the best course of action would be to ignore him. It would do no good to let Agent Gianetti gain the upper hand. That was abundantly clear now. Thank God she hadn't slept with him. It was bad enough she'd fancied herself falling in love with him.

"I'm not through with her yet," he insisted, his voice annoyingly determined. "Miss Moseby will be there in a minute."

He wasn't through with her? Well, she would just see about that. She moved around him, intent on showing him that she could bloody well speak for herself, thank you very much. "Nonsense, Charles, I'll come with—"

Luke grabbed her and yanked her back against him. "I said not yet," he muttered as his lips came down to cover hers.

She opened her mouth to protest and knew an instant later that it had been a colossal mistake. His mouth devoured hers. He used her lapse in judgment to his advantage and thrust his tongue in her mouth. Although her brain told her to fight the indignity, her body simply refused to cooperate. Oh, he tasted so good, his mouth so warm and insistent. She felt the blood drain out of her body, felt her bones dissolve to dust while he continued to kiss her senseless.

When he finally thrust her away from him, she staggered and had to grab one of his arms for support. She only had a moment to glimpse the molten heat in his eyes before he quickly shuttered his expression. He even managed to smile, although it wasn't a magnetic Luke Gianetti smile. It was a tight, frustrated, I-shouldn't-have-done-that smile. It was a put-her-in-her-place smile.

"Now you can go," he drawled.

She slapped his arm away, mortified when his smile deepened. The old arrogant, self-assured Luke was back, damn him. When her brain slowly began to function again, she discovered Agent Josephson had backed away, a rueful smile on his face. How would she face him? How would she face any of them? Her gaze flew to the window where the buzz of activity had all but stopped for their sideshow. Why he'd practically branded her as his property in front of everyone. Every last one of them was staring. And grinning.

She whirled on Luke. "Don't you ever touch me again, do you understand?"

He chuckled as she shoved past him. "Yeah. Right."

She'd only turned her back on him for a moment before she heard the most godawful noise from outside. It sounded like an explosion. Before she could turn to question Luke, she was bodyslammed from behind and sent crashing to the floor on the far side of the bed.

The scent of dust filled her nose as Luke threw himself down on top of her and pushed her face into the carpet. "Where are the boys?" she asked.

"Murphy's got 'em. Keep your head down," he ordered. "Don't move a muscle until I tell you to."

"What was that?" Her body frozen in fear, she could only listen to the commotion taking place near the door to their room. Petrie had moved swiftly to the door and launched himself out into the dark. She heard his footsteps clatter down the outside corridor, each step reverberating like gunshots as he took the stairs two at a time. Terrified, she wondered how an agent could manage to sneak up on anyone, being that noisy.

"Sounded like a rifle shot. Close range," he muttered in her ear. "I'm gonna have to go see what's happening." He slithered down her body, keeping his own close to the floor. "No matter what happens, don't freakin' move," he ordered. "Do you hear me, Jill? I mean it. Don't move an inch until I get back."

"Luke, please don't go," she pleaded.

"Promise, dammit."

"I swear. I swear I won't move." She wished desperately that she could turn, wished she could see his face, but she'd just given him her word that she wouldn't budge. "For God's sake, be careful."

Chapter 8

"A false alarm? A bloody false alarm?" A quarter hour later, Jillian sank onto the edge of the bed, her legs still trembling too badly to hold her weight.

"Yo, Jill, you okay?" Luke frowned as he crossed the room to check on her.

"I can't take this anymore, Luke. This is sheer madness." Despite her efforts to contain them, her eyes welled with tears.

"Hey, it's nothing, okay? A car backfired in the parking lot and the overhang on the motel made it echo like a shotgun." He sat beside her and patted her hand. "Look, we're all a little jumpy, but everything's going to be okay. Everything's back to normal." He shrugged his shoulders. "At least our plan worked."

"What plan?"

"If it had been real," he clarified. "If it had been a real shooter, everyone did exactly as they were supposed to do."

"If that's supposed to be comforting, it's not working."

Ignoring her sarcasm, he rose from the bed to give James a quick hug. "You guys did a great job."

Rather than terrified, the boys had been thrilled. It wasn't a life or death situation, it was like something out of a movie starring Luke Gianetti as the hero. As Luke had dived across the beds to send Jilly crashing to the floor, Murphy had done the same to Samuel and James. Josephson had covered the door. The boys had been practicing all evening and on Murphy's signal, they had eagerly slipped under the beds in the spare room, a heavily armed Josephson guarding all of them.

Sarah, bless her little heart, had slept through the whole episode in her portable crib that had been wedged deep inside the closet, all but hidden by the hanging clothes. Jillian shook her head and gazed down at Sarah who was finally awake. She picked up the baby and bounced her on her lap to Sarah's delight. Still reeling from the close call they'd averted, Jillian couldn't seem to shake her fear. Her head spinning, she wondered what would be left of the old Jillian when this mess was finally resolved. Already she felt changed. So far away from home—so far away from everything she'd known. Why, if all went well, in ten days she'd be working at a new job in a state hundreds of miles to the north in a town she hadn't ever seen. Living with her new children in a home she hadn't yet found.

And where would Luke be next week, or next month? She'd ignored him for the better part of the afternoon, unsure if she should be angry with him or with herself for being such a fool. Now it had gone dark and she was no closer to an answer. For his part Luke seemed as unaffected by the near death encounter as he had been moments earlier, when he'd kissed her senseless, she recalled with a frown, then set her on her feet and walked away.

She didn't want to feel anything for him. In a matter of days, hours, even, he'd be gone from their lives. And she'd never set eyes on him again. She could not fall for him, with his cocky attitude and his sexy good looks. She couldn't allow herself to care that he was so bloody wonderful with the boys, nor admire the fact that he handled Sarah like a professional father. She couldn't afford to forget how dangerous his life was, how often he'd been shot. How he seemed to thrive on the challenge of outwitting people who would kill him just as easily as drawing a breath. And how he deliberately held himself back, always keeping a certain distance from everyone around him.

Biting her lip, she allowed herself a moment of pity as she cautiously glanced across the room. Agent Josephson, a set of headphones covering his ears, was playing with the buttons on a console that looked like a stereo. Petrie was at the window, his body alert, his eyes continually scanning the night for signs of activity.

Everything had, indeed, returned to normal, if one could call a motel room crammed with federal agents "normal." Luke, as usual, was oblivious to her. Deep in conversation with the man named Murphy, he probably wouldn't have noticed if she'd set herself on fire.

She knew nothing about Luke Gianetti. Nothing, except that he wanted no part of a relationship. More specifically, he wanted no part of a relationship with her. He didn't want a family. He didn't want ties. He didn't want commitments. Her heart sank a little further into her stomach. Despite knowing all that, it was still too late.

She loved him, dammit.

How she had allowed it to happen so fast was absolutely beyond her.

"Hey, Jill."

The object of her misplaced affection dropped to a squat on the carpet in front of her, bringing himself to her eye level. "Yes, Luke?"

"Petrie and I are gonna run out for a few supplies. Since it looks like Sloan is gonna be a no-show, we need to get food and stuff. In any case, it's nearly time for another security check." He glanced down at Sarah and his gorgeous face creased with a soft, secret smile that had Jilly's heart pounding in reaction.

"Hey, beautiful. How are you?" Sarah turned toward his husky crooning voice and smiled in response. It took all the strength Jillian had not to cry. He was so tenderhearted. Under that gruff, surly exterior, Luke Gianetti was soft as butter. At least when it came to children.

"You need anything special?"

Her thoughts scattered abruptly as the blast force of his attention was turned on her. "I—I don't think so."

"Diapers? Wipes? Formula?" He ticked them off like a pro.

"Yes, of course." She swallowed hard and forced herself to concentrate. "I need all those things."

"Anything for the boys?"

"No—yes." Exasperated, she raised her gaze to meet his curious expression. "I don't know. Ask them."

"You okay?" His beautiful eyes flashed concern.

She steeled her resolve not to weep at his feet. "I—I'm fine. Just a little overwhelmed. D-don't let me keep you."

His eyes narrowed and he stood rather abruptly. "Right. Just wanted to let you know I was leaving. It's not like I'd expect you to be concerned or anything."

Now what the bloody hell was that supposed to mean?

"Ask Murphy if you need something." He turned on his heel and walked away. "I'll see you later."

She stared helplessly at his rigid, well-muscled back as he strode to the door and forcefully jerked it open. What was he doing to her? She'd never in all her life met a man as aggravating to deal with as Luke. The men at home bored her to tears. Luke, on the other hand, made her stark raving mad. Why couldn't she want someone less challenging? Perhaps some nice plodding academic?

Sarah burped and then sighed gustily, her eyes drooping with the exertion. Jillian gratefully shoved her wayward thoughts aside.

"Want a little help with her?" The man named Murphy watched her curiously.

"You don't mind?" She glanced beyond him to see Josephson busy scribbling notes at his station, his gun within reach.

"Heck no. I love babies."

"Thanks, Murphy. I think she's ready to go down for the night. I just need to find her jammies in this mess." She started toward the dresser and paused. "What's your first name?"

"It's Danny. But everyone calls me Murphy."

"Your wife, too?"

He grinned then and it absolutely transformed his face. Instead of sweet and unassuming, Danny Murphy's hulking frame became devilishly handsome, his eyes snapping with good humor.

"Nah, mostly Danny. Unless she's pis—excuse me, ma'am—ticked off at me. Then it's Daniel Joseph or something worse."

"Been married a long time?" She sounded wistful, even to herself, and smiled when Danny cradled Sarah in his big, burly arms.

"Yeah, forever. Met Lucy fifteen years ago." He glanced up, his expression suddenly thoughtful and she forced herself to move briskly over to the nightstand. "You know, Luke's a really good guy. He's just a little stressed right now."

"I'm certain he is. He just doesn't like me very much." She managed a smile, even though it nearly killed her. "I seem to rub him the wrong way."

Murphy chuckled at that. "The way I see it, you're rubbing him exactly the right way. He just doesn't like it very much."

"Yes, well, it doesn't matter, does it? After this is all over, I shan't be seeing him again."

"Wouldn't be too sure about that. I see the way he's watchin' you." He waggled his eyebrows and she felt the heat rise in her cheeks. "Reminds me of how I felt about Luce when we first met. Couldn't keep my hands off her."

"Did you look at Lucy like you wanted to strangle the life

out of her?'' She turned her back to him and pulled a diaper and fresh pajamas out of the drawer, fumbling with the clothes despite her attempt to look nonchalant.

Murphy's grin got wider. "He's got a lot on his plate right now. He's worried about you and the kids. It's worse because he likes you. It's a big risk, what we're doin', and there are complications you don't know about."

"Yes, I'm positive there are scads of details I don't know. Luke made that clear in no uncertain terms." Jilly raised angry eyes to meet his gaze. "I'm just along for the ride, like so much luggage."

"Cut him some slack, honey. He's feelin' stuff he hasn't felt in a long time."

"I believe you're way off the mark on that one." Her heart sank when she acknowledged the truth of her words.

"No." Murphy shook his head. "Trust me."

"Let's assume, for argument's sake, that you're correct. What's that got to do with anything?"

"His wife was no picnic."

She glanced up then. "He told me all about Linda."

"He did?" Murphy's eyes widened with disbelief. "Oh, he's got it worse than I thought. G never talks about her to anyone. I thought he'd never get over it when she killed hers—"

He heard her gasp of shock around the same time he must have seen the expression of horror in her eyes because he stopped midsentence. "Oh shit. He didn't tell you."

"I d-didn't know she was dead," she whispered. "I—I thought they divorced. He told me… He said she left him four years ago."

"Yeah, she left all right." Murphy glanced across the room at Josephson and lowered his voice. "G took it pretty bad."

"He loved her that much?" She took a few shuddering breaths to force back the tears. Poor Luke. That would certainly explain a great deal. He'd lost the woman he loved.

"Not quite. They hadn't been getting along for years."

"But you said…"

"He blamed himself. Still does, I think."

"What happened?" Her heart ached at the thought of the pain he had to have endured. No wonder he held himself apart.

"Big irony, she was addicted to prescription painkillers. She was always sort of a hypochondriac. Always whinin' to Luke about him being gone all the time." Murphy stroked Sarah's fuzzy head as he swayed back and forth. "God, I love this age. They're so sweet."

"Luke doesn't strike me as the type to complain," Jillian said and smiled when the giant man feigned a look of surprise. "Let me rephrase that. He complains about me incessantly. I meant that he keeps important things close to his chest."

"Yeah, you're right about that," Murphy admitted. "My wife's always gossipin' with the other wives, ya know? Some of the old-timers knew Linda pretty well. And—no offense—" He seemed to brace himself for her response. "But, when chicks say that about another chick…"

Jilly tried desperately to keep a straight face. "Indeed. A very credible source."

He paused to rub his chin over Sarah's soft curls. "Anyway, she'd been downing painkillers for a long time and G didn't know anything about it. Came home from an op and found her dead. She'd taken an overdose."

"Maybe it was a mistake?" She winced at the thought of Luke's reaction, of the agony he must have faced when he'd realized what she'd done. She knew him well enough to know that he would have felt completely responsible. Regardless of whether it was true or not.

"Nope. She made sure to leave a very detailed note. Because of the way it happened and because of who we are, the agency had to investigate her death, to rule out foul play. So the note… Well, G had to hand it over." Murphy shook his head sadly. "I've never seen it myself. Apparently it contained an extensive list of all his failings as a husband."

She felt the tears trickle down her face and knew this time she would be helpless to stop them. "How could she do that to him?" she whispered before clapping a hand to her mouth. Linda had to have known it would destroy him. How could anyone be so cruel? "Oh, Danny, she sounds bloody awful."

"So, now you know. Luke's been to hell. In four years, you're the first evidence I've seen to indicate that he might be finally comin' back." The burly agent lowered his gaze to the infant slumbering on his shoulder and carried Sarah to her crib. "Don't judge him too quickly. He's been in a very bad place. I don't know anyone who deserves a break more than him."

Luke was edgy, his gut strumming with uneasiness as they left the convenience store. At least they were only a couple miles from the motel. Petrie appeared alert but completely unfazed. Luke wondered which of them was off kilter and decided it must be him. He hadn't wanted to leave Jilly and the kids, not even under Murphy's watchful eye. That told him something he wasn't exactly sure he wanted to admit.

He'd been dying for a little breathing room, been relieved to get away. But now he was antsy to get back. His need to protect them at any cost was beginning to cloud his judgment. He hated waiting for the takedown. It required a degree of patience he found hard to maintain. And he hated it even more knowing Jilly and the kids would be in the thick of it when it finally went down. Grateful to have reinforcements, he was equally grateful for the buffer they created between him and Jilly. Yet it gnawed at him each time one of the guys was on the receiving end of one of her smiles.

He gave himself a mental head slap. It didn't help that he was forced to exert every ounce of discipline simply to keep his distance from her. Not touching her was nearly killing him. And damn, if he wasn't wasting precious time wondering what he'd done to make Lady Jillian pissed at him again.

He'd broken the cardinal rule. He'd let her creep under his

skin. He'd let her crawl into his head. And she'd filled it with thoughts he had no right to be thinking. Thoughts of a future together with her.

Crap. Luke shook his head in disgust. The way he was acting, he deserved to get shot tonight. A sudden awareness crawled up his spine and he skidded to a stop, gravel crunching under his feet, his gaze sweeping the parking lot.

"Yo, Pete. Everything look okay to you?"

"Yeah, man. Let's get back. You're next on watch."

Something was wrong. Luke felt it in every fiber of his being. His senses throbbed with the scent of danger. The westerly breeze that ruffled his hair carried the scent of honeysuckle and decaying mulch. And something else. Gunpowder.

"Pete, opposite side of the building. Something's going down," he whispered. Petrie gave him a questioning look, but moved quickly to the car where he dumped the groceries in the back seat. He withdrew his gun, then signaled Luke to take the lead.

Luke hadn't crept more than a dozen yards into the shadows before he saw the flash of weapon fire. He rolled to the ground and returned fire, hearing gravel scatter as Petrie dove for cover behind a car.

"Luke? You okay?"

"Yeah. You see anything?"

"Nope. I'm gonna head around the far side, see if I can shake 'em out before the locals get here. Cover me in three."

Petrie began to run as Luke fired a few warning rounds into the shadows, straining to see the flash of return fire. There wasn't any. He raised his eyebrows at that miracle, and then hunkered down, flattening himself into the mossy bank of the drainage ditch he'd landed in. He heard the faint sound of sirens and knew it was time to move. He took advantage of the noise and shimmied out on the other side of the ditch. Away from the washed-out lights of the parking lot, the heavy darkness swallowed him up. His eyes adjusted to the murky shadows and he found his visibility to be surprisingly good.

If he was quiet, he might be able to circle around the shooter to catch him from behind.

He listened intently to the sounds of the night. His heart drilled in his ears and he had to focus to hear over it. The soft, spongy earth muffled his steps as he moved through the woods, doubling back around the rear corner of the building. He scanned the opposite side for Petrie. He should be in position by now.

He froze at the sound of voices whispering at the edge of the clearing. Two—no, three—voices argued over where Luke had gone and about what to do next as the wail of sirens grew closer. He felt an adrenaline rush of shock when he recognized the voice of one of the shooters. It was only a split second later that his survival instinct kicked in. His gut told him to get the hell out of here.

Luke obeyed.

Sweat poured into his eyes as Luke staggered through the woods. The burning in his lungs told him he'd run at least two miles. The burning in his forearm told him he'd been shot. Again. He knew he had to reach Murphy. And he had to do it now. They'd seen him, but they didn't know which way he'd gone. Common sense would lead them back toward the motel. They had to know he'd warn the others.

He pulled out the borrowed cell phone, pausing only a moment to examine the sleeve of his jacket. The size of the hole indicated serious firepower. It was a miracle he'd only been grazed. But he had the gnawing suspicion he was running out of miracles.

Petrie was the leak, but was he the *only* leak? Pete was in it up to his neck with Sloan's bunch. But had he acted alone? Or could there be another mole on the task force? Damn, it just kept getting worse.

He'd run nearly all the way back to the motel and still hadn't seen evidence of a surveillance crew anywhere. Where the hell was their backup? Had the whole takedown been faked? Just to get him? This was no freakin' vendetta. For Sloan to risk everything, he wanted Luke dead in a big way. His brain flashed back over the past several weeks. What the hell had he seen in Sloan's operation that he shouldn't have?

Sweet Jesus. What if Josephson was in on it, too? He shuddered at the implication. What if he'd overpowered Murphy? What if they were all dead?

Had that been the plan all along? To separate them and take 'em out one at a time. He thought about the boys. They'd been playing with their cars on the beds when he'd left. And sweet little Sarah. She'd smiled at him. It was the most beautiful thing he'd ever seen. That couldn't have been the last time. And what about Jilly?

He was gonna be sick. Luke threw himself down on the mossy ground, his hands sinking in the decaying leaves as he forcefully lost the contents of his stomach. His hands were still shaking a few minutes later when he dialed his partner's cell phone. They couldn't be dead. Not now. Not when he'd only just realized how much he cared about them.

His knees buckled with relief when he recognized his partner's gruff voice. "Murph—don't say anything. Petrie's working for Sloan. He just tried to take me out."

"I understand, sir."

"Watch Joe," he ordered. "Watch your back. Petrie's probably on his way back to you."

He took several cleansing breaths while Murphy moved into the spare room away from Josephson. They were safe. They were alive. His brain knew it to be fact, but his nerves didn't seem to be comprehending. He'd worked with Danny Murphy long enough to know exactly what to expect from his partner and he waited impatiently for his friend to come back on the line.

"Make sure you keep an eye on Josephson," he said to his partner.

"Yes, sir." Murphy's crisp tone indicated Josephson was somewhere nearby. "What's the latest?"

"Petrie set me up at the convenience store. Two other shooters. I don't know if they're on their way back to you or not. I'm a quarter mile north of you in the woods."

"Hold on, sir. Let me get a pen." Murphy fumbled around for a moment, shuffling papers on the table, in the event Josephson became suspicious. It would appear to be a call from the field supervisor. "What do you want us to do?"

"Get Jill and the kids. I need the car and as many supplies as you can get together in a few minutes. Tell Joe we received new orders. Tell him we're moving them to a safe house and that he needs to wait there for me and Petrie to come back."

"Okay, sir. I think I've got it. We'll be outta here in twenty."

"Murph, make it fifteen. Jesus, make it ten if you can. I'll be there. I'll cover you from the woods just beyond the car."

"Yes, sir."

Jillian was still awake and lounging on the bed in the corner. She couldn't let herself fall asleep. Not yet. Not until Luke returned. They'd been gone an awfully long time. She rubbed at the goose bumps rising on her arms. What was keeping them?

She tried to block it out. Tried to focus on the inane program on the telly. Tried to swallow the irrational fear that something was terribly wrong. She hated feeling so vulnerable, hated needing Luke so very much. She couldn't shake the memory of him diving across the bed to protect her. When Petrie had sounded the alarm, Luke had reacted in a heartbeat, had been on top of her, covering her in seconds.

She'd watched him transform into a warrior, his eyes burning with a frightening intensity that she'd never seen before. His battle face was deadly calm as he'd focused completely on the task at hand. She knew in that moment that he would not hesitate to kill anyone foolish enough to cross the threshold of the door. She also knew he would not hesitate to die for her—for anyone he was forced to protect.

It was the dying part that bothered her most. She didn't want Luke to die. Even if she couldn't have him, she wanted him to live. He was fearlessly worthy of living. He deserved to find happiness with someone.

She glanced up when Murphy strolled over to the bed and sat on the edge.

"Hey, I need your help." His voice was casual, but his eyes weren't. His expression was rigidly serious and Jillian immediately sat up.

"What?"

"We just received word that I'm moving you outta here. Can you be ready in ten minutes?"

"Luke? What about Lu—"

"Once he's back, he'll join us." Murphy cocked his head slightly in the direction of Josephson who had methodically started packing toys and clothes into a suitcase. He lowered his voice and leaned into her as though he was about to brush something from her shoulder.

"Trust me."

Her eyes widened in understanding. Whatever was going on had something to do with Luke. She rose from the bed and began stuffing Sarah's diaper bag.

She shivered in spite of her heavy sweatshirt. The wind had turned chilly, the night damp and sinister as she crept along the outside corridor of their hotel. Someone had turned out the lights and it was difficult to see where she was going. Holding Sarah in her arms, she felt dangerously exposed. What if someone was out there watching them? Danny Murphy tugged gently on her arm, guiding her hurriedly through the shadows. He hadn't spoken since they'd left the room. She knew that just beyond the shadows, Josephson covered their backs, his weapon drawn and ready.

Poor Murphy would have to make yet another trip with James and Samuel. She prayed they would be quiet, prayed Samuel would remain asleep until they were safely away. She felt the rush of cool air hit her face when they emerged from the covered staircase and stumbled when Murphy quickened their pace. His hand squeezed her arm in signal as they approached the car.

A shadow loomed up from the darkness beyond the car. Before Jillian could shout a warning to Murphy, a hand clapped over her mouth, cutting off her scream.

Chapter 9

"Shh-hh. Jilly it's me."

She sagged against him, relief pouring through her veins when Luke gave her a quick hug and then pushed her into the car.

"You check the car?" She heard Murphy whispering to Luke.

"It's clean."

"Underneath?"

"Ditto. Are we worried about Joe?"

"Reacted fine. Didn't seem to have a problem." He actually smiled at Luke. "Guess I'll find out, huh?"

"Be careful. I'll keep an eye on him for you." Luke ducked back into the shadows as Murphy jogged across the parking lot and launched up the stairs.

Jillian sat in the back seat, Sarah still cradled against her chest. It was eerily quiet for several minutes and she turned in her seat. Luke was nowhere to be seen. Had she only imagined his presence? She heard a soft tap on her window and jumped. Lord, he was only a foot away and she hadn't heard a sound.

"Get down on the floor and stay down. Don't move around." He was gone again before she could respond. She squeezed herself onto the floor and tucked her head over Sarah's. A few minutes later she heard James slide into the back seat, heard Murphy order him to the floor. Still asleep, Samuel was laid across the seat and covered with a dark blanket.

"Jilly? You in here?"

She smiled. She would have sworn that James actually sounded nervous. "Yes, James," she whispered. "Stay down, love. We musn't talk."

She heard him shift quietly, heard the murmur of voices just outside her window. Not a minute later Luke slipped into the car and started the engine. He smelled of night air and sweat and gunpowder and tension, and she wondered what hell he had endured the past few hours.

"Luke?"

His gaze flicked down to meet hers for a scant moment. He shook his head as if to say "later," then winked at her and turned his attention back to the road.

"Not now, babe. Stay down." The quiet words belied the smile on his face. His voice sounded strained. The worry lines around his eyes only confirmed it. Something was wrong. Something was terribly wrong.

Drawing in a deep, shuddering breath of the damp night air, she blew it out to steady her nerves. Anything to relieve the strain of uncertainty. Though he didn't say a word, she knew Luke expected her to stay calm. Without having to look, she sensed him there, crouched low over the steering wheel. She could probably have reached out to touch him if she'd wanted but she didn't have to. She could feel the intensity radiating from him when he maneuvered the sedan out onto the road. He practically throbbed with awareness of his surroundings. And despite being virtually certain that Luke had more bad news to tell her, she relaxed. For the first time in the past several hours, she felt a sense of composure settle over her. They were with Luke. They were safe.

"Can I come out yet?" a voice piped up from the back seat.

"Not yet, Jimmy." They'd been on the road nearly forty minutes. Luke glanced in the rearview mirror and caught a flash of Murphy's headlights looming out of the darkness in the distance behind them. He listened to the engine of the overloaded Chevy as it hurtled up another strenuous climb through the mountains.

"But I'm all squished up. How come Samuel gets to—"

"Buddy, I need you to stay down for just a few more minutes, okay? Pretty soon it will be safe to come out." His gut was still on red-alert status. They'd travelled nearly twenty miles on the darkened backcountry roads without incident, but Luke didn't feel any better.

"Okay, Luke. I can do it."

"Thanks, pal." Their escape had been too easy. Why hadn't anyone tried to stop them? And where was their backup? According to Duncan, the task force had supposedly set up two different checkpoints. He'd been through hundreds of takedowns and he'd never not known where his surveillance team was located; he'd never not been able to spot them. Unless the group out of Charlotte were freaking magicians, he was beginning to wonder whether they'd ever been there in the first place. The whole thing was beginning to smell rank.

Questions shot through his mind and he hated admitting that he didn't have the answers. If Petrie was working for Sloan, then why hadn't he finished what he'd started? There had been three shooters at the convenience store. They'd had the opportunity to kill him. Why hadn't they? Dammit, what was he missing?

There were too many gaps in the puzzle. Was it possible

that by running, Luke had left them more vulnerable to attack? He felt guilty leaving Murphy behind to face God knew what. The scene had disaster written all over it. He shook his head in disgust. He didn't like chaos. He'd never forgive himself if Murphy got killed over this.

"Where are we going?"

He tensed at the sound of Jilly's worried voice. It was a damn good question. He wished he had an answer that made any sense. They were going nowhere. The Tennessee line was only a few more miles. Best he could do was try to get lost in the mountains. Of course, he then had to worry about staying in contact with Murphy.

"Don't know, babe. We're makin' good time, though." He heard her shift around in her tiny spot on the floor. She had to be uncomfortable, yet she didn't complain. She had to be thinking that he was a complete idiot and that he was no closer to solving their problem than he'd been four days ago when their odyssey had begun.

"Are we alone?"

"Murphy's tagging with us to make sure we're not being tailed. Then he'll head back."

"Then we'll be on our own?"

"Sort of. Murphy'll meet up with us tomorrow." He grinned at her lowered head. "Why? Don't tell me you're finally nervous?"

"Not really. If anything happens, I'm sure you'll think of something. You've managed pretty well so far."

He did a double take on that one, startled at her show of confidence. "Yeah, right. This is the most disorganized operation I've ever been involved in. I'm sorry I got you into it. If I had to do it over again, I'd have picked another car to jump into."

"And have me miss all this excitement?"

He glanced at the fuel gauge as they crossed the line into Tennessee and thought about his options. They'd need gas in another hour. While the highway would be faster, it would be safer to travel the back roads. And back roads meant gas stations would be closing soon. It would probably be wise to fill the tank and find a place to stop for a few hours. Jilly and the kids could sleep. He could take stock of his pathetic situation and try to get organized. If they left before dawn, he'd still have the cover of darkness working in his favor.

"We'll stop in about twenty minutes. Can you last that long?"

"Of course. Don't feel like you have to stop on my account."

His gaze dropped to her hiding place. With her head tucked down, she couldn't see him looking at her. Her Ladyship was proving to be quite resilient. Who'd have thought it?

"Tell Jimmy we're almost there."

"He's gone to sleep." Her voice floated up to him on a husky whisper. He studiously ignored the tingle of awareness that crawled up his spine. Instead of worrying about tomorrow, he should be concentrating on tonight. Another endless night alone with her. How would he handle it? Especially now.

There was a very distinct possibility he cared about her. He swallowed hard around the sudden constriction in his throat. The mere thought was enough to make him break out in a cold sweat.

Jillian didn't even wrinkle her nose at the smell of the damp, musty cabin. She waited patiently when Luke stepped in first, intent on protecting them from any gun-toting thugs who might be hiding in this very cabin. She even managed a smile as he carefully checked out the two small rooms and the attached bath. It was clear to her that the cabin hadn't been rented in months. The only thing he was likely to uncover would be a pack of marauding raccoons.

The thought of climbing between the sheets and stretching her cramped muscles was too good to think of anything else. The scent of cheap motel rooms was beginning to grow on her, she realized as she watched Luke bolt the door and re-position the furniture to block the draped window. She had the feeling she would remember this little hole-in-the-wall with fonder memories than all the holidays she'd ever experienced at the Savoy.

"Okay, we're good to go. Let's get the kids to bed." Luke materialized by her side in the space of a heartbeat and carried James into the adjoining room. He stripped off the little boy's shoes and socks and let them fall to the floor. Then he returned to scoop up Samuel from the chair where he'd deposited him and crossed the room, laying him gently next to James between the sheets.

"What will we do about Sarah? We left her crib behind."

He smiled and tugged Samuel's shoes off. "Got it covered. The guy in the office has a cradle. I'm sure it's probably ancient, judging from the looks of the place. But I'll make sure I get some clean blankets for it."

She smiled at the back of his head. He was so bloody organized. "That will be lovely. Are we staying here long?"

Luke glanced up from tucking the boys in. "Probably not even the whole night. You can take the spare bed in here with the kids. I'll grab an hour on the bed out there." He nodded to the next room. "I want to be near the door…just in case."

She stifled a yawn and tried not to jostle Sarah, but the desire to move and stretch was nearly overwhelming. Her body still felt as if it had been folded in two and she was dying to work the kinks out.

In no time Luke had the antique cradle assembled, wincing only once when it squeaked in protest. With fresh sheets and a worn, faded blanket, it didn't look half bad. Jillian wasted no time setting Sarah down and tucking her in.

"I'll wake you when it's time to go," he whispered as he turned to leave.

"Okay." Sighing with relief, she gave in to the urge to flex her aching muscles. Luke was halfway across the room before he turned back. Ignoring him, she continued to hop from one foot to the other, then waved her arms and bent from side to side. He was probably thinking that her thin veneer of sanity had finally cracked, but she couldn't summon the energy to care.

"What the hell are you doing?"

"My back is stiff from crouching so long," she whispered. "I'm just trying to loosen up." She noticed his frown and tried not to be annoyed with his impatience. "I'm sorry if I'm offending your sensibilities. I'll stop in a minute."

"I'm too tired to figure out what that means," he said wearily. "Why don't you have a seat on the bed out there and I'll rub your back. It'll work some of the kinks out."

She didn't need a second invitation. She remembered how good it felt the last time he'd rubbed her neck. Luke's hands were nothing short of miraculous. And with the room so dimly lit, he probably wouldn't be able to see her drool.

She left the door open a sliver, just in case the children woke up. Then she crossed the room and dropped down onto the edge of the ancient bed, rolling her neck in anticipation. The lumpy mattress shifted under his weight when Luke slid over behind her. She resisted the urge to groan as he placed his hands at the base of her neck and began kneading.

"Take your sweatshirt off."

Well, wasn't that a bloody fantasy come true? She started when she felt him tug it up over her head.

"It's getting in the way." He placed his warm hands on her shoulders and began rubbing her weary muscles through her T-shirt. "Man, you're tight," he acknowledged.

Jillian didn't know how much she could attribute to being folded up in the car and how much was from the knowledge that Agent Heartthrob was touching her. The thought of his hands on her body had her tightening with desire.

"Sorry about the close quarters in the car. I couldn't risk someone else getting shot."

"What happened back there?" She could barely form coherent words into a sentence, not when he stroked her like this. An involuntary shudder swept through her and her eyes flew open. Dear Lord, he was sure to have felt that.

"You okay? I'm not rubbing too hard, am I?"

She swallowed around the lump of panic rising in her throat. "I—I'm fine. It feels wonderful." Lord, her face was flaming. Even the sound of his voice had her stomach fisting in a knot of desire. It was gruff and edgy, as though he'd gone for days without sleep. Luke hadn't even touched her sexually and here she was on the verge of coming undone. If he so much as looked at her, he would see it. He would see the desperate need in her eyes. She only prayed he wouldn't see the love shining there or he'd run away for sure.

"We should get to bed soon. You're not gonna have very long to sleep."

Luke didn't wait for her response, but rose suddenly and headed for the bathroom. She shuddered, took a deep breath and rose unsteadily from the bed, her body still tingling from his touch.

"I've got the case out here," she called through the open door. A minute later she snatched up the toiletries bag and followed him. He would probably want to wash up before bed. She poked her head around the door and stifled a cry of horror when she saw him in the mirror.

"Good Lord, you've been shot again."

"It's not that bad. Just a graze." Their eyes met in the mirror and Jillian's widened as she read the pain and frustration mirrored in his.

"That's a bloody big hole in your jacket."

"Yeah. Lucky for me he missed." Luke rinsed out the washcloth he'd used to wash his face and neck.

"You didn't think to mention it before now? What the hell were you waiting for?" She dropped the bag on the counter with a thud and unzipped it angrily while she tried not to tremble with fear. Someone wanted them dead. Lord, what if they'd killed him? What if she'd never seen him again? "For the love of God, you could have bled to death."

"Jill, it's nothing."

"Give me your arm," she ordered. "Let's get it cleaned up." Her vision blurred as she dug through the bag for antiseptic and gauze. Her hands wouldn't stop shaking as she withdrew the mountain of supplies. She paused to wipe blindly at her eyes.

"Hey, are you okay? It's gonna be all right." Luke tipped her chin up, forcing her to look at him. "Jill, I'll keep you safe, I swear it. They'll have to kill me before I let them get to you or the kids."

Incredulous, she slapped his hand away, the tears coming faster now. "What about you, Luke? Who's going to keep you safe?"

His eyes registered shock and she could only assume it was over her emotional display. She was clearly violating one of his rules by having her meltdown in front of him.

"Don't cry, Jill. I can't handle crying."

"I can't help it. You're going to get yourself killed." The tears continued to pour out and she wiped her eyes on the tail of her shirt. "Take your blasted jacket off so I can clean that arm."

"Stop crying first," he ordered. "I don't want you touching me until you can see straight. You'll end up bandaging my elbow instead." He chuckled and pulled her roughly into his arms. "Babe, don't worry about me. I can take care of myself."

"I'm scared, Luke. I mean, I'm trying to hold it together, but I'm truly frightened." She burrowed against his chest and gulped in several shuddering breaths. His hands held her in place, slowly stroking her back while she battled for control. Lord, she wanted to stay in his arms forever. He was so solid, so strong and fearless. She wanted him more than she'd ever wanted anything in her whole life.

She wanted Luke forever, but knew in her heart that particular wish would never be granted. Luke didn't want to care about anyone. He would never allow himself to care. Linda had seen to that, making certain she'd destroyed him for anyone else who came after her.

"You're doing great. Better than I ever thought you would," he admitted. "It's okay to be scared, Jill. Just so long as you don't let the fear paralyze you. If you freeze up, you're as good as dead."

"What about you? Are you frightened?" She tipped her head back so she could see his expression.

He shook his head. "Not for me. I've never worried about dying. I knew the risks when I signed on. It's an occupational hazard," he explained, seeming to choose his words carefully. "I don't want anything to happen to you or the kids. The only thing I'm afraid of is letting my guard down. If that happens, I won't be able to protect you."

"Are we safe here?"

"Safe enough for tonight," he amended. "No one followed us. We're well hidden but I'm not taking any chances. With Petrie involved—"

"Petrie!" she interrupted. "The man who works with you? The man who was in our room tonight?"

"Yeah. He's the one who shot me. Him or one of the other guys I ran into. There was an ambush at the convenience store." He released her and tugged his jacket off, wincing as he pulled it gingerly from his wounded arm. "The problem is I can't be sure who else is involved. I doubt he was working alone. If Sloan got to him, he may have gotten to others."

"You've got that look on your face." She took a step closer, scrutinizing his expression. He was holding out on her. "Give me the rest of it."

"I'm beginning to think there may be others in the agency who might be involved." He seemed to choose his words carefully. "If that's the case, then I don't know how this will end."

"What does that mean?"

"It means that, aside from Murphy, I don't know who to trust."

"Danny feels this way, also?" He nodded. "What about Josephson?" She retrieved her scissors from the first-aid kit and carefully cut away his shirtsleeve at the elbow. Once she'd rid him of the sleeve she unbuttoned the rest of his shirt.

"I don't know. Murph seems to think Joe's not involved, but I had him lined up in my sight the whole time you were coming down to the car."

"And?" She bit her lip when she got a look at the torn flesh of his forearm. Lord, it looked as if he'd been attacked by a wild animal. He grunted when she applied antiseptic to the angry wound.

"Dammit, that stings." He would have tugged his hand away but she'd tucked his hand into her side and held it firmly in place with her free arm.

"Quit moving around," she ordered. "Really, Luke. This is nothing compared to your backside."

"Yeah? Speak for yourself." He was scowling when she glanced up at him and she couldn't help smiling.

"You were saying?"

"Oh, yeah, Joe. Believe me, I had my gun trained on him. One wrong move and he'd have been toast." He jerked his arm free when she turned back to the counter to get fresh gauze. "The damn thing's clean enough. Just wrap it up and let's get you to bed."

She frowned at him in the mirror but the argument died on her lips when she took in his haggard appearance. He was exhausted and hurting, his eyes red-rimmed with fatigue. And though he tried to hide it from her, he was worried about what was yet to come.

"I do believe I enjoyed patching up the other end better. You didn't talk back quite so much."

That remark brought a slow grin and she was relieved to see him smile. She hadn't realized how much she had grown to rely on his sense of humor to carry them through this ordeal.

"You've just got a thing for my butt, that's all."

"For a part of your anatomy you rarely see yourself, you're awfully hung up on it, don't you think?"

"Hey, I've seen the way you look at me."

She continued to wrap the gauze around his arm until it covered the wound completely, only glancing up after she'd taped it in place. He stared at her, his expression serious now and she swallowed around the sudden dryness in her throat.

"And just how is it that I look at you?"

He held her gaze, his golden eyes burning with an intensity that made her heart pound. "Like you want me to take all your clothes off and kiss every inch of you."

Jillian sucked in a ragged gasp and knew her eyes had widened in shock. She felt her face flush with embarrassment at the very same moment her body clenched with anticipation. He would never allow her to love him, of that she was absolutely certain. Luke would sooner run first than face the possibility of caring for her. The next best thing would be to love him for the few nights they had left. She could accept what he was willing to offer. All she had to do was keep the love to herself.

"You mean, like this?" She wrapped her arms around his neck and pulled his head down to hers. She felt his body tense, heard him take in a sharp rasp of air.

"Jill—"

The next best thing could very possibly be the worst—to know wholeheartedly the intimacy they shared would be beyond incredible and to know she'd never experience it again. But tonight, even that possibility didn't matter. To be sure, her heart would shatter into a million pieces, but she'd have the rest of her life to put it back together.

Before he could push her away, she leaned in and kissed him. It took only a moment before he was kissing her back, only a moment for the passion that simmered beneath the surface to ignite and flash over, melting her with its intensity. He crushed her against him and she groaned as their bodies collided. Luke's body was lean, corded muscle, all of it rock-hard and rigid with control.

"Baby, we—"

"No." She shook her head. "Please don't say it. I know it's wrong. I know you'll regret it, but I don't care anymore."

"You don't know what you're saying."

She never would have believed she could be so bold. A part of her stood to the side, mouth dropped open in disbelief, watching as the fearless Jillian tugged her T-shirt over her head, smiling brazenly when Luke's eyes darkened with passion. A part of her couldn't believe that she, Jillian Moseby, was the sole reason the intensely beautiful man standing in front of her was rasping in air as though he'd just run several miles.

"What I'll regret is waiting another second to make love with you."

He groaned and pulled her hard against him. She reveled in the way he kissed her, as though he'd been tested to the limits of his endurance, as though he'd waited all his life for this very moment. Luke devoured her, first with his mouth and then with his hands as they stroked her body into painful awareness of how desperately she needed him.

She leaned against the bathroom counter, her breath coming in short, shaky gasps while his lips trailed over the wildly beating pulse at the base of her throat. A sharp cry of longing tore from her lips a moment later when he released the front clasp on her bra and cupped her breasts in his hands. Her eyes fluttered open and she watched him stroke her nipples into tight, aching nubs. She could only moan when he lowered his mouth to her breast, tugging at her nipple until the coils of pleasure building inside of her finally tore free, nearly rocking her to the core.

"Luke, please tell me you're not going to stop this time."

"Not a chance, sweetheart."

"Bloody hell, I don't think I can stand up anymore." She sagged against him then and felt him lift her to the counter.

She pulled him back to her and kissed him again, all the while running her fingers over his clenched muscles. Her breasts were pressed tightly against his chest and, oh my, didn't it feel wonderful.

He had the most beautiful body she'd ever seen. She trailed her mouth along his jaw and dropped to the steely cords of his throat. She tasted the salt of his perspiration and buried her nose into his neck. She loved the clean male scent of him, loved how strong and sure of himself he was. She loved every damn thing about him.

Her hands fumbled with the button on his jeans. He groaned when she stopped to stroke him through the fabric. Luke was hot and hard and more than ready. She tugged the jeans down over his lean hips and bit back a cry of frustration when he took a step back.

"You're not leaving this time. I swear if you do, I'll shoot you myself."

He had the audacity to grin as he tugged off his jeans, returning to stand between her parted thighs as she watched him from her perch on the counter. "I'm not leaving. Not in a million years could I walk away from you tonight."

She reached for him again and Luke stepped into her embrace, eager to get his mouth on her again. His body was burning up for her and if he didn't take her soon, he knew for sure he would go mad. Her legs were locked around him and all he could feel was Jillian. Her mouth moving frantically under his, her arms wrapped tight around his neck and the moist hot center of her, thrust against his throbbing erection. His hands were wild in the frenzy to relieve her of her jeans. He lifted her off the counter and tugged them down her legs in one fluid motion borne of desperation. If he didn't get inside of her soon, he would die.

He relieved her of her panties before he set her back down on the counter. By then, Jillian was trembling in his arms and the soft whimpering sound she made in the back of her throat was making him crazy. The thought of her needing him as much as he wanted her was an incredible turn-on. The mental image of her going wild in his arms was almost more than he could stand.

"Now, Luke." She wrapped her arms around his waist and pulled him to her.

He was only too willing to comply. He meant to lift her from the counter and to carry her out to the empty bed. But in the recesses of his fragmented thoughts, he worried about the bedroom. They would have to be very quiet so as not to wake the kids and he wasn't quite sure that was possible. When he finally came inside of her, it would be all he could do not to shout. He'd only carried her a step when her low, husky voice stopped him.

"Bloody hell, Luke. I mean, right now."

He opened his mouth to explain and she tugged his head down to meet hers. And the raw, sensual heat she displayed nearly made his knees buckle. When her hand dropped down to stroke him, Luke knew he was utterly lost. With a sharp cry he tightened his hold on her waist and drove himself into her.

He took a shaky breath once he was imbedded deep inside her, the gratification almost too exquisite to live through. He had waited too long for this moment, wanted her far too much to last very long. He prayed he hadn't hurt her with the force he'd used in taking her. And then he heard Jilly's ragged moan, felt her move against him, and he withdrew and entered again. She cried out this time and the sound sent a rush of sweet agony jagging down his spine.

She writhed in his arms, slowly driving him wild with the movement. He took her nipple into his mouth, tugging hard as he felt her tighten around him, her luscious body contracting on a wave of pleasure. She sobbed his name and he thrust once more before he was rocketed by his own splintering release. Luke staggered against the counter as he lost control, the white-hot intensity so blindingly perfect it was almost too much to bear. His last coherent thought was one of bewilderment. He'd never come close to experiencing anything like this before.

Still joined together, his arms still wrapped tightly around her, he leaned back against the counter. His brain reeling from the force of his mind-blowing release, all he could think was that he didn't want to drop her. He was relieved to note that Jillian wasn't faring much better. She lay slack in his arms, her breath shuddering out as she kissed the side of his neck, her slender body still trembling as she spun back down to earth. His strength sapped, he clutched her tightly against him and tried to convince himself it was only so he wouldn't lose his grip. But damn, she felt so unbelievably good in his arms. He loved the way she melted against him when he kissed her, loved how she held him as though he were the single most important person in her world—loved how she clung to him still.

Jillian finally raised her head to stare at him. Her eyes were still cloudy with passion but her smile was one of sleepy satisfaction. "Wow."

"Is that all you can say?" He felt her throaty chuckle all the way down to where they were still connected. A part of him wanted to stay that way. He longed to hold her in his arms for the rest of the night. This was as close to another human being as he'd been in the last several years. And a part of him didn't want to give that up again so soon, didn't want to return to being numb. He felt alive—for the first time in years. This situation with Jilly and the kids made him feel challenged. She made him…feel. She forced him to connect with her in a way that for too long he'd been happy to avoid.

But when his brain finished short-circuiting a minute later, another more urgent part of him wanted to put Jilly down and run. And if he didn't do it soon, he was going to want her all over again. He set her gently on the counter and carefully disengaged, keeping his head down when he heard her soft mew of disappointment.

Sweet Jesus… What did that mean? His heart started

pounding in reaction to her little sigh and Luke groped nervously for a rational reason how he could excuse his desperate need to pull away. He had to put some distance between them—quickly. He didn't want her thinking anything had changed between them. Because nothing had. He couldn't offer Jilly more than what they'd just experienced and he didn't want more.

In his line of work a family was nothing but trouble. He scowled away the thought of Murphy with his wife and kids. All right, so some of the guys had families. But he couldn't be one of them. He didn't *want* to be one of them. End of subject. He'd screwed it up too badly the first time around. He couldn't afford to chance it again.

"Honey, we'd better get you to bed. You're not going to have long to sleep." And he wouldn't have enough time to recover from what just happened. To get his head screwed back on straight he needed distance. A lot of it.

"Will you come, too?"

The uncertainty in her voice crawled through his system. He heard hope in the husky timbre and felt the answering call in his gut. And his blood ran cold. He swallowed the fear that wanted to pound through him and carefully masked his expression when he raised his gaze to meet hers. He would not run. He would not leave them. And he would not—God help him—touch her again.

"No, baby. I have to keep watch."

Chapter 10

She was still awake. Her frustrated sigh reached out to torture him each time she twisted restlessly under the sheets and it took every ounce of strength left in him to stay in his chair by the window. Luke cursed his stupidity. How could he have been so weak? He knew better than to give in to the temptation Jillian offered. Yet he'd done it anyway. Even more pathetic was that he wanted her more now than he had before. He wanted to pull back the blankets and climb in beside her. He wanted to take her into his arms and never let go.

He stood abruptly and stretched the tension from his muscles. It was only sex, he reminded himself. Incredible, heart-stopping sex. His reaction to Jilly was physical, strictly a reflex to a need he'd denied for too long. He hadn't had a one-night stand in more than two years. What did he expect? He was a normal, healthy male. Of course he wanted her again.

Taking a deep breath, he sat again, his mind whirring with a list of perfectly plausible excuses. After Linda's death he'd isolated himself, accepting any assignment that took him away from Washington. His guilt over her death had existed on many levels. Their marriage had been shaky from the start. She'd driven him crazy with her neediness, a trait he'd tolerated during college but found smothering once they'd married. Her nearly obsessive desire for a child had been another weight he'd carried. Out of loyalty, he'd agreed to try, but deep down, he'd been uncertain whether Linda could handle motherhood. A part of him had wondered if she would use a baby as another weapon in her battle to make him quit the agency.

It had been an unnecessary worry. He'd failed to give his wife the one single thing she'd claimed to need most. The one thing that could have saved her from the dark cloud of sadness that had clung to her. What he alone had to offer his wife simply hadn't been enough. And Linda had left him, preferring to take her own life rather than spend the remainder of it with him.

He hadn't been there to stop her overdose. He hadn't even noticed she'd had a problem. After he'd worked through her death, he'd been troubled by a new discovery. Luke was startled to realize that he was relieved to be alone. And a new wave of guilt had threatened to drown him. What did that say about him? Had he ever really loved Linda at all?

"Luke?" Jilly sighed and thumped the pillow.

"Why aren't you sleeping? You're gonna be sorry later."

"Can we talk for a minute?"

Her breathy whisper reached out to sucker punch him. He studiously ignored the clenching sensation in his gut. "No. Go to sleep."

"Please? It'll only take a minute." Jillian held her breath in the dark, her body crying out for sleep. But her brain crackled with an awareness that would not allow her to rest. They'd made love again in the shower. And all the while, she'd sensed Luke's regret. It bothered him tremendously that he wanted her. Even as they'd climaxed, as he'd poured himself into her and groaned her name. Even when he'd kissed her with a sweet longing that made her want to weep, he'd held back. His eyes had mirrored passion but nothing more. He'd let her know that his body wanted her desperately but his heart would have no part of her.

She shouldn't have cared so much when he'd withdrawn into his shell. If nothing else, he'd been honest with her. She'd known it would happen, had expected it. What she hadn't known was how much it would hurt. Her body ached from the force of their lovemaking, but it was no match for the ache in her heart.

"Jill, I don't want to have this discussion. I told you…" She heard a slight creak as he rose from his seat by the window. She didn't hear another sound until he materialized by the side of the bed.

"I told you this would be a mistake. I told you exactly how it would be…and you agreed." His voice was low and insistent and just a little bit angry.

She sat up hastily. "And I'm not asking you to change how you feel," she quickly reassured. "I, um, just wanted to thank you for…you know—earlier. I really needed someone and I'm glad it was you, that's all."

"You're thanking me for having sex with you?"

She lifted her hands to her cheeks and felt them burning and was grateful for the darkened room. She knew she wouldn't have the courage come daylight. "Well, yes. It was more than that for me."

"I don't need to hear any more," he interrupted. "You're welcome."

She could sense his body stiffening with tension and chuckled in spite of her sinking heart. "Don't worry, Luke. I'm not going to get all emotional. Frankly, if it weren't so dark in here, I wouldn't have the courage to say this."

"Don't do it on my account."

"I don't particularly care if you want to hear this. It's something I have to tell you. You'll simply have to be tough."

His sigh told her he was clearly aggravated, but he didn't try to stop her.

"Despite your claims to the contrary, you are a sensitive and kind man, Agent Gianetti. Whether or not you regret tonight, I wanted to state for the record that I do not, nor will I ever, regret it. I needed you desperately and you were there for me. And for *that*," she emphasized, "I thank you."

His silence reached out and wrapped around her. He was watching her. She could feel his eyes on her, could sense his alertness each time she moved. She waited another moment before she sank back against the pillows.

She had been so completely, utterly wrong.

She couldn't make love to Luke and then pretend the act meant nothing. Not when her heart felt as though it was ready to burst. The moment he'd withdrawn, she'd wanted him back. She'd wanted to stroke and to soothe him, to take him in her arms and to never let him go. She wanted to shout at him that she wasn't like Linda, wanted to convince him that she would never, ever hurt him.

But that was the last thing he would wish to hear.

"You can relax now, Luke. I've finished declaring my undying devotion to you. I wouldn't want to overwhelm you with too many emotional outbursts in one night."

"You need to remember why we're here," he muttered. "The only reason we're still together is because I'm protecting you. Once this is done—that's it. There won't be a repeat of tonight's performance, Jilly. You need to get that through your head. As soon as we nail Sloan, it's over. You'll never see me again."

Her heart pounded with a dull, stabbing pain and she wanted to shout in frustration. Why couldn't he admit that what they'd shared was incredible? Luke Gianetti would take a bullet for her, yet he lived in absolute fear of the possibility that she might want to see him again.

"Not every woman is like your wife, Luke." She bit her

lip while he digested her remark and knew, despite the darkness, that she had startled him.

"What the hell do you know about my wife?" He didn't wait for her to answer. He leaped up from his perch near the bed and began pacing the room, his movements nearly undetectable despite his anger.

"Murphy had no business discussing my personal life with you."

"He didn't. Murphy thought I knew." She was quick to defend his friend. "He never would have said anything...except he thought you'd told me."

"Why would I tell you? I haven't spoken with anyone about her." She felt his edginess from across the room. "Look, she's dead. Despite what you think you may know, I don't want to discuss her."

"I'm just stating a simple fact. You obviously had a terrible experience and you have every right to be afraid of ever wanting to try again."

"Wait a minute. I'm not afraid."

"Yes, you are," she said. "You're terrified by the mere thought of loving another woman."

"You're really something." He laughed then, but it was a cold, bitter sound. "Let's get one thing straight. I don't love you, Jill. I don't even know you."

She steeled herself against the pain his words caused. She'd asked for this. By provoking him, she was taking a huge risk. She was risking not only her pride, but his, as well.

"Yes, Luke. I know that."

"Don't get me wrong, I like you, Jilly. You're a nice person. You'll make a wonderful mother to those kids. But that's where it ends. I don't want to hurt your feelings, but tonight was just sex, all right? You offered. I took."

She felt the chill of his anger as it radiated out to wash over her and wondered how the same person could have been so loving only hours earlier. "It was just sex for you, and that's fine. But don't put words in my mouth. I don't have sex with every man I meet.''

"I never thought you did.''

"You act like it's a crime to care about someone. I care about you, Luke. Is that so terrible?''

She shook her head in dismay when the silence wore on. He was worse than she had imagined. Dammit, this was all her fault. He'd warned her nothing could come of it, but she'd blithely gone along and done it anyway. Luke Gianetti may very well be a lost cause. And the thought of that had sheer frustration pumping through her veins.

There had been stark terror in his eyes when he'd realized they'd forgotten to use a condom. The package had been inches away from them both times. Yet she hadn't given it a moment's thought. Jillian wasn't insulted by his fear, only saddened. She probably should have been more concerned about having unprotected sex, but found she simply couldn't work up a head of steam for it. She knew there'd be no risk of pregnancy. And somehow Luke didn't strike her as the type of man to sleep around. She was more upset by the fact that he was so bloody furious with himself…and with her, too.

"How can you be so brave and so willing to die for a cause you believe in, yet so frightened of the least little expression of emotion? It won't kill you, you know.''

"I'm not gonna listen to this. You think by spending four days with me that somehow you know what makes me tick? You don't know anything about me.''

"I know enough after four days to know that you're a wonderful, considerate man.''

"If you think that—'' he laughed derisively ''—honey, you don't know anything.''

"I know that you love children, that is, if you'd let yourself love them. And that they love you back. I know that underneath that strong, gruff exterior you're kind and gentle.''

"Look, let's clarify something here. I'm nice to your kids because it's easier that way. I'm stuck with you and you're stuck with me. If I could be a father, which I can't, I would be a terrible one. I have a dangerous job. One that requires me to be away from home for weeks at a time. Sometimes months. And I'm not willing to change any of that. Not for you. Not for your kids.''

"Have I asked you to change?"

He snorted. ''No, but you would. My wife thought she could handle it, too. Then I come home one day and find her dead.'' His voice grew colder, quieter. ''Not dead from an accident. Linda chose dying over living with me. Not divorce. Death.''

"Her death must have been awful for you. I can only imagine—"

"You can't begin to imagine," he interrupted. "That's how wonderful a guy I am. I ruined her life. You stick around long enough, I'll ruin yours, too.''

"Did you ever, just once, think she might be to blame? She was a grown woman, Luke, fully responsible for her own actions.''

That stopped him in his tracks. If she could have seen his face, she knew his expression would have scared her to death. But this could very well be the only chance she would ever get to offer her opinion. She swallowed her fear and continued.

"Did you ever think maybe she was weak? That instead of admitting she had a problem, she chose to blame you instead?''

"You don't know anything about it," he said, his voice rigid with resentment.

"She was drowning, Luke. But she didn't want you to save her. She wanted to hold you under with her. It was easier to blame you for her unhappiness. Then she wouldn't have to try to fix it herself. She wanted to hurt you…because she was hurting.''

"That's enough. I don't need your dime-store analysis. I accept full responsibility for what happened. I killed Linda.

Me!'' He swore viciously when he bumped into the corner of her bed. ''I know it was my fault. If I'd quit my job when she asked me to, she'd still be alive.''

''And would you be happy if you'd let her manipulate you? If she'd forced you to change into something you're not? Would you still be together under those circumstances?'' Jilly clutched the blankets to her chest. She knew he'd never hurt her with his fists, but he could slice her down with his words if he chose to.

''It doesn't matter now, does it? I never should have gotten married in the first place. I made the mistake of thinking you could have everything. Well, I learned the hard way that you can't. I don't need anyone and I don't want anyone needing me.''

He strode to the door and jerked it open. ''I've got a job to do. This discussion is over.''

''Murph, thank God you're here.'' Luke bounded down the steps of the narrow porch. He'd spent the remaining few hours of the night outside, away from the claustrophobic cabin and away from Jillian. He watched his friend grab a shotgun from the trunk. Murphy slung it over his shoulder to make room for the box of provisions he had perched in one arm.

His partner had arrived in the nick of time. If Luke had spent one more second analyzing how he felt about Jillian, he would go freaking nuts. And it was getting a little awkward staying out on the porch. If the kids weren't up yet, they would be soon. He should be inside helping, not hiding out on the porch.

''You know, instead of watchin' me, you could help with some of this stuff.''

''But it's more fun to watch you.'' He sauntered down to the car and grabbed the box from his friend. He'd decided during the night to let Murphy take over Jillian's protection. That way he'd be able to keep his distance without hurting her feelings. His partner would act as a buffer between them.

"Jesus. What happened to you? You look like shit."

Luke held up his arm and winced at the twinge of pain, grateful that it wasn't his shooting arm. "Shot again. Petrie, or one of his guys, nicked me. It's still pretty sore."

"I wasn't talkin' about your arm. You look like you haven't slept in a week." Murphy did a slow double take and then grinned. "You finally got some, didn't you? Mary Poppins proved to be too much for your vow of celibacy, eh? I knew you wouldn't last long. Not the way you were droolin' over her."

His heart started pounding and he wasn't quite sure whether he was more angry about the insult to Jilly or the fact that he'd been so easy to read. "Shut up, you idiot. Do I talk about you and Lucy that way?"

"Lucy?" Murphy shifted his load so he could get a good look at him. "Damn. You're serious about this one? You thinkin' a' marrying this girl?"

"Damn, Murphy. That's not what I meant and you know it." He felt the beads of sweat start to form on his forehead. He was definitely not up to a verbal boxing match with his partner. Not after the night he'd had. He'd lost Round One to Jilly. Her words had etched into his brain and, as hard as he'd tried, he couldn't stop thinking about what she'd said.

His partner chuckled. "Well, what did you mean?"

Hell if he knew. Jilly'd voiced thoughts about Linda he'd been too ashamed to admit. It *had* crossed his mind that she'd been manipulating him. As a result, along with the guilt he'd felt over his dead wife, there'd been a residue of smoldering anger toward her, as well. She'd never wanted to go for counseling, steadfastly clinging to the belief that he was the sole cause of their marital problems. Her only solution had been for him to quit—for him to change—for him to give up everything. After a few years he'd sincerely doubted that any action on his part would have pleased her.

"Can we please talk about anything else? Like maybe what the hell's goin' down with this op?"

"Yeah, all right. But you're more fun." Murphy set the box on the bottom step of the porch.

He forced back a sigh of relief. "What happened? We get him?" He didn't really hold out any hope that Sloan and his supplier would walk into the poorly set trap.

"Okay. Here's the rundown. Sloan was a no-show. Big surprise there. He's the freakin' Invisible Man. Petrie's disappeared. Joe's still on our side. He's runnin' the slug from your ass through ballistics. Might have something when he gets here later."

"I thought we were giving that bullet to someone outside the agency?"

"We don't have that luxury, my friend. We've got to trust somebody."

"And you think Joe's on our side?"

"Well, he didn't shoot me last night. That says something. The last thing we need is to get paranoid." Murphy scratched his chin and looked thoughtful. "Not that I'm expecting any surprises from ballistics. Sloan hasn't made many mistakes so far. I can't imagine we'll get lucky."

"Anything on the leak?"

Murphy shook his head. "And if that ain't enough bad news for you, I've got some more. Duncan's pissed at you, my friend. Big-time pissed. He's on his way down here. Said he'll be here around noon."

"Perfect. What the hell will that accomplish?"

"He wants this resolved. Said you've dragged it out for too long."

"Like this mess is my fault? It was inside leaks that got us here in the first place." He kicked a pinecone and watched it skitter across the soft mossy ground. He turned back to face his friend. "I'm starting to think we were made four days ago—when the building went up with us inside it. The whole thing felt wrong." A sudden thought made his blood run cold. "Where was Petrie during that mess?"

"No dice." Murphy shook his head. "I thought of that,

too, so I checked on it. He wasn't even in the area. He got sent down from Charlotte two days ago.''

"Then who leaked our safe house location?"

"Hell if I know. Duncan ain't too concerned about the leak—"

"Well he should be," Luke interrupted.

"He figures we can handle that in-house. He's pissed about her." Murphy tipped his head in the direction of the cabin door. "What the hell were you holdin' out for? You shoulda let Duncan know about Jilly."

Luke fought to hold on to his temper. "Let him know what? He knew I had four people in protective custody. Names, ages, sex. What'd he turn up on her? A parking ticket?"

The rich baritone laugh rumbled up from the depths of Murphy's chest and, under normal circumstances, it was a contagious sound. When Danny Murphy started laughing, you couldn't help but join in. Except this time. This time, Luke had a hard time not taking a swing at him.

"You really don't know?"

"No, but I have the feeling you're gonna tell me soon or in about five seconds you're gonna lose all your teeth."

"Duncan got his ass chewed out this morning by the SAC, who got *his* ass chewed by the director himself. And the director got reamed by State."

"The director? What the hell for?" Luke felt his gut go to DEFCON 5. He had the sinking feeling his career was about to implode. Damn if he knew why.

"The British consulate has been swarmin' the place."

"Yeah, she's British. Big deal. Duncan knew all about it. What happened? Her mother finally pitch a fit?"

"That's puttin' it mildly. The old lady had a meltdown. Apparently, Jilly forgot to call home."

"Last I checked, she was over twenty-one," he argued. "From what I've gathered, her mother told her she was on her own. She refused to help. She left Jilly by herself to fly over here, bury Annie and adopt her kids.''

"Well, G-Man, the duchess has apparently had a slight change of heart.''

"Duchess?''

"Yeah. A duchess. Not ten feet away from here. Your lady love is friggin' royalty.''

Luke shook his head in disgust. "What are you talking about? She's going to work for Dartmouth College as a librarian or something.''

"Guess again, G. Her sister, the murdered one, was named Annie.''

"Yeah, I know,'' Luke said impatiently. "Annie Moseby, remember? We had this conversation yesterday? You said you were too busy to look into it?''

"Uh-huh. That changed in a hurry, too. Wanna know Annie Moseby's official name?''

He tried to dispel the impending sense of doom that clutched his stomach. "Well, go ahead,'' he said irritably.

"Lady Anna Rose Winthrop Moseby, Duchess of Sussex.'' Murphy grinned and bent at the waist, performing a low bow for his partner.

Luke continued to shake his head in spite of the sledge-hammer shock that had just nailed him in the chest. No way. No freakin' way. If that were true about Annie, then…

Sweet Jesus. Then Lady Jillian really *was* Lady Jillian. He heard a roaring sound in his ears and immediately felt the blood rush from his head. He quickly sat on the bottom step. It was either that or collapse.

"Then who's…you mean Jilly's really—''

"Lady Jillian Marie Winthrop Moseby. Did you know she's thirty-ninth in line for the British throne?'' Murphy had the nerve to smile. "Yup. Who woulda thought? You're really moving up in the world, G. You just slept with a freakin' duchess.''

"Shut up, Murphy. Not another word about her.'' He gritted his teeth against the verbal abuse he wanted to sling at his friend and swallowed hard around the hot burst of anger that threatened to crush his chest. He launched himself off the steps and strode down to the car.

A duchess. What the hell had she been playing him for? What could she possibly have gained by lying? Unless she'd been out to humiliate him just for the fun of it. Miss High Society out for a stroll with a lowly commoner. Maybe she just liked the idea of getting it on with the pool boy. Her comments came rushing back to him all at once: how she'd spoken of finally being free to make her own decisions, about breaking free from her mother and the man she'd chosen for Jilly to marry.

Damn, she was probably supposed to have an arranged marriage. She'd mentioned that her schedule was planned from morning until night. But he'd taken her remarks in stride. Everyone he knew was overcommitted. Most people had too much going on in their lives to enjoy anything. None of those comments added together would have remotely suggested she was freaking royalty. She'd deliberately withheld the information.

His brain pounded viciously inside his skull and he took a deep breath. God damn. She sure hadn't acted like royalty. Whatever she was, he couldn't fault her for being a snob. In fact, she'd been the polar opposite. Jillian was the most down-to-earth woman he'd ever known.

He shouldn't care that she'd played him. They'd agreed to no strings. Hell, he'd practically insulted her after they'd made love—when he'd bluntly told her it was just sex. And she'd been okay. He knew her feelings were hurt, but she hadn't tried to change his mind. She hadn't pleaded, hadn't tried to use sex as her bargaining tool.

Only an hour ago he'd been freaked out by the thought that Jilly might care. He'd been afraid she'd push for something more, that she'd beg him for some kind of relationship. He'd been worried he'd have to hurt her, that he'd be forced to say no. While an even bigger part of him had been afraid he'd say yes.

And when the conversation turned difficult, he'd been the one to run away. He'd kept his anger at Linda well hidden behind a screen of guilt. For too many years it had fueled him and kept him company. It had become his excuse for not taking chances. Letting go of it now meant he'd be free to try again with someone new. Releasing his guilt meant risking himself all over again. And where would that get him? What did a DEA agent from Chicago have to offer that would be good enough for a damn duchess?

What a joke. All the while, Jillian had wanted nothing more from him. It really had been "just sex" for her. Luke closed his eyes and willed away the pain, his chest aching with something alarmingly close to despair. This was a perfect example of what went wrong when you let your guard down. He'd let himself get emotionally attached to her and the kids. It was all the proof he needed that he wasn't meant for a relationship. Caring made him weak. Need would make him do stupid things.

This was a valuable lesson. He'd get over her. He'd get over the kids. And then he'd be good for another decade.

Why, then, did it feel as though the bottom had just fallen out? He tried to summon a reserve of anger to cover for the pain, but couldn't seem to find anything but anguish. And he knew the reason why. He'd known it for days. Hell, he'd known it from the very start. He wanted her, dammit. He wanted the flaky, fiery, stubborn free spirit he'd spent the last several days trying to run away from.

He wanted Jilly.

Forever.

"Yo, G? You okay, man?" Murphy huffed down the hill after him.

Luke glanced up and cringed when he saw the sympathy in his partner's eyes. God, he was pathetic. If Murphy could see it, then Jillian surely would, too. And he would never allow that to happen. It was one thing to be humiliated, but he'd be damned to the fires of hell before he'd let her see that she'd gotten to him.

"I'm fine. Let's get to work." Finally he felt the anger begin to pump through him. Anger was good. That he could handle. Bottled-up rage would work far better than hurt. He was gonna end this thing today, one way or another. And then he was gonna take a long, long vacation. There were a million women out there. Once he'd had a few of them, Lady Jillian Moseby would be nothing to him. Nothing except a distant memory.

Jillian glanced up from making the bed when she heard voices on the front porch. Samuel and James bounded off the bed, still in their clothes from the previous night.

Danny Murphy was back and he was involved in an intense debate with Luke. "Are you sure you wanna do it this way?" Murphy's voice sounded more than just a bit skeptical. His eyes met hers briefly and he flashed a smile. "Hey, Jilly."

"Good morning, Mr. Murphy."

"I'm positive. You can handle the protection detail from here," Luke explained. "The mood I'm in, I don't want to get within twenty feet of Duncan. This thing has been mishandled from the start and I'll be damned if I'm gonna stand here and take a lecture from that asshole."

"That's Sir Asshole," Murphy corrected with a grin. He must have sensed Jillian's curiosity because he winked in her general direction. "Luke's got a problem with our ASAC."

"Is that the same thing as the SAC he spoke of earlier?"

"Close. Duncan is the Assistant Special Agent in Charge. For this op, it means he's the boss."

"I see. And Luke doesn't like him?" She noticed that the subject of their conversation was carefully avoiding any sort of contact with her, including making eye contact. She wondered how he would react if she walked over to the table where he was cleaning and loading a deadly looking gun and threw her arms around his neck. What would Agent Heart-throb do if she dropped into his lap and gave him a resounding kiss? Jilly suppressed a smile and refocused her attention on his partner.

"Nah. Luke suffers from an aversion to authority figures." Murphy winked again. "I think it stems back to childhood. Something about taking orders from all those nuns in school."

Luke glared at him in response, refusing to rise to the bait. "I can handle the sisters. It's just the boneheads I have trouble with."

"Wow. That's a Glock, isn't it?" James leaned over his forearm to get a better look. Luke's surprised gaze shot over the little boy's head to finally acknowledge Jillian's presence. She noticed that even Murphy had been temporarily stunned silent.

"Yeah, kid. How'd you know?"

"Oh, that." James puffed out his chest, incredibly proud to be right. "Sarah's daddy had some of those. And so do all his friends. His friends had all different kinds." He bent over to take a closer look, his nose scrunched up in concentration, completely missing the stunned looks that passed between the adults. "His gun had a thing on the end of it, though," he continued. "It made a poof sound when he used it. He always promised he'd show me how to shoot it, but he never did. He never kept promises."

"That was probably a good thing, Jimmy. Guns are very dangerous. They should never be left around small children," Luke explained. "Bad things can happen with a loaded gun."

"Slow had a whole closetful of 'em." James settled into the chair opposite Luke, continuing to watch as he loaded the clip. "I always made sure to keep Sammy away from them. He's too little to know better."

"Slow? Did I miss somethin'? Who's Slow?" Murphy set his box of supplies down and then carefully placed his shot-gun on the high bureau in the corner of the room, far away from the kids.

"Slow's Sarah's daddy."

Chapter 11

Slow's Sarah's daddy. Luke felt the air rush out of his chest and his heart started racing a mile a minute. He flashed back over his conversations with James. *Once she an' Slow left us for four whole days.* Slow. *Sarah's daddy was Slow. He was real mean to us.*

James's singsong voice came back to haunt him and his photographic memory began placing missing puzzle pieces into the correct slots. It wasn't possible. If he'd only been paying closer attention to the kid. He'd had access to critical information for the past four days.

Slow.

Sloan.

"Sloan," he rasped. "You mean Sloan, don't you, Jimmy?" He rose from the table and shoved the gun into his waistband.

"Yeah, that's his name. That's what Mommy called him."

"Damn. I can't believe I didn't put it together before now." He glanced at Murphy and saw the dawning understanding in his partner's eyes. He turned on Jilly then, anger throbbing through him at the knowledge that he'd been played by her, not once but twice. The princess had held out on him again.

"When the hell were you going to tell us that your sister was screwing one of the biggest drug dealers on the east coast?"

Jillian took two steps back and bumped into the bed. Her face drained of color and her smoky-blue eyes filled with tears. He didn't miss how her mouth quivered before she bit down on her lip and composed herself. Dammit, he refused to let her tears get to him this time. She turned them on and off like a faucet.

"Luke, hey! It's not her fault." Murphy stepped between them, intent on protecting Jillian from his wrath. "How the hell would she know?"

"She knew. She had to know." Luke refused to believe that she was the innocent in all of this. "Just like she knew she was a freakin' duchess all this time that she's been yanking my chain."

"Oh, Lord," she whispered, comprehension flaring in her eyes. "How did you find out?" She sagged to the bed and stared woodenly out the window. Sarah chose that moment to begin fussing. On automatic pilot, Jilly got to her feet and walked over to the ancient cradle.

"Your mummy was looking for her precious daughter. You forgot to phone home." He knew he'd hit his mark when she visibly winced, but it didn't make him feel any better. In fact, it made him feel foolish.

"I don't care for your tone, Luke. Who I am is not pertinent to our situation. Being a bloody duchess is hard enough without having to announce it to the world. Besides, it only would have made you worry more."

"I should have been the one to decide that."

Something flashed in her eyes and Luke watched as angry color flowed back into her cheeks. She hoisted Sarah from the cradle and yanked the diaper bag from its perch on the chest of drawers.

"My being a duchess didn't foul up this operation, Luke. You boys did that all by yourselves. Therefore, I would greatly appreciate it if you would refrain from taking out your wretched temper on me."

She advanced on him then, her eyes sparking with fury while her hands carefully cradled Sarah to her chest, her fingers stroking the baby's back. Despite his anger, Luke found the contrast fascinating.

"For your information, I didn't know anything about this Sloan person. Your memory is obviously selective when it comes to me. I clearly remember telling you that I didn't even know about Sarah's existence until two weeks ago. How the hell was I supposed to know who her bloody father was? The man who tried to claim paternity after I got here wasn't named Sloan. *That* I would have remembered."

"What are you talking about? What man?"

She took a deep breath and let it out slowly. "Two days after I arrived, I had to go to court because some man wanted to take Sarah away from me. I had to hire an American lawyer and we went to the judge...and I got her back."

"What happened? Who was he?"

"I don't remember. Everything happened so blasted quickly." Her lower lip began trembling and Luke felt his heart drop to his feet. When she was furious—hell, even when she was crying—she was still the most beautiful woman he'd ever known.

"I mean, I buried my sister one day and the next day I tried to pick up the kids from social services and..."

She turned her back on all of them, pretending she wasn't really crying as she pulled out a diaper and set about changing Sarah. Luke watched Samuel cross the room to sit next to her, one thumb stuck in his mouth and the other chubby little arm wrapped around Jilly. She gave him a watery smile and tousled his still messy hair. Even James gave Luke a bewildered look and shrugged his shoulders in confusion. Then, as casually as he could manage, he slid out of his chair and went to sit with her, too.

It was Murphy who finally broke the awkward silence. "So then what happened? When did you go to court?"

"They told me I could have the boys, but someone was trying to claim Sarah. So I got out a phone book, found a solicitor and we went to see the judge the next day. All the court papers are buried somewhere in that blasted car of yours." She flung her finger toward the curtained window. "That's assuming we didn't leave them in one of the umpteen motels we've lived in over the past week. But if you want to tear apart the car looking for them, be my guest."

Luke glanced at Murphy and looked quickly away, ashamed that he'd let his anger get the best of him. Ashamed that he'd ripped into Jilly. She hadn't deserved it. He'd been frustrated on so many levels that he wasn't seeing anything clearly. His feelings for her were too intertwined with the case. But that still didn't make it her fault.

He made a mental note to apologize before he left and then his brain clicked back to the business at hand. He crossed the room and snatched the diaper bag from the corner of the bed. Jillian's eyes questioned his actions, but he wasn't willing to meet her gaze, not after the way he'd treated her.

"You done with this?" His voice sounded gruff to his own ears.

"Yes."

"Is this the only suitcase of your sister's?" Luke asked.

"No. There's one other."

He riffled through the bag before turning back to face Murphy. "If Sloan is Sarah's father, then Annie Moseby is—"

"Winnie." Murphy's eyes widened in comprehension. "Winthrop—Winnie. Makes sense now. The missing money—"

Luke nodded, his eyes narrowed and purposeful. His gut tightened noticeably as another of the puzzle pieces fell into place as they always did when a case was about to explode.

Jimmy's story about his mother having money came back to gnaw at his brain.

"Is probably right here." He unzipped the outside pocket of the diaperbag and ran his hand along the lining. Finding nothing, he flipped it over and checked the seams. "That's what Sloan wants. Not Jilly. Not me. He's after the money Annie took from him."

Murphy shook his head in disbelief. "Where's the other bag?"

Jilly spoke from her perch on the bed. "Did we bring everything with us or did our bags get left behind last night?"

"After you left last night, I cleared out the car Luke drove yesterday. When you switched vehicles, I took everything with me."

"Then they're still in the boot." She tickled Sarah and set her on the floor to play with Samuel before walking over to Murphy. Luke noticed that she gave him a very wide berth, skirting around the far bed to avoid him. And even while his gut twisted into a knot of regret, he didn't blame her one bit. He'd acted like an idiot. Again.

"I can show you which case is hers if you'd like."

Her voice was all sweet helpfulness and it served to make him feel even worse about the accusations he'd flung at her. He'd blown it with the one woman he wanted more than anything. But royalty or not, it would have ended between them anyway.

He couldn't handle a woman like Jillian. Couldn't handle all the damn emotion and tears. Couldn't handle loving her kids. They were sweet and precious and in need of so much more than he could offer. He wasn't up to it. He was far from qualified to become a dad.

"I don't want you leaving this cabin." He made the announcement to Jillian, but kept his gaze on Murphy.

She whirled to face him, hands on hips, and frowned. "Well, then how will he know which case is Annie's?"

"You can describe the shade of periwinkle to him. I'm sure he'll catch on faster than I did."

"What's this about periwinkle? Damn, not a discussion about colors." He threw his hands up in the air. "I don't know what it is, all right? I've been married fifteen years and I still don't know what color that is." Murphy rolled his eyes and headed for the bathroom. "I'll be back in an hour when the two of you have resolved this. G, you gonna call Duncan or you want me to?"

Luke didn't take his eyes off Jillian. "You do it."

She waited until she heard the bathroom door close before she approached him. "Don't you think you're being just a tad unreasonable? Murphy's car is about twenty feet away." She'd folded her arms across her chest and was heading for the door when he cut her off.

"Princess, you're not going anywhere until I say you can."

"I'm not a bloody princess. I'm a duchess." Not that it mattered anyway. "I knew you'd find something—some excuse to stop seeing me." She glanced at the kids and dropped her voice to a whisper before advancing on him.

"This has nothing to do with us," he snapped back. "There is no 'us,' remember? This is about your failure to communicate a vital piece of information during an ongoing investigation."

"You don't give a damn that I'm a duchess. It has no bearing on this investigation whatsoever. You're simply too afraid to see what might happen if we continue to see each other." She ran a disapproving gaze down his face. "You'd sooner take a bullet than have a serious conversation with me. You'd rather run away than face the fact that we could be great together."

"You don't know what you're talking about." He knew she had to see his heart pounding, knew she must see his hands shaking. He folded his arms across his chest and fisted his hands.

She shook her head sadly. "You're such a liar. And I am,

too. I love you, Luke. Last night was the most incredible night of my life. I could try to pretend otherwise, but why should I? These past four days with you have made me realize what my life could be like."

"You've been chased and shot at—"

"Stop it," she interrupted forcefully. "That's not what I meant and you know it. Despite all your efforts to keep me at bay, I've gone and fallen in love with you. How sorry is that?"

"Don't say anything else," he warned, wincing at the desperate sound of his voice. He could not cave in on this. He only had to hang on a little while longer and then he could retreat to safety. "You don't love me. If you knew me, you'd realize that you're wasting your time."

"I *do* know you," she argued. "I know everything that's important. I've already seen most of your faults. You're incredibly foul-tempered. You get easily frustrated."

She'd evidently thought long and hard, he realized as he watched her tick them off on her fingers. "Easily frustrated? You'd try the patience of a saint."

Unfazed, she continued with her list. "You have to think through every bloody angle before you make a decision. I have several perfectly normal habits that seem to drive you completely mad—"

"Jill. God, don't do this. Please? I'm sorry for what I said earlier about you and about your sister. I was angry and I didn't mean it. That's no excuse. But I don't… I can't—"

Luke felt as though he were drowning, that each time she spoke, another huge wave crashed down over his head. If she persisted in trying to convince him, he knew he'd go under and he'd never come up for air. He'd be lost for sure, because if he gave in, he would never let her go. She couldn't love him. Not really. Those feelings didn't last. He'd believed that he loved Linda. What if he fell for Jilly and then she came to her senses? She'd leave him, too.

"You're always bragging about your gut instinct. What

does your gut tell you about me?'' Her wistful smile faltered when she saw the panic that must be visible in his expression.

The million-dollar question. Luke dragged his fingers through his hair and looked away. He couldn't risk it. Not when it meant losing everything. His jaw clenched, he turned back and looked her straight in the eye. And lied.

''My gut is telling me to walk away and never look back.''

Her face remained stoic, a true testament to her ironclad control. But her eyes, her eyes told him a different story. Where a moment before there had been a defiant hope, the spark of her eternal optimism, now there was emptiness. She had her answer and she would live with it. He knew her well enough to know she wouldn't ask him again. The crushing weight of reality sat heavy on his chest. There would be no second chances after this. She'd laid herself out on the floor and he'd wiped his feet on her.

''I see. Well then, I guess that's settled.'' Her beautiful eyes filled with tears and she dashed them away with her fingers. Several teardrops still sparkled on her lashes and it was all he could do not to wipe them away.

''I still love you. I know it doesn't change anything. I can't make you feel the way I do. And it's okay. I'll survive this.'' She gave him a watery smile. ''Maybe not completely happily, but I'll make it. *We'll* make it just fine,'' she emphasized. ''I just…wanted you to know how I truly felt. So when you're off on your next adventure and you're far, far away, you can know with absolute certainty that someone, somewhere…''

A desperate bubble of laughter surfaced through her tears and the sound sent a knife into his chest. It made him want to take her in his arms and hold her forever.

''That someone in New Hampshire loves you very much,'' she finished bravely. She wiped her eyes again and took a deep breath. ''That's all.''

''Jill.'' He swallowed hard, completely uncertain of what to say. She surprised him again by reaching her fingers up to press them against his lips. He was helpless to control the shudder that tore through him with the simple contact.

"Don't say anything, all right?"

He heard the bathroom door open and Jillian jerked away from him, pasting on a smile for the benefit of Murphy and the children, who were now watching TV and clamoring for something to eat. He realized as he watched her that she had as much, or maybe even more control than he did. Her upbringing had forced her to hide behind a smile, no matter how she was really feeling.

More than anything else, Luke couldn't handle what he felt for her. He'd never imagined he could love someone again. Never imagined he'd experience the tidal wave of emotion that he felt when he thought of her. Panic and hope intermingled. Loving Jilly and losing her would kill him. Ending it this way was better in the long run. He could start nursing the pain now.

Murphy finished his conversation with Duncan and flipped his cell phone closed. "Well, that went well. *Not.* Instead of heralding our major breakthrough, Duncan is twice as determined to come down here and take over." He flicked a glance at his watch. "Chopper's gonna drop him around ten miles from here. Should be here in about half an hour."

Sensing the tension throbbing in the room, he glanced from Luke to Jilly and back. Jillian pretended to be oblivious, busying herself with feeding the kids the fruit and cereal Murphy had brought with him. He raised an eyebrow toward Jillian, questioning him with his eyes. Luke shook his head and Murphy shrugged his shoulders in what appeared to be exasperation.

"G, he wants one of us to pick him up at the airstrip. Actually, he wants you. You want me to go instead?"

"No. I'll do it." Too quickly he responded. "You stay here with the rest of them."

James glanced up, seeming to tune in to the conversation. "Can I go with you, Luke?"

"I don't know, kid." He was desperate to leave the claustrophobic cabin. If he stayed any longer, he would end up throwing himself at Jilly's feet—an embarrassing scene that would be too little, too late.

"Please, Luke? You said it's just a quick ride. Lemme go, too! I can help."

"Should be safe," Murphy pointed out.

"All right, Jimmy." At this point, it was easier to cave in than to stand around arguing. "Go brush your teeth and then we'll get outta here."

They'd been gone for ages when Jillian remembered the other suitcase. She left her spot at the window and flopped on the end of the bed. There was no use feeling sorry for herself. With any luck, the whole sorry affair would be over today. She and the children would finally be free to go. She would make a beeline for New Hampshire. The sooner they were settled and busy with other things, the sooner the children would establish a routine and the sooner she could start repairing the damage to her heart.

Despite Luke's reaction, she was still glad she'd been honest with him. She took a deep breath and let it out. It had been a small step toward independence. She'd seen something she'd wanted desperately and she'd gone after it. Of course the failure part was pretty hard to swallow. In this particular instance, the failure felt quite devastating. She'd seen the fear in his eyes when she'd told him she loved him…seen the disbelief. And she'd seen regret. She wasn't sure if it was because he'd said no or because she'd told him in the first place. And at this point, what difference did it make?

She loved him enough to let him go. She absently rubbed the tender spot over her heart. It was a dull ache now, compared to the stabbing pain she'd felt only an hour earlier when he'd rejected her offer. Even in a disaster, she told herself, the human heart recovered. It was deflated, but still pumping. Truth be told, it hurt to breathe. Her heart felt as though it had been stepped on. But she was a Moseby. They had never been the type to plead or to beg or to negotiate. If Luke didn't want her, she would get along without him. The ordeal he'd been through with Linda had obviously left him too emotionally scarred to try again. It was either that or he simply didn't want her enough to make the effort. Jillian wished desperately that it was the first reason.

"Danny, didn't Luke want to take a look at that other suitcase in the boot? I can show you which one it is. That way, when your lieutenant or major or whatever-he-is gets here, you might have something more to show him."

Murphy sat back in his chair by the window, stretching his long legs. "I don't see why not. It's quiet as a tomb out there." He rose to his feet, stretched again and double checked his holster before heading for the door.

"Yeah, let's do it." He checked the porch and scanned the deserted road leading back to the motel office before he let Jilly pass. "What about the little ones? They gonna be okay for a minute?"

Jillian checked on Sarah. She was still napping in the ancient cradle. She sat on the bed near Samuel where he was busy playing with his cars. "Samuel? I want you to be a very good boy. Stay on this bed and don't move until I come back in with Mr. Murphy. I'll only be a moment."

She stood then and went swiftly to the bathroom where she closed the door tight. He wouldn't be able to turn the handle by himself. Then she rechecked Murphy's shotgun. Even with a chair, he couldn't climb up to reach it.

Murphy caught her perusal and chuckled. "That's right. You're thinkin' like a mom now. No matter how well you check, it's pretty much guaranteed that he'll find something you didn't think about."

"Perhaps I should stay."

"Tell ya what. You run down there with me real fast. Point out the suitcase and then run right back up here. You'll be gone maybe a minute or two. That's about as safe as it's gonna get. Otherwise, we can wait for G to come back.''

She bit her lip, torn by the desire to be in two places at one time. ''No,'' she finally decided. ''I want to look myself. I haven't had a moment to even think about my sister. What if she left me a letter? I'd like to be the one who sees it first, if you don't mind.''

''I can understand that, but Jilly if we find a letter we're gonna have to take it as evidence, especially if it says anything about Sloan,'' he warned.

''I know, Danny. Perhaps I could have a copy of it? That is, if we even find anything.''

He smiled at her persistence. ''Yeah, I think I can arrange somethin' like that. Remember though there will be no touching until I give you the all-clear. I'll have to preserve any fingerprints.''

''It's a deal.''

''You see anything yet?'' Luke was impatient to get back. His gut was strumming again with an edgy uneasiness that grew stronger with each passing minute. Despite his earlier eagerness to gain some distance from Jilly, he was distinctly uncomfortable with the separation. There was safety in numbers.

He glanced in the rearview mirror at Jimmy as he bounced from one side of the car to the other, a pair of high-powered binoculars in his hands. Watching him go from window to window for the past half hour was giving him a case of whiplash.

''Where is he? Shouldn't the man be here by now? I wanna see the helicopter.''

Luke checked his watch and frowned. Fifteen minutes overdue and still no sign of the chopper. It wasn't like the anal Duncan to be late for anything. In fact, the opposite usually held true. His boss had an annoying habit of showing up early for meetings and then criticizing everyone for keeping him waiting.

He'd had trouble finding the isolated airstrip and he'd half expected Duncan to be waiting when he finally pulled up with Jimmy. "Strip" was the operative word. The runway consisted of two dirt tracks down the middle of a long field of wavering grass. Anything smaller than a chopper might have had trouble with the rutted tracks and the rough terrain. The regional airport had been a mere fifteen minutes away—in the opposite direction from the cabin. Why the hell hadn't Duncan chosen to land there? He wondered about the sudden secrecy.

"Hang on there, bud. He'll be here all too soon." He shook his head ruefully. As if the day wasn't progressing poorly enough already. He still had a butt-chewing waiting with his name on it. His head still ached from his run-in with Jilly and just thinking about her now made his gut tighten like a vise.

He was grateful it would end today. Grateful even, that Duncan was coming down to take charge. That meant she'd be off his hands—permanently. The ASAC would move her to a safe house and he could stop worrying about her. He could head back down to Charleston for cleanup duty—a duty that would include finding Sloan and taking him out for good. It was the only way he knew of to guarantee Jilly's and the kids' safety. The last thing he wanted was her feeling she had to look over her shoulder for the rest of her life. And he realized that he didn't much care what the duty would entail. If it meant dying, then so be it.

For a long time after Linda died, he hadn't really cared if he died in the line of duty. He'd felt in some convoluted way that it would be suitable punishment for failing to help her, for failing to care enough. Only now did he realize what a waste it would have been. Luke smiled for the first time in a long while. Finally, he'd found something that really *was* worth dying for.

And if he lived, then just as soon as he'd accomplished his

mission, he could post out to an assignment that would take him as far away from the east coast as he could get.

Through the crack in the window, Luke heard the distant whine of an approaching aircraft. "Here it comes, Jimbo. Look around. You see it yet?"

"Nope. Wait! I see it," he cried. "It's a tiny little speck and it's getting bigger." He continued to squint through the binoculars for another minute as the chopper came closer. "Hey, there's a couple guys in there."

"Well, yeah. Did you think my boss was gonna fly it all by himself?"

"I mean in the back seats. There's two— No, there's three guys sittin' in the back seat.

The thump of the propeller blades grew louder with every passing second. Luke frowned over the information. What the hell was Duncan up to? He and Murphy had worked the investigation for months. Now that they'd had a huge break, the pinhead was sending in replacements? It was bad enough the ASAC had screwed up with Petrie. The bastard might've killed them all. And why wasn't he more concerned about the leak? Any safe house Duncan took Jilly to would still be unsafe in his mind. Until they found the leak and shut it down.

He felt the wind howl against the car, heard sand skitter against the windshield as the helicopter set down across the field, a few hundred yards away.

"Now do you see why I didn't want you playing outside when the chopper flew in?" He had to shout to Jimmy over the screaming noise of the engine. He strained to see through the clouds of dust and made out two figures as they alighted from the chopper.

"Uh-oh. Luke, this is bad."

Luke took his gaze off the helicopter and glanced in the rearview mirror. Jimmy was perched in his spot, his binoculars trained on the men who were still a football field away. "What's up, pal? Can you see the color of their neckties yet?" The damn suits.

Jimmy dropped the field glasses from his eyes and glanced up to meet his gaze in the mirror. The terror he found there made his blood run cold. His gut tightened instinctively and he whirled around to face the little boy. "What? What is it, Jimmy? What did you see?"

James shuddered once and then brought the binoculars back up to his eyes for confirmation.

"Dammit, what the hell do you see?" He snatched the binoculars away from James and quickly adjusted the sights. Duncan walked toward him, his trenchcoat blowing in the wind from the chopper. He was just wondering why his boss would be wearing a trenchcoat this late in the season when he shifted his gaze to the other man. And his heart dropped like a stone.

Sloan.

Duncan was walking toward the car with Sloan. A drumbeat of warning pounding in his ears, Luke gunned the engine and jerked the wheel to the left as he saw the ASAC raise his arm and reach inside his coat.

"Get down, Jimmy. On the floor right now. And don't come up unless I say so." He lost precious seconds keeping his eyes trained on the back seat to make sure the kid followed orders and then jerked the wheel as a shotgun blast took out the windshield. Wincing as shards of glass rained down upon him, panic blinded him for an instant and then he reacted, accelerating as fast as the car would go. He bounced down the main road, praying that his erratic driving would keep them out of range.

"Jimmy," he barked. "You okay back there?"

"Yup. You okay?"

"Stay down on the floor." He took several deep breaths as he concentrated on the rutted one-lane road. He should slow down. If they blew a tire, they'd be in big trouble. And Lord help them if anyone was heading toward them on the narrow pass. At this speed the crash alone would probably kill them. "And hold on tight."

Chunks of tree bark flew at him from the left side of the road, from a shot that had gone wide and missed the car. Duncan was still firing at them. Luke wondered if he'd inadvertently entered a trap. Would Petrie be positioned up around the next bend? It's what he would have done if he'd been setting up an ambush.

"Jimmy, listen up. Anything happens to me, if we have to pull over, I want you to run. Take the cell phone—" he groped around on the seat and found it with his hand "—and run into the woods. You'll have to hide for at least an hour or two. They don't know you're with me. You can call the police and get help for Jilly and the kids."

"No, Luke! I wanna stay with you," his muffled voice protested from the floor.

"I know, pal. I want that, too." He jerked the wheel to the left to avoid a fallen tree and felt the car shimmy in protest.

"Are we gonna die?"

"Not if I can help it, Jimbo. But just in case…" His brain fired rapidly now, knowing that he had very little time before Duncan returned to the chopper and came after him. He knew Duncan had been too far away to have seen Jimmy. Hadn't he? Sweet Jesus. They would hunt Jimmy down until they found him. The kid would be as good as dead.

Jesus— Duncan. Duncan was the leak. Or worse, Duncan was Castillo? Duncan was the drug dealer, the king of heroin on the east coast. Everything made sense now. The safe house blowing, the failed bust on Tuesday. Duncan had pulled the strings on all of it. He'd watched and waited for the right moment to kill them all. No wonder he wanted the operation shut down. No wonder he wanted Luke dead. They were getting too close to Sloan's source. Way too close for comfort. Way too close to Duncan.

He fumbled with the phone and managed to hit the speed dial as the car lurched over another pothole. He had to warn Murphy. His partner would be no match for a surprise attack—especially one from the most unlikely source possible—from the person who was supposed to be helping them.

He brought the phone to his ear and held his breath while it connected. It was taking forever. Please, God. Don't let them be in a dead spot. "C'mon, ring!"

He exhaled as the call finally went through. "Now pick it up," he ordered.

"Did ya see him, Luke? Did ya see him? He's the one who shot my mom," Jimmy cried. "I saw him from my hiding place, but he didn't see me."

"What do you mean, you saw him?"

"The day he shot my mom. I was hiding behind the big chair and I heard them fightin' about money."

Luke's heart began beating wildly. They'd been going about it all wrong. When it came to his drug empire, Sloan had been nothing short of Teflon. Throughout the investigation, he hadn't been able to make so much as a parking ticket stick. But now...

Forget the drugs. With an eyewitness, maybe they could get Sloan on a murder charge instead. Trouble was, the witness would be Jimmy. The thought of him in the same courtroom with Sloan, of knowing how ruthless the drug dealer could be, of the violence he was all too capable of committing. He shook his head. He didn't want Jimmy within a thousand miles of Sloan. The kid would need twenty-four-hour protection. For their own safety, Jilly and the kids would have to all but go into hiding. And what about after he testified? Sloan could still have them taken out, even from behind bars, assuming they got lucky enough to finally nail him. Impatiently he dragged the phone away from his mouth. Where the hell was Murphy?

"Let me get this straight. You saw Sloan shoot your mom?"

"No, not Slow. The other guy. Slow's friend."

Chapter 12

The breeze lifted the collar of her jacket and whipped Jillian's hair around her face. With all the excitement, she'd forgotten to pull it back in a ponytail this morning. She dragged the cool mountain air into her lungs and immediately felt her head begin to clear. She'd been stuck indoors for far too long.

Not a soul was in sight as she skipped down the porch steps with Murphy by her side. There were other cabins visible in the distance, but all of them appeared to be vacant. The stillness was almost eerie in its serenity. Sunlight filtered through the tall Southern pine trees creating patches of light on the mossy carpet that seemed to sway and move with the wind. It felt as though they were the only two people for miles around. Jilly smiled at the foolish thought. Why, not a mile down the road a restaurant claimed in rather glaring neon that it was the biscuit capital of the southeast.

"Lord, Danny. It's really beautiful here. It was dark as a pocket when we arrived last night."

"Seems kinda isolated if you ask me. It's too quiet."

"Are you one of those men who can only relax when you're near a major sports park? Your poor wife."

"Nah. I'm one of those guys who likes to plop down at the beach and watch all the women in bikinis walk by. And when I get bored with that, then I go fishing."

She raised an eyebrow at his confession. "How long did you say you've been married?"

He laughed at her outraged look. "I'm just kiddin'. It's Lucy's fault. She likes to check out all the guys. She thinks it's good for me to feel a little threatened. Says it keeps me in line."

She turned slowly around to admire the mountainous terrain and realized their cabin was perched on the side of a hill. Murphy had taken a step toward the car when she took a quick detour around the back of the cabin and discovered the hill was actually a mountain. They were at the edge of a small clearing that quickly went straight up. Just past the treeline behind the cabin, she could see the rock formations that rose above.

"Hey, get back here." Murphy caught up with her a moment later. "Just because we're out in the middle of nowhere doesn't mean you can walk around whenever you feel like it."

"But it's over, isn't it? Sort of?"

He snorted in response. "Honey, nothin's over until we bust up Sloan's operation. We still gotta catch him and Petrie and whoever else is involved. Are you forgetting Luke got shot again last night?"

"Of course I haven't forgotten. I assumed with your boss coming and everything…" She trailed off, aware of how that probably sounded to Murphy. "What I meant was, with all these new clues, doesn't that mean you've wrapped it up?"

"No. It means that we're one step closer, that's all. It doesn't give you license to be out here wandering around." He jerked his head in the direction of his car. "Now, come on. Let's get movin'."

They'd nearly reached the car when Murphy jerked her by the arm and shoved her to the ground.

"Get down." Before she'd had the chance to speak, he rolled over her and withdrew his gun. She could barely breathe under his crushing weight.

"Danny?" She stopped when she heard a rustling sound in the woods beyond the car and then watched as a large chunk of earth exploded out of the ground about ten feet to their right.

"Stay down." He hissed in her ear, "Someone's shootin' at us."

"Ohmigod. Samuel." Instinct made her clamber to her feet before Murphy slammed her back down to the mossy ground.

"Dammit, I said don't move. You'll be dead before you get to the door."

Murphy's gaze never left the cluster of trees fifty yards south of their position. The moment he detected movement, he squeezed off a round. Her heart in her throat, Jillian shut her eyes against the deafening reverberation and prayed that Samuel wouldn't come to the door to see what was happening. Sarah was due to awaken soon. What if she began crying? Samuel would try to find her. Dear Lord, why, oh, why, had she left them alone?

She opened her eyes when she heard Danny start cursing a blue streak. "What is it? Have you been shot?"

"I left my freaking phone in the cabin," he growled. "Luke's gonna drive right back into the middle of it."

She shook her head, terrified at the thought of losing Luke. And then she moaned when she remembered who was with him. "Lord, no. He has James."

"Right now, we've gotta worry about ourselves. If this guy isn't alone, we're pretty much screwed. He's got us pinned down damn good. The bastard."

She couldn't help but notice a certain admiration in Murphy's tone and fleetingly wondered at his sanity. She lifted her head a fraction of an inch and then yelped when a shot rang out almost simultaneously.

"Aha. Just what I was waiting for," he muttered and pulled the trigger several times. She heard a shout of pain. Several seconds passed before she heard a crashing sound as someone staggered out of the brush and fell to the ground with a lifeless thud.

She took an unsteady breath. Her heart was about to gallop straight out of her chest and no amount of deep breathing would ever make it slow down. "Is it over?"

"Dunno." Still lying on his side, Murphy reached into his back pocket and withdrew another clip. He slammed it into place before doing anything else. "Don't move a muscle. I'm gonna check out the shooter. I want you to take this pistol."

"I can't," Jillian said. "I've never even held a gun before." Well, that wasn't exactly true. But she didn't think skeet shooting would count for very much right now.

"You may have to." His eyes had gone cold and he was deadly serious. "I need you to watch out for me. There's no one else. If something happens to me, you run like hell to the cabin as fast as you can get there. Don't stop and don't look back. Lock the door and call for help."

"But what about you?"

"Go straight to the cabin," he repeated, ignoring her question. "You gotta warn Luke and you've got to call for help." He grabbed her arm to quiet her and they both listened to the stillness for what seemed like a lifetime. When he seemed satisfied there was no one else out there, he motioned to her that they were about to move. He handed her the gun and she tried not to cringe at the heavy weight of the handle in her grasp.

"Hold it steady, aim and shoot. There's barely even a kick to it."

"What am I looking for?" She tasted blood on her lip and realized she'd chewed through several layers of skin.

"Any sudden movement. Shoot first and ask questions

later. Just make sure you don't blast me." He rolled into a crouch and indicated she should do the same. "I'm goin' over to check him out. You watch my back until I give you the all-clear. Then I want you to run like hell up to the cabin. Don't wait for me, you got it?"

She nodded and said a silent prayer as he launched out of their hiding place. She got to her feet and scanned the area where the dead man had fallen and saw nothing. Her gaze traveled first to the left and then to the right of his hiding place. Then she turned her attention toward the cabin.

Murphy was nearly there. He'd crossed the clearing without incident when she saw a flash of movement. A flock of birds alighted from a tree near the cabin, squawking in protest over being disturbed. Murphy must have seen it, too, for he spun toward the cabin, raising his gun as he reached the prone man on the ground.

She nearly had heart failure a moment later when she saw the cabin door open out of the corner of her eye. Samuel's little blond head peeked around the door frame, his startled eyes searching for Jillian.

"Mama? Where you are? I come out an' find you."

"Get back inside and close the door." She shrieked the warning at the top of her lungs. A split second later, Jilly's eyes snapped the pictures as though they were a camera filming a movie. She saw the shiny flash of a gun barrel appear out of the shrubbery at the base of the tree. Without stopping to think, she raised the gun that was clutched in her hand and fired in the direction of the movement.

She didn't realize she was screaming until she ran out of bullets. Hers was the only voice in the suddenly desolate silence. When she came to her senses, there were bodies everywhere. Another man had fallen out of the shrubs. And Murphy was lying on the ground near the first dead man.

"Danny!" She staggered out from behind the car, tears blinding her eyes as she ran toward her friend. Halfway there, she remembered his words. Luke. She had to warn Luke. But, dear Lord, she had to get Murphy, too.

"Samuel, get in the house straightaway." She turned then, propelling herself toward the cabin, her legs trembling so badly she didn't think they would support her weight.

He handed her Murphy's cell phone after she stumbled up the porch steps. "Mama, Luke's on the phone."

He thought he would die while he listened to the gun battle taking place back at the cabin. He was still in shock over Jimmy's announcement. His boss, the ASAC of one of the largest DEA offices in the country, was also one of the biggest drug smugglers in U.S. history. He was also a murderer. He and Murphy were seriously outmanned and outgunned. What was worse, he'd placed Jilly and the kids in terrible danger.

Luke mopped his forehead with his bad arm, wincing at the sharp twinge of pain. When he pulled his arm back he was surprised to find blood. His hair was loaded with glass from the windshield, and apparently, so was his scalp. Dismissing it, he kept his grip tight on the phone. Despite his efforts, sweat still poured into his eyes, making it harder to drive the car at their current eighty-mile-an-hour speed. His eyes watered from the air streaming in through the shattered windshield. He'd finally cleared the airstrip road and was back out on the main drag. Which meant they were in even more danger from the helicopter that was sure to show up at any moment.

Please don't let them be dead, he prayed fervently. He'd nearly had a heart attack when Samuel answered the phone and told him Mama and Murphy were shooting people. He could have sworn he'd just heard Jillian scream, but prayed fervently that it was the wind howling past his ears.

"Pick up the phone. Pick up the phone." He heard Jilly sobbing and shouting at Samuel to get back in the cabin, heard the clatter as she stumbled into the cabin and slammed the door shut. And felt his heart start beating again. Relief poured through him and he clenched the wheel in an effort to regain control. He'd never been more relieved in his entire life. She was safe. She was alive. For the moment.

"Luke? Are you there?"

"Baby, I'm here. Are you all right?"

"Murphy's shot. He's lying out there with the others." He heard her taking in great shaking gulps of air. "I've got to go back out and get him."

"No," he yelled, panic seeping into his voice as he swerved to miss an oncoming car. He was driving on the wrong side of the road. What others? How the hell many shooters were there?

"I'm ordering you to stay inside. The police are on their way. Just stay put until they get there."

"Luke, I hear the helicopter. It's comin' up behind us," James announced from his position on the floor.

"Stay down, Jimmy. Make yourself as small as you can get," he shouted over the roar of the wind. Into the phone, he issued another order. "Jill, dammit, you stay inside. Get my other gun out of the top drawer of the bureau. Take it out and get ready to use it."

"Does it have a kick like Murphy's?"

She'd stopped crying and, in fact, sounded almost icily calm. Luke wondered at the change. It was probably due to all the noise on his end because she'd been nearly hysterical only moments before.

"It'll be a bigger kick. The Glock has more power."

She was gone for a second, during which time Luke forced himself to focus on his own precarious situation. If he didn't have Jimmy with him, he could have used himself as bait and lured Duncan away from the cabin. But with Murphy down, they were still in danger.

She came back on the line. "I've got it."

"Get the extra clips, too. You pull out the spent one and shove in the new one. Once you hear it click, you're good to go." He heard the faint sound of sirens and prayed they were on her end. But his car was so freakin' noisy he couldn't tell if they were behind him or coming toward him.

All he knew was that he wanted her safe, dammit. He loved her. He loved her kids. And as long as he were wishing for things that could never be, he wanted help for his partner. He prayed Murphy was still able to defend them.

The fragment of a plan began to formulate. He would slow down enough to drop Jimmy somewhere safe and then he would keep going. The trick would be in making sure Duncan didn't see the little boy. The ASAC would be forced to follow him until he was sure Luke was out of commission. With any luck he could keep them occupied for another fifteen minutes or so. He glanced at the gas gauge. He'd run out of time before he ran out of fuel. The strategy had switched from trying to win to simply staying in the game long enough. All he had to do was stay alive long enough to buy Murphy some time for the locals to arrive.

"I'm about seven minutes from you. Is that sirens I hear on your end?" She paused a moment and came back on the line.

"Nothing yet. It's pretty quiet. I'm going to check on Danny. I think I can drag him up on the porch," she announced.

A swift, sharp burst of paralyzing fear knifed through his chest when his brain filtered her words. God, no. "No, dammit—"

He resisted the urge to smash the phone against the dashboard while he filled the car with an angry tirade of curses. She'd hung up on him. "You'd better be alive when I get there," he vowed.

James's disgusted voice floated up from the back seat. "Yeah, and she better have that bar of soap ready."

Jillian shivered and cracked the door open again. The woods were dangerously quiet as she took a step out onto the porch, Luke's gun clutched tightly in her shaking hand. She'd changed her mind about the dangers of the bathroom and had locked Samuel and the baby inside, instructing him to sit in the bottom of the tub until she returned. She'd placed Sarah's cradle in the corner under the vanity and retrieved a fresh bottle for when she awoke. If she ended up dead, at least Samuel would be able to feed his sister. She prayed they would be safe in there, prayed no one would find them until the shooting stopped.

Nothing happened after her first step, so she carefully took another, her eyes scanning the area in front of her. Murphy hadn't moved from the spot where he'd fallen and she quickly blinked back the hot tears that wanted desperately to fall.

"You can't cry," she muttered. She had to stay cool. She had to be calm. Her heart pounded violently, its rhythm matching the pulsing tempo of the roar in her ears. Dear Lord, she felt as though she were about to faint. She took several cleansing breaths, all the while keeping her gaze moving over the landscape. Once she'd cleared the porch, she half walked, half staggered over to where Murphy lay curled up on his side.

"Danny? Danny, love. Can you hear me?" She pried the gun from her trembling fingers and set it on the ground to run her hands lightly over the huge man. She felt quickly for a pulse and found a faint, thready beat in the side of his neck.

"Jill? Get back inside." His voice was weak, but it was an order nonetheless.

"Not without you. Can you move at all? I don't know if I can lift you."

"Can't move. Shot."

"Where, Danny? Where are you shot?" Her gaze ran the length of him and she saw the blood pooling under his side. She took a deep breath and blew it out. Dear Lord, don't let him die. Where the hell were the police?

"Leg…stomach," he rasped. He tried to speak again and began coughing. Panic flared through her and for a dreadful moment she thought he was dying.

"Don't die, Danny. Stay with me." His eyes fluttered open again and he jerked her down toward him with surprising strength.

"Gun."

Sweet Mother of God, couldn't they think of anything else? "I've got the bloody gun. Stop worrying."

"No." He closed his eyes for a moment. "Get your freakin' gun. Someone's coming."

Her heart all but stopped when she heard the snap of a dry twig. Someone was coming up the trail. Her eyes wide with shock, she snatched up Luke's gun and glanced down at Danny. Wincing in pain, he nodded and then jerked his head toward the car. He wanted her to hide behind the car. But that would leave him exposed in the clearing. She shook her head and he glared up at her.

"Do it now, dammit."

She crawled over to the car and crouched by the front fender. Her insides felt as though she'd swallowed cement. If she were forced to run away, she knew her legs wouldn't carry her. They'd all but locked up. The only part of her body that seemed to be working was her heart and it was pumping overtime. Any second now it would surely burst free from her chest. She forced herself to take in shallow breaths, forced herself to keep her eyes open when she wanted to scrunch them closed and hide. Biting her lip, she turned to glance at Danny and watched in amazement when he pulled his gun out from under him. Stifling an audible groan, he loaded a clip and slammed it home.

She heard the faint sound of sirens off in the distance but had no idea of which direction to look. Instead she focused her attention on the dirt road beyond the car. Whoever was coming was getting closer. Part of her wanted desperately to peer around the end of the car, wanted to believe the person would be a friend. Please let it be someone who could help. A police officer perhaps. Maybe the cabin owner, come to check out all the noise.

The realist in her remained glued to the grill of the car, flattened as small as she could get. The muscles in her thighs knotted agonizingly, crying out for movement. She felt a trickle of sweat course down her back and into her pants and shivered when the breeze blew through her too thin jacket and cooled her overheated skin. The scent of gunpowder still hung in the air when she took a great shuddering breath. She wanted to scrub at the goose bumps that had raised on her arms. Instead she held tight to the pistol clenched in her perspiring fist and waited.

"Murphy, good God."

She heard the man's footsteps pound the rest of the way up the trail after he made his discovery. He flashed by the car, skittering pebbles when he veered toward the center of the clearing where Murphy lay prone on his side, raised up on one elbow.

"Jesus, are you all right?"

Jillian didn't hear Murphy's response. She was too busy concentrating on the broad back of the man bending over Murphy, a man he clearly knew. She waited for Danny to call out to her. Why hadn't he given her some sign that it was okay to come out of hiding? She felt the shudder of fear course through her, felt the rush of blood sing through her veins when he didn't. And knew with overwhelming certainty that something was very wrong. When Murphy's signal didn't come, she pressed herself more firmly against the car and quietly raised her shooting hand up over the hood.

The whirring thump of a helicopter grew louder in the distance and she realized it was about to pass directly overhead. She watched the man tilt his head back at the sound, smiling as he withdrew a gun from his jacket. He lurched up from his squatting position on the ground to stand tall over Danny. When he leveled his gun at her friend, Jillian gasped in recognition.

Josephson couldn't have heard her cry of outrage, not over the deafening sound of the chopper overhead. No, he had to have sensed her startled movement because he swung around to face her, his gun already raised and locked on her. She fired the Glock and felt the tremendous pull as she was jerked back off her feet. Her head spinning, she landed hard on the ground a few feet away and somehow managed to scramble around to the passenger side of the car. Her body felt as if it was moving in slow motion despite the danger. Her brain was working but her legs didn't want to respond. When her brain told her to dive for cover, she threw herself to the ground and rolled under the car. She bit back a moan of agony when her shoulder protested the sudden movement.

Dear God, what should she do now? Had she hit Josephson or not? Where was he? This very moment, he could be walking this way, intent on killing her, and she couldn't hear a bloody thing. The commotion from the chopper was unbearably loud and her head vibrated with the excruciating sound. Her panicky sobs were swallowed up while she choked on the great clouds of dust that swirled overhead, her eyes burned as the sun-dappled forest turned into a thundering rain of earth and sticks and scattering tree limbs. Tasting dirt, she tucked her head down to the ground in a pathetic attempt to find clean air. She rubbed at the grit in her eyes, ignoring the white-hot pain that shafted through her arm and tried to locate Murphy from her new position under the car.

Mercifully, the helicopter lifted higher, hovered for a moment and then twisted toward the east. But there wasn't to be any relief. She cringed at the screaming sound of another chopper moving fast across the sky. Her ears still ringing from the first wave of sound, she could have sworn she heard sirens blaring up the narrow dirt road.

She swallowed hard and gagged on the dust. Dear Lord, she felt light-headed but she couldn't take the time to rest yet. She had to find Danny. What if Josephson found the babies? He had a gun, didn't he? Yet, try as she might, she could barely keep her eyes open in the swirling clouds. The ground pitched and swayed each time she raised her head and the movement was driving her mad. This was it, she realized. She'd obviously snapped from all the stress. She'd finally gone 'round the bloody bend.

As the sound of helicopters finally faded, Jillian forced herself to listen. There were more ear-splitting noises. Sirens. Lots of them. She winced when car doors slammed, each one louder than the next. And then there were footsteps and voices...strident, arguing voices. All the sounds blurred together and she smiled at the softer, muted sound. Now everyone sounded as though they were inside a tunnel. And the loudest noise of all was someone calling—no, he was bloody shouting her name at the top of his lungs. And cursing a blue streak.

Luke.

"What do you mean you don't know where she is?"

"She's somewhere around here, dammit."

Danny's voice was gravelly with pain. Jillian lifted her head and scowled in the direction of the sound. Why the hell didn't Luke leave the poor man alone? Didn't he know Murphy'd been shot? She watched owlishly as pairs of legs milled around on the other side of the car and chuckled at the thought of grabbing their feet. Wouldn't that scare the life out of them?

"Time to get up," she muttered and then scooted her body into a crawling position. She licked her lips and tasted dirt against her teeth. She was so bloody thirsty. The absolute first thing she was going to do was get a large glass of water— the very moment she stood up.

She lurched to her feet and was surprised when she staggered against the car door and a frisson of fear pumped through her cloudy brain. Was she paralyzed? Why was she having so much trouble walking? She'd only taken a step when she heard all the shouting start again and felt her legs buckle under her weight. She slid along the car and flopped onto the hood for a rest.

"Jill! God, no. Jill."

She frowned at the hoarse sound of his voice. Luke was upset. The forest was still so damn dusty. He must be choking on it, too.

"Baby, can you move?" His hands shook when he gently lifted her from the hood of the car. There was blood everywhere. Jillian's face was ghostly white and her eyes didn't seem to recognize him when they fluttered open. Fear like he'd never known before knifed through his chest, nearly immobilizing him.

"Medic! I need a medic over here," he shouted in a voice he knew was dangerously close to hysteria. His grip tightened reflexively and he forced himself to loosen it. His fingers found hers and he took immeasurable comfort that they were still warm. She was so damn fragile. So helpless. He blinked back the tears that burned in his eyes. Dear God, he couldn't lose her. He heard the medic drop down near him, watched while he carefully cut Jilly's jacket away from her and grimaced at the amount of blood that seeped from her shoulder.

He was helpless to stop the muted groan of anguish. "Help her. You've got to hurry. Can you stop the bleeding?"

"Sir, you need medical attention. Sit down over there until we can get to you."

"Is she—" He sank to the ground, his heart in his throat. His hand shook violently when he raised her fingers to his lips. God, he couldn't even think it, never mind say the words. "Tell me she's gonna be all right."

"Took one in the shoulder. Close range." The paramedic's skillful hands got busy, clinically and methodically preparing Jillian for transport to the hospital.

Her eyes fluttered open and his limbs went liquid with fear when she bit back a sharp cry of pain. "Christ…go easy with her." He swallowed hard and dropped his head to his hand. "I'm sorry. I—"

"Luke? Is that you?" Her voice was weak and thready and it terrified him to realize how vulnerable she was.

"Yeah, honey. I'm here."

Her fingers tightened in his hand and she managed a wan smile. "Your Glock has quite a kick. My shoulder hurts a bit. I think I grazed it when I fell down." Her words slurred together and her eyes clouded while she tried to remember what she was saying. "Be a love and get out the first-aid kit for me, won't you?"

He exchanged glances with the paramedic who shook his head in disbelief and Luke felt a volcanic fury begin to build inside of him.

"It's not a freakin' graze when you take a bullet in your shoulder," he argued. "Why the hell didn't you stay inside?"

Josephson had blasted her from close range...and missed. Luke knew he'd aimed to kill. He should be thanking God that he had only caught her in the shoulder, but the murderous rage that welled up inside of him left no room to be thankful. He wanted to tear Josephson apart with his bare hands. But he was already dead. Unbelievably, both Jilly and Murphy had gotten off a round. It would take ballistics to figure out who'd delivered the lethal blow.

"Danny needed me."

"I need you." Luke sank back on his haunches and relived the drive back. He never should have left her. Never. Never. His mistake had nearly killed her. He'd seen Joe with the gun as he'd bounced up the trail on two flat tires—and the realization had hit him that he'd be too late. Again.

He was always too late.

He swallowed convulsively and tightened his grip on Jilly's fingers. God, how he needed her in his life. She sighed when the pain finally became too much to bear and his heart dropped to his feet when her fingers went limp in his hand. She'd fainted.

"I love you." He stared down at her face, at the freckles that now stood in stark contrast to the translucent paleness of her skin and wondered how he would ever be able to let her go.

* * *

Luke rubbed his bleary, overtired eyes and set the pizza on the table.

"Okay, guys. Dinner is served." Jimmy and Samuel rushed over to get a slice. He dragged himself over to check on Sarah and was relieved to find her still asleep in the super-deluxe travel crib. Maybe he'd have time for a quick shower before they headed back to the hospital.

"All set, Mr. Gianetti?"

"Yeah. Thanks for staying with them today." For the life of him he couldn't remember her name. The Knoxville office had sent her over to watch the kids but he hadn't paid attention when she'd introduced herself. All he could think about was getting back to the hospital where he'd nervously paced while Jillian had the bullet removed from her shoulder and his best friend had undergone surgery to repair the damage to his stomach before they went to work on his leg.

"No problem. We got a great deal of information from the older one." She nodded toward James and lowered her voice. "Apparently he ID'ed Duncan as his mother's killer?"

Luke nodded, his eyes never leaving James's face, a surge of protectiveness flooding through him. The poor kid had been through enough. He didn't need a bunch of strangers talking about his mother like she was just another Jane Doe.

"Yeah. I was with him."

"We're pretty much done with him for now. Unless Duncan lives. Then we'll need to talk to him in greater detail. Will you need someone to watch the kids tomorrow?"

Excellent question. He wished he had an answer. He doubted Jilly would be out of the hospital. And her mother wouldn't arrive for several days. Apparently the Duchess of Sussex had quite the busy schedule.

"Yeah, probably. I'd appreciate it if you could send someone over." He thanked her again and walked her to the door. Leaning back against it, he rested his eyes for a moment before the chaos of the evening began. He couldn't remember the last time he'd slept. He'd had no real excuse the previous night. The room was large, the bed comfortable, the children exhausted from the terror they'd experienced during the day. And he'd spent the night pacing the floor, his brain unwilling to release him from the nightmare of seeing Jilly, bleeding and half dead as she fell onto the hood of Murphy's car.

She and Murphy were in the hospital across the street. Duncan and Petrie had been taken to a more secure facility where, under heavy guard, they still clung to life. Sloan hadn't lived through the helicopter crash. Josephson and the still unnamed shooter had been killed by Murphy and Jill. Jillian Moseby, the Duchess of Sussex, had blown away possibly two of the biggest drug dealers on the east coast. His Jillian.

"Luke? You gonna eat wif us?"

He forced his eyes open and found them both staring at him, mouths full of pizza. He knew they were anxious to see Jill. Especially Jimmy. She would be pleased, he thought, to know that James had worried himself sick over her. She'd finally won him over. Then he shook his head. Knowing Jilly, the fact that he'd been scared would probably make her feel horribly guilty. She'd always been confident that James would come around eventually. She wouldn't want him to love her out of fear.

"Yeah. Let's eat and then we can go across the street to see Jilly." He pulled out a chair and grabbed a slice of pizza, unable to get the picture of her out of his head. If she could see what he'd been feeding them she'd be having fits. He took a healthy bite and grinned.

"Remember, guys, when we see Jilly, don't say anything about the junk food."

"Can we go see Murphy, too?"

He glanced at Samuel who was already nodding his head in agreement and remembered how pale his friend had appeared. "We'll have to see how he's feeling first. He might not be well enough for visitors yet."

Lucy Murphy had arrived during the night on a company

Lear. She'd spoken only briefly with him before rushing off to spend the rest of the day by her husband's side. He'd checked on them several hours later, peeking through the window of the intensive care unit and had gotten a lump in his throat when he saw her dark head resting on the blanket, her hand tucked into Murphy's. Fifteen years. And they still adored each other.

"I wanna tell him about the money. The lady tol' us that they found a bunch a' money in our suitcase."

When they began to argue, Luke winced. "You can both tell him about it."

It had been right where they'd thought it would be, a tightly wrapped package tucked inside Sarah's footed pajamas. The suitcase had been packed not in haste, but methodically, with clothes for the kids that crossed several seasons. It was pretty obvious that Annie Moseby had been plotting her escape from Sloan for some time. It was also beginning to look as though she'd been the one to kill Sloan's lieutenant, Gomez. That action had inadvertently helped Luke's sting operation. If he'd only known then what he knew now... Perhaps Annie would be alive today.

But then he never would have met Jillian.

He'd held her hand in the recovery room when she'd first awakened and then fallen promptly back to sleep. She'd slept fitfully throughout the day, waking briefly to mutter incoherent words and phrases. And since he was the only person she knew on this side of the Atlantic, Luke had used that as his excuse to stay with her. She'd smile at him each time she awoke, even spoke his name, but he knew she would remember very little of it.

He'd used the time to memorize everything about her. Every feature. Every expression. The soft, scented skin. The stormy gray eyes. Her full, ripe mouth that was nearly always twitching into a smile. She was a beautiful woman. But when the beauty blended together with a strong sense of purpose, with her resounding love for her sister's children and her passion for living, she was damned close to irresistible.

Very soon he realized, he would have to say goodbye. To her and the kids. He glanced across the table at the boys and smiled. After spending so many days with them, he wasn't sure who would be harder to leave.

The ache in his chest for Jillian had been there almost from the start. The twinge he felt for the kids was something more recent. He would miss them. Their smiles, their silly expressions, the fascinating conversations he'd overheard between Sam and Jimmy, the love he saw between them and for their baby sister. He'd gotten used to having them around all the time. And he felt a hollow regret over all the everyday things he would never experience with them.

Their lives would go on. With Jilly in the picture, he knew they would have full, rich lives, ripe with laughter and fun and love. Each day would be a new adventure. And he would miss out on all of them. She'd asked him to be a part of it. By some miracle, she thought she loved him enough to allow him entry—into their family and into her heart.

And he'd declined.

Who cared if it might have only been for a little while? It didn't matter if she were the queen. He should have said yes. It would have been worth the risk. It would have been incredible. And he wouldn't have ever wanted to leave. He thought of Murphy, of Lucy sitting with him, holding his hand. He wanted that, too. He wanted the comfort of knowing someone cared for him more than he cared about himself. He wanted the comfort of loving her more than his own life.

Jilly's words came back to haunt him. No matter where he was, he would always know someone loved him. The irony was that if he had Jillian, he wouldn't ever want to go away again. He would want to see them every single day. He wanted to cuddle Sarah in the middle of the night. He wanted to watch Jimmy play baseball and push Sam on the swings at the park. And Jill. He wanted to go to sleep with her every night, certain in the knowledge that he would wake up every morning and feel her in his arms.

A shiver jagged down his spine catching him unaware and he dropped the slice of pizza he'd been eating, suddenly sick to his stomach. He'd turned down the offer of a lifetime. The question now was whether or not he would be too late to change her mind.

"Mama!" Sam's exuberant cry seemed to rattle the quiet stillness of the stark hospital room.

"Take it easy, champ. Let me lift you up to see her." Luke swung the little boy's legs up from the floor before he leaped onto the bed and jarred Jillian's shoulder. With one arm, he set him gently on the end of the bed and smiled at Jilly while Sam eagerly scrambled into her good arm. She smiled a greeting at Sarah who was kicking madly in his other arm.

"How're you feeling?" Now that he knew what he had to say to her, Luke felt ridiculously self-conscious yet confident that he would be able to fix it. She loved him. She'd already admitted that she loved him, he reminded himself. It shouldn't take much to convince her that he felt the same.

"Rather well, thank you."

He wasn't put off by her cautious response. After all, he'd been the one to put the damper there. He'd damn well be the one to remove it. He'd plotted for the last hour how he would approach her and had decided to wait until he could get her alone. And then he'd tell her. That he loved her. That he always had. That he wanted to spend the rest of his life with her. Duchess or not, he wanted her—badly. Desperately.

His eyes never left her face. Luke wanted her to know his feelings now. He wanted her to see the love in his eyes, wanted to see the flare of acknowledgment in hers. But she was already looking beyond him, a smile of encouragement on her beautiful lips.

"James, love. Why are you hiding?" She patted the spot on the bed near her legs.

"Jimmy, buddy? Did you want to say hello?" Luke gave him a little nudge forward.

His slender shoulders hunched, he sat tentatively and allowed himself to be drawn up against her chest. "You're not gonna die, are ya?"

"No, love. I'm going to be just fine." Her eyes misted with tears and she blinked them away. "As soon as I get out of here, we can finally go home."

"Where's home?"

She pulled him tighter against her and laughed when James yelped. "You're squishin' me."

"Home is wherever we're all together." She dropped a kiss on his forehead before glancing over his head to meet Luke's gaze. "Home will be in New Hampshire, if we're finally free to leave, that is."

"Not quite yet. Duncan is still—"

"I see," she interrupted. She dropped her gaze to Jimmy. "Well, just as soon as we're able to leave, we'll finish our drive north. Better yet, I think it'll be much easier if we fly."

"Cool! You mean it? I've never flown in an airplane before."

"It'll be our next adventure." She laughed and snuggled them close to her chest. "I missed you all so much."

His blood iced over at the finality in her expression and his gut tightened with warning. She was shutting him out. She'd laid it on the line and now it was over. She wasn't about to give him a second chance. Was it too late? Not now. Not without a chance to fix it.

"Jilly, we need to talk."

"Let's not, shall we? I think we've said everything that needed to be said. No sense rehashing it."

He saw the flash of pain in her eyes and knew she held her emotions in tight control. He just wasn't sure if the hurt was physical from the gunshot wound or from the emotional pain he'd inflicted. But it was pretty clear that she didn't want to be hurt any more. In one short week he'd taken a vibrant, loving, free spirit and twisted her into a wounded, guarded shell of her former self. He'd succeeded in turning Jilly into a carbon copy of him.

"Look, I've been thinking about us." His heart began pounding and he was certain that she could hear the thumping across the bed. "I was really wrong. I think we should try—"

He scowled when her gaze drifted past him to rest on the person entering her room. Couldn't she let him finish? This was the most important speech of his life. Didn't she care to hear what he had to say? His frown intensified when he saw the flash of recognition light her features. His grip tightened on Sarah as he turned and his free hand went reflexively for his holster.

"Ian! What are you doing here?"

"Hello, darling. What in God's name are you doing in this backwoods hellhole?"

Luke's mouth dropped open when an expensively dressed, perfectly groomed, too pale, too tall jerk strode into the room and disrupted his train of thought.

"For the love of God, Jillian, I'm staying in a bloody motel. You've been gone for what? Two weeks? And you've been reduced to this? These accommodations are appalling." He turned to eye the hospital room with dismay. "Lord only knows what caliber the surgeons are in this backwater. Dear Lord, if the duchess could see you… Why, we've simply got to get you back home. Immediately. I've assured your mother that I will stand by and offer my services as your escort."

"Ian, allow me to introduce you. This is Luke Gianetti. He's an agent with the DEA. He's been taking care of the children and me."

He did everything but click his stupid shiny heels together. Like an automaton, Luke stuck his hand out and nodded at the distinguished-looking snob in the suit. His fingers were cold, his grip just this side of wimpy. And he'd be willing to bet that Ian's nails were manicured. A moment later his lordship dismissed him. Just like that, with an arrogant little nod of his neatly combed head. He felt the knife in his gut twist a little harder when Ian leaned over Jillian and kissed her cheek.

"Well, good job, chap. I'm here now, though. I'll be taking care of Lady Jillian from here on in. Thanks for all your help."

"Ian, don't be ridiculous." Jillian intervened, blushing with embarrassment. "Agent Gianetti saved our lives. We surely would have been killed if he hadn't protected us."

Ian turned back, carefully sizing him up. Loverboy wasn't as stupid as he looked. He'd recognized the admiration in Jillian's voice.

"Of course, love." His expression clearly condescending, Ian deigned to speak to him again. "Well see here, we'll make sure that you're properly recognized. I'll get the paperwork going with the consulate. The duchess will be very pleased to hear that her daughter's all right."

"That's not necessary."

"But I can take it from here," he continued loftily. "I'm here representing the Duchess of Sussex. As I've already indicated, I've been charged with acting on her behalf. You're free to go," he said, dismissively.

Luke stood frozen to the spot, his gaze locked on Jilly's as his blood began to boil. He noticed that Ian hadn't even acknowledged the two little boys who clung protectively to their mother. He hadn't made the slightest effort to smile at Sarah. His hand tightened reflexively into a fist. This was the man her mother had picked for Jilly? This was the wimp she'd contemplated marrying?

"'Fraid I can't do that, Ian, old boy. Until I say so, Jilly and the kids are still under my protection."

Ian stiffened in protest. "That's Lady Jillian to you, sir."

"Whatever." He shot an annoyed look in her direction and was surprised to see her lips twitching into a smile. When Ian turned to her, his expression appalled, she buried her face in Sam's hair in an attempt to choke back her laughter.

Luke felt a trickle of warmth spread through his frozen

limbs. She was so clearly not one of them. And he was sure she never had been. She was still Jilly. No matter what this prissy snob said and no matter what her title claimed, Jilly was the very real woman he'd fallen in love with. With that knowledge in hand, he knew he'd never enjoy putting someone in their place more than this very moment.

"This is still an ongoing investigation, Ian. Jilly *and* the kids," he repeated, "are under my protection for the next few days. If that's too inconvenient for you, then you're certainly free to go."

Prissy boy glared at him then, the white gloves coming off his manicured fingers for the first time. "Well, Mr. Gianetti, we'll just have to see about that, now, shan't we?"

Chapter 13

Jillian sighed when she heard the hesitant knock on her door. What in blazes could he possibly want now? Rolling her eyes, she jerked the door open with unnecessary force.

"Bloody hell, Ian. I said I'd think—" She tightened her grip on the knob and a tiny squeak of surprise escaped her lips. "—About it."

Her heart pounding, she raised her free hand to her throat. "L—Luke, what are you—I mean, h-how are you?" Her gaze swept him from head to toe and came back to rest on his face. His beautiful, tired eyes watched her assessment. He looked horrible. And wonderful. She clutched the door handle while every single nerve ending in her body exploded at the sight of him. "You're not shot again, are you?"

Unsmiling, he shook his head and stood awkwardly in her doorway. "I, uh… Can I come in?"

Her eyes widened in sudden comprehension and she pulled the door open. She was acting like a complete ninny. "Yes, of course. Please."

She somehow managed to lead him to the sofa in the cluttered living room. Her eyes scanned the room, imagining what he was seeing. There were boxes piled in one corner, still waiting to be unpacked if she ever managed to find the time, pictures leaning against the wall, waiting to be hung.

"Sorry for the mess. We've only been here a couple of weeks." She wished her heart would slow from its current gallop. Dammit, it had been nearly three weeks. She'd gotten along without him. Her nightly cry in the shower was working. She knew it was only a matter of time before she would start sleeping again.

Feeling a bit dizzy, she flopped into the nearest chair and shored up her resolve. He'd abandoned her in Tennessee. For all his challenging words to Ian that night, he'd left and he hadn't returned. Up until the moment they'd boarded the plane for New Hampshire, she'd held out hope that he would show up at the airport—and had sobbed like a bloody fool when he hadn't.

It was time to move on. She'd already made a complete and total idiot of herself over Luke Gianetti. She would not embarrass herself further by repeating those actions today.

"How are you? How's your shoulder?"

His voice sounded strained and she braced herself for what would surely be an awkward visit. She wondered why he'd decided to seek her out now. She followed his gaze to her shoulder sling and waggled it in response.

"I told you it would be fine. It's hardly been a bother. A simple graze…just like yours."

"Jill, for God's sake, you took a bullet to the shoulder at close range. There's nothing simple about it." He sat in the chair across from her and continued to fidget with his shirt collar. "Where are the kids?"

His eyes missed nothing. They never had. She had the uncomfortable feeling that he knew how edgy he was making her. He was stunning in his expensive suit, his golden tan set off to drooling perfection against the snowy white shirt. And he'd cut his hair. The beautiful honeyed strands only reached his collar now.

"Sarah's napping upstairs and the boys are up in their room. Can you stay for a while? I know they'd love to see you." She nearly leaped from her chair and headed for the stairs. Breathing room. She needed a little breathing room. There was far less chance of embarrassing herself with witnesses in the room. Leaning into the stairwell, she was intent on calling them down when he stopped her.

"Not yet. Please? I—I wanted to talk with you first."

He'd followed her. She winced at the husky sound of his voice. She'd dreamed of that voice and now it was only inches away from her. Lord, it was so good to see him. She nearly ached with the need to touch him. "All right. Why don't we sit down?"

He sat heavily in the armchair and continued to stare at her. Jillian swallowed nervously, her throat as parched as though she'd walked in the desert for days. She was unable to still her nervous fingers and finally clasped them together in her lap.

"Why are you here, Luke?"

"I—I'm on special assignment. I, um, just got here today." He ran one hand over his face and for a fraction of a second she witnessed a flicker of uncertainty in the tawny depths of his eyes. And her pulse rate tripled. Good Lord, maybe he did care?

"I see. Going to be here long, are you?"

"I—I don't know yet. That depends."

Oh, yes. Agent Heartthrob was sweating. His expression was the same one he'd worn on the day they'd met. It was the grim look of pain and frustration and edgy fear. He looked as if he'd been shot in the butt all over again. Jillian schooled her expression carefully even though her heart felt as though it was about to soar straight out of her chest. She wouldn't give herself away this time, dammit.

"Is it a big case? If you're going to be around, I know the children would love to see you."

"Jilly, we need to talk." He fumbled with a necktie that appeared to be choking him and finally gave in to his burning need to remove his suit jacket. He resisted what appeared to be an urge to ball it up and throw it in her dustbin. Instead he stood and heaved it on the back of the chair he'd just been sitting in. "I saw your friend Ian down in the lobby."

"I thought you were him again at the door. He just left. I assumed he'd forgotten something."

"What's he doing here? He been around a lot?"

Luke was pacing now, his back to her, so it was safe to grin. "He arrived a few days ago. My mum sent him to check up on me."

He turned suddenly and she wiped the smile from her lips. It was all she could do not to dance a jig around the living room.

"What did you mean when you opened the door? You said you'd think about it. What's he want?"

"Oh, that," she drawled. "Ian still wants me to marry him. He said he's willing to keep the kids if I really want them, but only if we return to England. Ian refuses to live here. Says it's too inconvenient for him."

"Inconvenient?" Luke's eyes blazed a golden fury. "He's *willing* to keep them? They're not freakin' house plants. What about the kids? Does he care about them? Does he even know their names? Dammit, Jill, you're not seriously considering his offer, are you?"

It took every morsel of strength she had not to shout with joy. He was jealous. Luke Gianetti was stark raving mad. For her.

"Well, I—"

"You're not going," he announced, folding his arms across his chest as he glared at her.

"How dare you? You don't know the first thing about it."

"You can't go. The kids would hate it over there."

"You've been there before? That's funny…you never mentioned it."

"Well, no. Not yet." He hesitated, his footing clearly uncertain. "It's just…they've already been moved so many times. You're already here. I mean, I think you should stay here."

"Really? Ian's not all that bad, you know."

"That wimp."

She had all she could do to keep a straight face. At six years old, James was nearly as bad as Luke. He'd already started referring to Ian as the wimp. "You're a fine one to talk," she reminded him. "You left me to fend for myself. All alone with three children—whom you never said goodbye to, I might add."

"I left you? Try the other way around, honey. I came back and you were gone. Your prissy boyfriend made sure I couldn't get anywhere near you."

"What?" A shudder raced down her spine. It wasn't possible. Was it? Had he really tried to find them?

"Yeah," he confirmed. "The jerk must know people in very high places because I couldn't even get close enough to get a message through to you. Duncan never regained consciousness," he explained. "Once he was dead, I knew for sure you'd be safe. I had to be certain that Jimmy wouldn't be required to testify."

"He's the one I saw in the papers," she muttered.

Luke nodded. "He's the one who shot me the first time. My own boss. We finally got the ballistics report back. The bullet was fired from Duncan's service revolver. Murphy and I were getting too close to the source of all the heroin. He had to take us out. But then it mushroomed when I involved you."

"Duncan was the man I saw in the courtroom that day. He's the one who tried to take Sarah away from me."

"Except he really didn't want Sarah," he corrected. "He'd probably already figured out that Annie might have stashed the money with the kids. He planned to swipe it back and you'd be none the wiser.''

She shuddered to think what would have become of Sarah if she hadn't been there to stop him. "What about Danny? Is he all right?''

"He's fine. He's already home. Lucy's taking good care of him. He should be back in another month or so.''

He continued to stare at her while the silence lengthened awkwardly. He still hadn't told her why he was here. She decided to throw him a bone. "So, Ian was the only reason you didn't say goodbye? You would have come to see us off?''

"Hell, yes. I couldn't even find out where the bastard took you. The DEA brass had a big enough scandal on their hands with Duncan without risking another headline about a missing duchess. They put a muzzle on me.''

"You have no idea how difficult the past three weeks have been.'' She gripped the arm of the chair, too edgy to sit still. "It's bloody hard work being a single mother. I'm not sure I can handle it alone. I work all day and then I work all night. Sarah and the boys spend all the day in child care.''

"You do need help,'' he agreed. His eyes registered surprise when she launched out of the chair and charged at him.

"And I suppose you've got all the answers?'' Jillian stood, hands on her hips, not three feet away from the man she loved more than life itself. She couldn't cave in—not yet. This was too important. "I suppose you're going to tell me what I should do?''

"Damn straight, I am.'' He took a step closer, his eyes more desperate than ever. He raised one hand to his face and she saw the way it trembled. He was in agony. Still, she held her breath and waited for him to speak.

"God, Jill, I missed you.'' His voice was grim with misery as he made the admission. "I missed you so much.''

She couldn't wait another blasted minute. Her eyes blurred with tears and she launched herself into his arms. Luke groaned when he caught her and held her, as though his very life depended on it. She felt him shudder with relief, could hear the pounding of his heart under her ear, and rejoiced at the depth of his feelings. Whether or not he ever spoke the words, she knew how he felt. Knowing he loved her was enough.

She blinked back her tears as she wrapped her arms around his neck and brought his mouth down to hers. "I missed you, too. What took you so bloody long?"

She kissed him with all the stored-up passion she'd foolishly thought she could banish at will. And he responded with such urgency that Jilly came up gasping. "Lord, we've got to stop. The boys—"

He captured her mouth again and she melted against him while the outside world went totally hazy. Breathing hard, Luke pulled back and loosened his clasp. His eyes had gone molten with desire, but his expression was still grimly intense.

A shiver of worry snaked down her spine and she took a step back. "Oh, Lord. You're not leaving me again? It's your blasted stomach, isn't it?"

He had the gall to laugh even though his eyes were still wary. "I—no. My gut is never wrong," he reminded.

"But you said—"

"I know what I said," he interrupted. "But it was *me* who was wrong, not my gut. My gut told me to grab hold of you and never let you go."

She took in a startled breath and held it.

"I did something I've never, ever done. I went against my gut."

She released the whoosh of air in her lungs at his surprising admission. And smiled when his gaze met and held hers. "You did?"

"And I've been miserable ever since." He winced and began pacing again, pausing only to loosen his tie. "I was wondering if maybe you'd…that is, if we could—"

"Yes, Luke?"

He took a deep breath. "I'll move up here. The royalty thing…I can handle it. I should tell you, though, I'll need lessons on how to act around those pompous, arrogant—" He glanced at her anxiously. "I don't even own a tuxedo."

"Bloody hell, Luke." What was he talking about? "There's nothing to handle."

He waved away the argument she wanted to start. "You were right. I was looking for an excuse. Any stupid reason I could find to run away. I used the only thing I had."

"And now you don't feel like running?"

He grimaced as he looked away. "How do I run away from myself? From what I want more than anything?"

He had to be able to see her heart beating through the wall of her chest. It was tripping along like a freight train, out of control. She cleared her throat nervously. "What do you want?"

"I was offered another promotion. I'm seriously considering it this time, but it's based in D.C."

"I see. Is that what you'd like?"

Luke ignored her question, intent on his explanation. "I even went house shopping. How presumptuous was that?" He shook his head derisively. "I thought…"

Jillian held her breath as his pause lengthened, dying to know what thoughts raced through his enigmatic brain. "You thought…"

"I thought I'd come up here and convince you to move to Washington. I thought—" He reached out to gently tuck a strand of hair behind her ear. "I talked to my friend at the Smithsonian. I had it all planned out. I'd get you a job…find us a house and…"

His voice lowered to a painful whisper. "God, Jill. I love you so much. Please, please don't go back to England."

The tears were pouring down her face when she stepped into his embrace. His arms tightened around her as though he would never let her go. "I never wanted to go back," she admitted, sniffing. "As long as I'm with you, I don't care where we live."

"Then you don't mind? Moving, I mean? You—you'll marry me?"

She opened her mouth to answer and was startled by the voice at the top of the stairs. Two little faces peered down at them from between the railings. James's eyes appeared to be especially worried.

"Bloody hell, Jilly. You're gonna say yes, aren't you?"

Luke checked his watch and frowned. She was late again. He sighed and opened the screen door and stepped back into the kitchen. "Yo, Jimmy, come here a minute."

"Yeah, Dad?" James ran in from the living room, with Samuel perpetually two steps behind.

"Fire up the computer. Mommy's lost again." He smiled distractedly down at Sarah while she crept along the kitchen floor, moving from chair to chair until she could reach out and grab hold of his leg. He scooped her up and gave her a kiss before shifting her to one arm. With his free hand, he pulled out his cell phone and dialed Jillian's number.

"Babe, where are you?"

"Dammit, Luke. I know I'm close this time. These houses look familiar."

He smiled at the waspish sound of her voice. "Honey, you're making progress. You're only getting lost twice a week now."

"That's because you drove me every day for two bloody months." He heard her curse as she shuffled the map he knew was sitting in her lap. "All right. I give up. Where am I?"

"Jimbo, where's Mommy?"

James checked the red blip on the screen. He loved when Jillian got lost because he got to pretend she was a spy that he and Samuel were tracking. "Tell her to take her next left." He paused while Luke directed her and watched the blip move around the corner. "Okay. She's one street over. Next left, then right. That's our street."

He snapped off the screen as Luke gave Jilly the directions. "Can we go outside now?"

Luke nodded and flipped his phone closed. "Don't forget you've got a ball game at six-thirty. Get your uniform on. Dinner's almost ready." He smiled at Sarah and ruffled her soft curls. "Wanna go wait for Mommy?"

He pushed the screen door open and strolled out into the yard. His yard. Luke Gianetti had a yard. He had a flower garden, too. Jilly had even convinced him he was capable of growing tomatoes. They spilled from their brightly colored pots on the deck out back. He had a deck. He shook his head in disbelief, something he still did at least once a week. Next, they'd probably get a dog.

His smile widened as Jilly's car rounded the corner. The tracking software had been the best investment he'd made in recent years. The transponder worked like a charm. Even if she ever tried, she'd never be able to lose him. He watched her get out of the car, a sweet smile on her beautiful face and told himself for the hundredth time that he was the luckiest man on the planet.

"Sorry I'm late." She kissed him, lingering a moment over the task, and he sighed with satisfaction. She scooped Sarah from his arms and nuzzled her neck, much to the little girl's delight. They strolled up the driveway together, his hand at her back as she climbed the steps.

"Work late?"

"No. I had an appointment."

The tone of her voice had him instantly curious. "Okay, what's up?" She removed her sunglasses and he knew immediately that she was nervous. "What sort of appointment? You didn't mention it this morning."

"I, um, had a doctor's appointment. I've been so bloody tired. I wanted to make sure nothing—"

"Jilly, for Pete's sake. In the last seven months you've

moved twice—once across the damn ocean—you've been shot and nearly killed, you inherited three children, started two new jobs and married me. You've earned the right to be tired.''

''Yes, well, I just thought—''

''What'd he say?'' Luke moved closer, suddenly suspicious. ''You're all right, aren't you?'' His gut tightened to red-alert status when she refused to look at him. He promptly stepped in front of her and forced her chin up with his finger. ''What the hell did he say?''

When her eyes filled with tears, he didn't know whether to comfort her or to throw up in the kitchen sink. Sweet Jesus, something was wrong with her.

''Tell me, Jill. Whatever it is. Tell me right now!''

She nodded and took a deep breath. ''He told me we're pregnant.''

A lightning bolt zagged through him and detonated in his chest, the explosion reverberating in his ears. ''That's not p-possible,'' he managed to croak. ''I told you—''

She recovered quickly, her eyes flashing angrily. ''I know what you bloody told me. And I'm here to tell you Linda was wrong.''

He shook his head, his brain firing too rapidly for him to form words. He'd had tests…she'd delighted in taunting him.

''The only logical answer is that she lied to you.'' Jillian took a step closer, her expression worried. ''I— Luke, how do you feel about this?''

''How do *I* feel? How do *you* feel?'' He winced at the gritty sound of his voice and swallowed hard in an attempt to rid the lump from his throat.

''I'm…thrilled. And overwhelmed. But you…you only signed on for three children, not four.''

Sweet Jesus…he felt as though he could leap a tall building in a single bound. ''Who said anything about stopping at four?'' He smiled and placed his still shaking hand on her stomach. ''Baby, you and me, we're just getting started.''

*　*　*　*　*

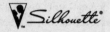

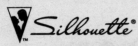

#1321 NOTHING TO LOSE—RaeAnne Thayne
The Searchers

Taylor Bradshaw was determined to save her brother from death row.
Bestselling author Wyatt McKinnon intended only to write about the
case, but ended up joining Taylor's fight for justice. As time ticked
down their mutual attraction rose, and with everything already on the
line, they had nothing to lose….

#1322 LIVE TO TELL—Valerie Parv
Code of the Outback

Blake Stirton recognized a city girl when he saw one, but leaving
Jo Francis stranded in the bush wasn't an option. She had information
he needed to find his family's diamond mine before a greedy neighbor
foreclosed on their ranch. When his feelings for her distract him, it puts
them both in danger. And the explosive secrets they uncover as they work
together up the stakes—for their relationship…and his family's
fortune—exponentially.

#1323 IN SIGHT OF THE ENEMY—Kylie Brant
Family Secrets: The Next Generation

Cassie Donovan's ability to forecast the future had driven a wedge into
her relationship with Shane Farhold, until, finally, his skepticism had
torn them apart. But when a madman saw her ability as a gift worth
killing for, Shane took her and their unborn child on the run. And not
even Cassie could predict when the danger would end….

#1324 HER MAN TO REMEMBER—Suzanne McMinn

Roman Bradshaw thought his wife was dead—until he found her again
eighteen months later. But Leah didn't remember him—or the divorce
papers she'd been carrying the night of her accident. Now Roman has a
chance to seduce her all over again. But could he win her love a second
time before the past caught up with them?

#1325 RACING AGAINST THE CLOCK—Lori Wilde

Scientist Hannah Zachary was on the brink of a breakthrough that
dangerous men would kill to possess. After an escape from certain
death sent her to the hospital, she felt an instant connection to her
sexy surgeon, Dr. Tyler Fresno. But with a madman stalking her, how
could she ask Tyler to risk his life—and heart—for her?

#1326 SAFE PASSAGE—Loreth Anne White

Agent Scott Armstrong was used to hunting enemies of the state, not
warding off imaginary threats to beautiful, enigmatic scientists like
Dr. Skye Van Rijn. Then a terrorist turned his safe mission into a
deadly battle to keep her out of the wrong hands. Would Skye's secrets
jeopardize not only their feelings for each other but their lives, as well?